**From a USA To
and 5 time RITA aw**

He paid a high price to serve his country, and has no plans to risk his heart...

The man known only as Flynn lives on the periphery of life. Until the day a little girl drops into his life, on a quest for the dragon of Dragon Hill, the billionaire's estate where he acts as caretaker. She charms him with her cleverness and bright curiosity, and reaches a place in his heart he thought long hardened to stone. When her lovely, courageous mother appears, that place in his heart is shattered forever. But his barriers are high, and strong.

Riley West has dealt with the worst life has thrown at her with the same determination she passed on to her daughter. When Gracie becomes fascinated with Flynn, a distrustful Riley tries to intervene. She has been running from her past for too long to let down her guard, even for this man who, after stealing her little girl's heart, is working his way into hers.

Can tough, hardened Flynn believe enough to let them into his life? Can Riley finally stop running, and accept the help only he has ever offered?

FOR THE LOVE
OF A CHILD

A Wild Oak Romance

Justine Davis

SxNW PUBLISHING

ISBN: 978-1-946331-36-6

CHAPTER ONE

Flynn saw the woman looking at him across the begonias. When she saw him notice she smiled, in that way women used to smile at him. Invitation, or at least welcome in their eyes. To talk, even flirt a little. Test the waters for more. A suggestion of coffee from the stand next door to the garden shop. Which could lead to...anything.

He knew all he would have to do was turn his head to end it. He didn't have the energy to do even that. He was in no mood to see shock roll over her pretty face at his destroyed one. No mood to see the way she would back away, wishing she'd never even looked. No mood to—

"You're loaded up, Mr. Flynn."

He turned to look at the lanky young man who had been putting the flats of plants into his truck. "Thanks, Kevin." He hesitated, then reached into his pocket and pulled out the gift card he'd acquired this morning. "You have any use for this?"

The boy—Flynn guessed he was about nineteen, but he looked younger—blinked. "The Oak Tree? My mom loves that place."

"Here, then." He smiled. "Take her to dinner."

"Oh, wow. But you—"

"I'll never use it. Take it."

The boy was still staring after him when he pulled out. He knew Kevin was working two part-time jobs after school to help out his mom after his dad had been killed, but that wasn't the only reason he'd stopped and bought the gift card on his way here. The main reason was the memory of the first time he'd run into the kid. Kevin had looked at his scarred face, calmly said, "Wow, that must have hurt," and never mentioned it—or stared at it—again.

He knew what John would say, since they'd had the discussion not long ago.

You haven't shaken the sheepdog mentality, the taking care of others thing.

Like you have?

Probably never will. But now I see to my own.

And that was the big difference between him and the man he'd once sworn to follow into hell if need be. The man he had followed into just that, more than once. The man he respected above all others. The man he owed his life to, three times over. Although John quibbled over one of those. But then, Army Rangers didn't generally argue about credit as long as the job got done.

They had both taken off the uniform nearly five years ago, but some things weren't so easily shed.

Like scars?

They both had their share—okay, John would say Flynn had more, but his were just more visible. Hard to hide them when half of your face looked like it had lost a fight with that lawnmower in the back of his truck.

He made the turn onto Oak Tree Road. For two years, his more frequent turn had been the other way, toward Jake's place. Now Jake and Rachel and Cammie's place. The thought of the now one-year-old made him smile, not only because she was an adorable, happy child, but because it made him think of John nervously helping to look after her—made more amusing by the fact that he had delivered her—in preparation for the birth of his own child any day now. The sight of John Reese nervous about anything was enough to entertain anyone who knew him.

But that brought on thoughts that made Flynn shiver slightly. Not because he wasn't glad for John, because he was. The man deserved every good thing he'd gotten, and Flynn knew how hard he'd worked to rebuild his life after the disaster it had become because he'd been determined to do his duty. A duty no one else could have done. But John had done it, at the cost of everything he'd held dear, and saved likely thousands of lives in the process.

No, the shiver was because of the request John had made. It was a small one, in light of what he owed the man. And yet it had made him recoil at the very idea. Because if there was anything on earth he was not equipped to handle, it was being godfather to his best friend's firstborn child.

It didn't matter that John's life was different now, that the likelihood of it being anything more than a ceremonial role was slim. Flynn had seen too much death to think it always announced its arrival in some obvious way. And he just wasn't the man for the job of taking care of a child.

He made the turn onto Dragon Hill Road. He'd use the main gate today, instead of the back gate that was actually closer to his place, only because the owner of the place and his main boss—Shan Kelleher, billionaire head of the Kelleher

3

Company—and his girlfriend Juliette were visiting her parents in Idaho.

The flicker of movement at the edge of the road had him easing up on the accelerator. Last thing he wanted to do was run over some critter. Then he spotted what had made the brush move and amended the thought. Second to last thing.

He saw the small human shape behind the spring green of the New River bougainvillea bushes that were already growing like mad along the fence. With luck, there would be a riot of bright purple before the summer was over. But right now, there was this little trespasser to deal with.

He slowed to a stop. The shape behind the bush froze. Flynn considered getting out of the truck, but didn't want to spook his quarry. So instead he just called out cheerfully, "You might want to rethink hiding there. Those bushes have nasty thorns."

A small, rueful voice came back at him. "I know, now."

"Ouch." He kept his tone light, although now he was concerned; some people had a nasty reaction to a scratch by those thorns. "Any blood?"

"I...a little."

A girl, he thought. "I've got some bandages and stuff, if you want."

Finally, a face popped out from behind the burgeoning leaves. Definitely female. Long, dark hair in a braid. Delicate, heart-shaped face. Bright blue eyes. He wasn't that good at guessing kid's ages, but he thought less than ten. And she was looking at him assessingly, with a touch of suspicion he was glad to see. Even if some of it did have to do with the scars.

She was also holding one arm as if she'd been looking at it, and he could see the bloody scratch that ran about an inch up from her wrist.

He didn't know much about kids, just what the son of a friend had taught him, and what he remembered from dealing with kids overseas. But that was different; all they had seen was the uniform, and they'd grown up in a harsh, often cruel manner, far too quickly. But he gave it his best shot.

"Tell you what, why don't I stay right here in the truck, and I'll hand you the stuff to clean that up and stop the bleeding."

She looked at him steadily, tilting her head, still assessing. "You look like Snowball."

He was almost afraid to ask. "Who's Snowball?"

"My teddy bear." He blinked. He'd been called a lot of things, but this was a new one. "He got hurt, too," she went on. "I was afraid he couldn't be fixed, but my mom sewed him up."

"Good for her," he said, not knowing what else to say. But he felt none of the weariness he felt when adults' gazes skated away from him, or worse, when they actually turned away, apparently unable to stand the sight of him. He'd take the honest curiosity of a child any day over that.

"Did someone sew you up?"

"Yes." *Eventually*.

She nodded, then shrugged slightly. "At least it's only the outside. Like Snowball. My mom says his heart is just the same, and that's what matters."

He couldn't stop himself from smiling at that. "Your mother is very wise. Shall we call her to come get you?"

The blue eyes widened. "No. Thanks."

Oops. He couldn't miss the reaction. And he wondered if he'd just wandered into some family chaos he didn't really want to get involved in. But he didn't want the girl to run until that scratch was handled. Some people reacted badly to the substance that coated the bougainvillea stems and thorns.

"Okay, just the first-aid stuff, then," he said easily, and reached back into the compartment behind the driver's seat. She didn't take off, in fact came almost up to the truck, so he guessed the scratch was stinging a bit. He handed her gauze first. She was short enough that she had to reach up for it, but tall enough that it wasn't a stretch.

"Stop the bleeding and clean it up first. Then—" he pulled the tube he'd located out "—put some of this on it. Some people are kind of allergic to the coating on those thorns, so you may develop a rash."

"Ew."

He almost smiled at the way her nose wrinkled. But she took the hydrocortisone cream and smeared some on. Finally, he got out an adhesive bandage that was wide enough to cover the scratch.

"It'd be easier to get it on right if I did it, but I understand that you're probably not supposed to trust strangers."

Again she gave him that assessing look. "I've seen you before. And your truck."

He nodded, unsurprised. "I work around here, mostly."

"You work at Jimmy's house sometimes."

"Jimmy McLane? Yes, I do. His dad's a friend."

"He's a fireman."

Trick question, to find out if he really knew Matt McLane. Oh, this one was smart. Very smart. "Hmm. Can you be both a fireman and a policeman?"

"And he's going to marry some lady named Karen."

"Then Kelly will be very upset."

She smiled then. "You do know him."

"I do." He grinned at her. "Did I pass?"

She grinned back. "You did. You can put the bandage on."

Still smiling, he got out of the truck. He tore the end off the wrapper, then peeled the paper off the adhesive. The top of her head came up to about the bottom of his chest, so he had to bend to place it carefully over the scratch. And all the while he was wondering what she was doing out here, away from most of the tract homes, by herself.

"You go to school with Jimmy?" he asked as he smoothed the tape ends down.

"Yeah. He's a year older than I am, but he got behind because he was sick and all."

"I know," Flynn said, feeling the little tug he always felt when thinking about that, and imagining how much worse it must be for Matt. No wonder he freaked every time Jimmy wanted to do something Matt thought risky. But Kelly, Matt's fiancée and a former championship equestrienne, was helping them both get past that.

So given Jimmy was now—thankfully—nine, that would make her about eight. That fit his first estimate.

"Do you live near Jimmy?"

"Sort of. I live over there." She gestured to the east, toward where the more condensed residential areas were. She clearly wasn't about to tell him exactly where. He wasn't sure her caution was in the right place, but he understood and appreciated it anyway.

"But you're over here, by yourself?"

She looked a little uneasy, but answered. "My mom's sick. She's got the flu. And I have to be super quiet so she can rest, so I decided I could be most quiet if I wasn't there."

It was all he could do not to laugh. "I follow your logic. But did you tell her you were leaving the house?"

"I left her a note," the girl explained. "I didn't want her to worry. But I really wanted to see the dragon."

He went still. "The dragon?"

She nodded eagerly. "Jimmy says there really is one, that that's why this is Dragon Hill." She frowned. "He said his friend Jake made it, but I don't know if I believe that."

"Believe it. He did."

The frown vanished. "You know where it is?"

"I do."

"Will you show me? Pleeease?" She drew the word out cajolingly. "I really, really want to see it."

He gave her a considering look. Felt an odd sort of inner tug at the hopefulness in her eyes. Stalled long enough to make it seem like a harder decision than it was. Because he flat didn't like the idea of her walking home. Wild Oak was a pleasant, peaceful place—one reason he'd decided to stay—but people did tend to race up and down Oak Tree Road a bit, since it was more country than city. So he'd use what little leverage he had to solve that problem.

"I'll make you a deal. I'll introduce you, and you let me take you home after you meet him."

She seemed intrigued by the way he put it. But she was still wary. "I can't get in your truck. I can't ride with anyone my mom hasn't met."

"I'm liking your mom more and more," he said, meaning it. "We can walk. You did, after all."

"Cool!" She was excited now. It fairly sparked off of her. They started up the hill. "Thanks," she added politely.

"You're welcome. He does require the full name of anyone he meets, though."

She laughed, a girlish little giggle that made him smile again. This almost made up for his sucky morning. "Gracie West. It's really Gracelyn, but that usually means I'm in trouble, so I don't like it so much."

He thought it lovely, but understood. "It could be worse.

You could have my name." He was startled at himself; he never brought this up, with anyone.

She danced ahead of him and walked backward as she looked at him. "What's yours?"

"Finnbar. With two Ns."

She blinked. "That's a funny name."

"The original Finnbar was the patron saint of the county in Ireland my grandfather came from."

"Oh. One of those names. Mine was my great-grandmother's. We called her Gran, and I got Gracelyn. I guess it's not so bad." She gave him a mischievous grin. "Compared to Finnbar, I mean."

"Oh, it gets worse," he said sourly.

"How?"

"My last name's Flynn. And my father used to call me Finn."

It took her only an instant to get there. "So you were Finn Flynn?"

"Told you it was worse. That's why I never tell anyone."

Still walking backward with the ease of childhood, she was laughing out loud now. And he didn't mind it a bit. Especially since the exchange had kept her focused on him, and not what was just ahead of them now.

"All right, Miss Gracelyn West," he said formally, "meet The Dragon of Dragon Hill."

He gestured past her and she whirled around. And the look of wonder on her face when she saw the towering creature carved in such beautiful, intricate, real-seeming detail gave him a feeling he hadn't had since...ever.

And scarred, life-battered, battle-hardened, dancing-with-embittered Finnbar Flynn melted a little inside.

CHAPTER TWO

Riley West rolled over in bed, fumbling as she tried to find the thermometer without opening her eyes. She wasn't sure why she was bothering. She knew the fever still had hold, but she was hoping it might have dropped a little. A half a degree would do. She'd been fighting this for two days, hadn't slept more than three hours at a time, couldn't keep food or liquids down, and she was about played out. Not to mention missing both Wednesday and today at work. Work, where the tests they'd acquired had at least proven to her this was only the garden variety of annual flu.

She finally pried her right eye open enough to see the little digital device. Grabbed it and closed the protesting eye again. Pressed the button by feel and stuck the thing in her mouth. While she was waiting for the chirp to indicate it had registered, she listened for other sounds. Nothing. No television going, no sounds of movement. For a moment, she felt badly for the parents for whom that likely meant trouble. With Gracie, it meant she was probably deep in a book. Either a schoolbook where she was dashing off homework that would win her another high mark, or some tome of fiction that was far beyond what the "experts" said should be her reading level.

The chirp came, and she pulled out the thermometer. She pried the other eye open this time—equal time—and looked. And sighed. A tenth of a degree did not signify a break in her view.

She had to get up and head for the bathroom, so she forced the other eye open. She sat up slowly, until she was certain she was steady, then stood up. She sensed she was a little wobbly, but she made it. She avoided looking in the mirror, knowing exactly how bad she looked—no make-up, flushed, her blue eyes bloodshot. She was grateful that she'd braided her hair before she'd collapsed into bed, or the long mass of it would be impossibly tangled by now.

When she was done, she splashed cold water on her face, did it again when it felt good, then straightened. Too quickly, because her head started to spin and she had to grab a towel rack for balance.

Once she was steady again, she headed out into the hall. She doubted she would be functional by tonight, so she would check on Gracie and make sure she knew there was leftover pizza—that's how sick she'd been last night, to resort to that—in the fridge.

Her daughter's room was empty. She paused just a moment to marvel at the wonder that was her child. She had posters on her walls like any preteen girl, but hers were not of the current pop idols, but of her vast array of interests, from the real aurora borealis to an unreal, fantastical dragon. The bookshelf over her small desk was full of the few books she owned—if there was anything she regretted about her finances nearly as much as the condition of her car, it was that she couldn't buy Gracie any book she wanted—and the maximum allowed by the library. The child read so much that researching those books took a great deal of her mother's time. Which she didn't really mind, and since Gracie was so far ahead of her age, Riley often found herself caught up in reading the same books.

She went down the hall to the living room, assuming Gracie was there. It was also empty. A glance into the kitchen told her that was also deserted. For a moment she just stood there, trying to process this through her sluggish brain. And when it finally got there, she felt the sudden acceleration of her pulse. She called out her daughter's name. There was no answer.

Gracie was gone.

She couldn't believe it. She retraced her steps, checking every room including Gracie's closet and the coat closet in the entry. That did it. There was simply no place else in the small apartment for her to be. When Riley finally had to accept the truth, her pulse kicked up again.

She ran back to her bedroom, bouncing off the wall once as her ailing body protested. She had to get dressed and go find Gracie, no matter how she felt. She pulled on a pair of jeans, grabbed the first bra in the drawer and a T-shirt that had seen better days, then went back toward the bed for the running shoes that hadn't seen her in three days.

It was only then she saw the note.

She recognized the writing before she was close enough to read it, knew it was Gracie, and she was able to breathe again. She sank down on the edge of the bed and picked it up in the same motion.

Mom, I know you need quiet, so I'm going over to find the dragon. Be home soon. Love, G.

She wasn't sure if she was more relieved or angry. How like her clever daughter to somehow turn doing what she wanted to do into a good deed. No, that wasn't fair, Gracie was ever kind. She worried about her mom almost as much as Riley worried about her. Leaving the apartment just to get outside was one thing, walking all the way to Dragon Hill, where it was rumored there was an actual dragon, was something else completely.

Shaking off the wave of weariness that had her wanting to crawl right back into bed, she stood up. Not trusting her foggy brain at the moment, she chanted, *driver's license, keys, lock the door, driver's license, keys, lock the door...*

A few minutes later, she was out in the old sedan that had seen better days. She drove slowly, both so she could scan the streets looking for that familiar, beloved, quicksilver child and in deference to her probable slowed reaction time. She was familiar with their neighborhood, less familiar with this area on the outskirts. She knew where the stables were, and had heard that the famous wood sculptor Jake Stone lived out here somewhere, and of course had heard the rumors that billion-aire entrepreneur Shan Kelleher's estate was out here. Rumors that said all of Dragon Hill, that the road was named for, belonged to him.

And that, of course, had started the rumors, particularly popular among the local kids, that there was an actual dragon. Which had in turn set Gracie off on her mission. Her brilliant daughter had the intelligence not to expect a real, fire-breathing dragon, but had somehow hung onto the wishful whimsy that there just might be one. That was one of the things she treasured most about her child, this precious gift that had turned ugliness into beauty.

She turned on to Oak Tree Road, thankful there was little traffic at the moment. Compared to the city she'd come from, which she tried never to think about, there was practically no traffic at all. The small-town atmosphere was one of the main reasons she'd decided the randomly chosen Wild Oak was the place to finally settle. The others were that she loved the countryside feel out here, that the people were friendly, the schools excellent.

And of course, it checked the most important box of all: it was far enough away from everything—and everyone—she wanted to be away from.

She slowed as she neared Dragon Hill Road. She hadn't known, when they'd moved here, that this was the home turf of world-famous billionaire Shan Kelleher. She'd gotten her first clue when she'd driven past the ten-story building downtown discreetly labeled with the Kelleher name. Then someone in the grocery store had mentioned him in conjunction with the Wild Oak Children's Cancer Clinic, and she'd been curious enough to do some research. What she'd found had moved her to tears, and she had sat there for a long time simply hoping the man had found some kind of peace.

Part of that was likely his privacy, she thought now with an inward grimace as she turned onto the road that was essentially the man's driveway. Normally, she would never dream of trespassing, but these were special circumstances. And if Gracie had done so, she was going to get a lecture on private property she wouldn't soon forget. She would—

She slowed even more, frowning at the big, dark blue truck parked at the side of the road. Well, almost at the side, it was mostly on the road itself. But given it was on private property, there wouldn't be much traffic. Besides, the truck, with all the gardening equipment in the back, looked familiar. She'd seen it around, she was sure.

And then she spotted Gracie. Walking along the road. With a man. A stranger. A big, powerful-looking stranger. Her pulse ratcheted up into high gear. She slammed on the brakes, threw the car in park, and jumped out. She started running toward the pair. Gracie spotted her.

"Mom!" the girl cried out, and started running toward her. The man beside her made no effort to stop her, which, had she been thinking more clearly, probably would have relieved her.

Gracie came to a stop in front of her. Riley grabbed her shoulders. "Are you all right?"

"Of course I am. Mom, I got to meet him, the dragon!"

She was all right. She was clearly all right. Relief flooded her. And on its heels came a wave of light-headedness that made the light fade around her. She tried to maintain her balance, to stay upright, but the world had gone crazy and began to spin wildly. She didn't know which way was up any longer. She had to close her eyes because it was making her nauseous.

And then there was a low, deep, comforting voice in her ear.

"Easy, now, I've got you." Then all she knew was a warm presence as a pair of strong arms caught her.

She vaguely heard her daughter's worried voice. "Is she all right, Flynn?"

"She will be," that voice rumbled again. And in that moment, the spinning didn't matter because she knew those arms wouldn't let her fall.

CHAPTER THREE

For a fairly tall woman, Gracie's mother was a lightweight. Which made Flynn wonder when the woman he held in his arms had last eaten a full meal. Or slept. He'd seen some weary eyes in his time, but few worse than this. He couldn't quite believe that in her condition, she'd trekked out in search of the kid.

"How long has she been sick?" he asked Gracie.

"This is the third day," the child said worriedly. "She hasn't eaten, 'cuz if she does, she throws up." That answered that. And probably explained the weakness.

"Has she been to the doctor?"

"No. She said she'd go Monday if she wasn't better."

"Should we call someone? Your dad?"

"Don't have one."

The girl said it easily, as if it didn't matter, so he left it there. "The emergency room isn't too far—"

"No. No."

The woman he was holding stirred, and when he looked down, those thick lashes lifted. Gracie definitely had gotten those blue eyes from her. They were crystalline, and reminded him of a lake he'd seen once, such a deep, bottomless, clear blue that it had struck him speechless.

Of course, that was his natural state most of the time these days. Or it had been until he'd found this little trespasser.

"Please, no," she said this time.

"Easy," he murmured.

"She hates doctors and hospitals," Gracie explained.

Flynn glanced at the girl. "On that," he said wryly, "we agree."

"Home," the woman said, still sounding groggy. Then, after a moment, she added another "Please."

He would have felt better if she saw a doctor right now, but he certainly wasn't going to force the issue. Not when she was at least coherent enough to comprehend what was going on. He looked back at Gracie.

"Can you show me the way?" The girl nodded. "All right. I'll drive her car back."

Gracie frowned. "But how will you get back to your truck?"

For some reason, that that was her first thought made him want to smile. Again. "Same way you got here."

"Oh. Okay."

"If I put her in the back seat, can you watch her and give me directions at the same time?"

The child drew herself up. "I can," she said firmly. He liked that, too.

And so, a couple of minutes later, with the feverish woman in the back, her head in her daughter's lap, he drove the dinged sedan back down Oak Tree Road. And after about the first quarter mile, he was hoping they'd make it; the thing ran like it hadn't seen a wrench since it rolled off the assembly line.

He was making a mental list of the things it likely needed when Gracie called out the first turn.

"Then go down to Grove Street and turn right. It's the apartment building on the right a block down." He heard a murmuring from behind him, but couldn't make out the words, or Gracie's whispered answer.

He'd gone by that building before. "The blue one?"

"Yes."

"All right," he answered. The older, somewhat tired-looking building went with the older, very tired-looking vehicle. "How is she?"

"I think she fell asleep. She said she's sorry for all the trouble, though."

"And what do you say to that?"

He heard the child's sigh. "That's it's my fault. I shouldn't have left her. She'd never leave me if I was sick."

He smiled inwardly. Yet again. "Lesson learned, then."

"No lecture?"

He glanced back over his shoulder at her. "Expecting one?"

"My grandmother would."

He went back to the road ahead. "Last time I checked, I bore no resemblance to anyone's grandmother."

"No, you don't," Gracie agreed. Then, in an impish tone, she added, "You're a lot prettier." If he'd been able to look away, he probably would have gaped at her. "Well, you are," she said, as if he'd done it.

"It's been a long time since anybody called me that." Five years, anyway.

"Then they're stupid," she pronounced.

And suddenly Flynn understood why the woman had dragged herself out of her sickbed to make sure her little girl was all right. Because already he would do the same thing.

RILEY ROUSED in time to welcome the ease of lying down again, and savored the warmth of soft covers being tucked around her.

"Thanks, honey," she murmured sleepily.

"You're welcome," came a deep, slightly rough, and very, very male voice. Her eyes snapped open. It was most definitely a man looking down at her, clearly amused judging by his crooked smile.

"Oh!" If she wasn't already feverish, her cheeks would be flaming now. "I thought...Gracie."

"She's in the kitchen, fixing you something to drink."

Belatedly, the mother wolf in her stirred. She tried to ignore her spinning head. "I need to see her."

"You need to rest," he corrected. "And drink. You're dehydrated. That's probably why you're dizzy."

"And who are you?" She was studying him warily, thinking he looked familiar but unable to place him.

"He's Flynn, Mom. He works at Dragon Hill."

Gracie's voice came from behind him as her daughter came in carrying a large glass. From the slightly greenish cast of the liquid, Riley guessed it was the watered-down sports drink she'd been trying to drink. Watered down because it was expensive, and she was hoping it would last through the cycle of this darn flu. She tried to sit up, to take the glass, but the spinning started again. And the next thing she knew the man was sitting on the edge of the bed, propping her up with a strong hand at her back. She would have protested, but she didn't have the energy, and she knew she probably needed the aspirin Gracie was also holding out.

She managed to get the pills down, and about half of the

glass of liquid. Then the man Gracie called only Flynn eased her back down onto the pillows. For a moment, she stared up at him. He was really almost annoyingly good-looking. Obviously tall and very fit, sandy brown hair that was a little long and tousled, falling down over his forehead in a way she liked, and eyes that could be green, or gold, or some combination she supposed would be hazel.

She started to focus on something about him, but then he turned his head and her muddled brain lost it.

"Thank you," she said, wanting to get that done before she did something stupid like passed out on him. Again.

He gave her a sideways look. "What, no 'honey' this time?" he asked, one brow arching upward. It was so obvious he was teasing her that she couldn't help smiling.

"Sorry. I was a little out of it." Then, very, very belatedly she realized what must have transpired to get her here. And remembered that lovely, safe feeling of being carried by strong arms.

"You were. But that makes you charging to your daughter's rescue even more admirable."

"Given what you've done for us, obviously it wasn't necessary."

"You couldn't have known that." He gave her that crooked smile again. "In fact, you probably should have stayed in the car when you got there, so if I'd made a wrong move with Gracie you could have run me down."

She blinked. "That's...thinking ahead."

"I'm all for using the biggest weapon you've got when necessary," he said. "Now, rest." She couldn't help but smile. He'd sounded almost...concerned. She saw him look at Gracie. "And you'll be here to watch out for her, right?" he said rather pointedly.

"Yes, sir," her daughter, her always sassy, often too smart for her own good daughter said meekly.

"And you've got the number. If you need anything."

"Yes, sir," Gracie said again.

Whoever this Flynn was, he'd made quite an impression, Riley thought as she fought to keep her eyes open. *And not just on Gracie.*

He put a gentle hand on the child's shoulder, nodded, then turned to go. Something caught her heavy-eyed gaze, but before she could focus or fix it in her mind, it all caught up with her and she slid into sleep.

CHAPTER FOUR

"Who was he, Gracie? What were you doing with him?"

It was easier for Riley to stay calm, with her child right in front of her, unharmed. But no matter how sick she'd been, she would never forget that moment when she'd seen her little girl walking with that strange man. She'd barely had a chance to notice him before the panic became too much for her feverish mind to fight off. But she knew enough. She didn't know him. He was with her little girl. Had apparently charmed her.

And he was a man strong enough to pick Riley up as if she weighed nothing.

She was feeling almost herself again, finally. It had only taken two days and almost twenty-four hours of sleep to do it. And she made a mental note to thank their neighbor, Mrs. Kemp. At least, she assumed that's where the nourishing, delicious soup Gracie had warmed up for her had come from. The older woman was so kind, and had seen that Gracie had gotten to school the two days Riley had been too sick to get her there.

"I told you, his name is Flynn." Gracie grinned. "I'd tell you his first name, but he wouldn't like it."

Riley's instincts woke back up in a rush. "He said not to tell me his first name?"

"No, Mom, it's just that with his last name it's kind of silly sounding."

She must have still looked wary, because Gracie, in that manner she had that seemed far beyond her years, said soothingly, "He works for Jimmy's dad, Mom."

"Jimmy McLane?" When Gracie nodded, she felt a rush of relief. Jimmy's dad was a cop; surely he wouldn't hire someone untrustworthy.

Assuming he knows...

"Yeah. I've seen his truck there. He's their gardener. But Jimmy says he used to be in the Army with Mr. Reese."

Well, in the service was another point in his favor but… "Who's Mr. Reese?"

"He's a friend of Jimmy's dad's too," Gracie explained patiently. "He works for Mr. K."

"Oh."

She may not have been here long, but long enough to know there wasn't a bigger name in Wild Oak—heck, on the west coast, maybe the country, maybe half the world—than Shan Kelleher. She hadn't known much about him before they'd moved here, but she'd quickly liked how many referred to him with that familiar, affectionate nickname. No doubt because he'd done so much for their town.

"I like him, Mom. And not because he looks like Snowball."

Riley blinked. Gave her head a sharp shake. Snowball? Gracie was saying this man Flynn looked like her much loved and very worn teddy bear? The somewhat blurry images played back in her mind. She remembered sandy-colored hair, and light eyes, but that was about it. Well, except for the way he moved, with that same sort of male grace and power her father had always had.

And that strength. She was pretty slim, but, at five-feet-eight, she was hardly small. But he'd carried her, all the way back to her car, as if he did such things every day.

Maybe he did. Not people, necessarily but bags of...whatever gardeners used. And tools.

None of which explained why her daughter had made the comparison she had.

"Why are you comparing him to Snowball?"

Gracie's forehead furrowed. She did that sometimes, when Riley was slow on the uptake of whatever it was Gracie's clever mind had latched onto. "Because of his face."

It was Riley's turn to furrow her brow. "His face?" She had only a vague image in her mind, but what she did have seemed quite...nice. No, better than nice. Handsome. As in catch-your-eye, head-turning handsome.

"The scars," Gracie said patiently.

Again she blinked. "He had scars?"

"Like Snowball," Gracie repeated, starting to sound a bit impatient.

"I was really sick, honey, and I couldn't focus too well."

The little girl looked immediately contrite. "I'm sorry I made you worry. But Flynn brought you home safe. He even tucked you in, like you do for me."

Dear God, could this get any more embarrassing? And if she'd looked as bad as she had when she'd finally looked in a mirror this morning...

Riley laughed at herself, finally. If she could start worrying about her appearance, she knew she was feeling better.

"That was incredibly nice of him," she said.

"Yeah." Gracie looked suddenly alert. "We should thank him, shouldn't we? I mean, I don't know how we would have gotten home without him."

Riley sighed. She could hardly fault her daughter for wanting to say thank you. "I suppose so. And Mrs. Kemp too." Gracie looked puzzled. "For the soup."

"But she didn't bring the soup. Flynn did."

Riley blinked. "Your Mr. Flynn brought soup? Here?"

Gracie nodded. "This morning, while you were still asleep. He said he wanted to be sure everything was okay. And he brought the soup. He said he thought it might be good if your stomach was...touchy, I think he said."

Riley let out a long breath. Thank you, it seemed, was definitely in order.

FLYNN GATHERED up the trimmings from the hedge near the road and dumped them into the bin for later composting. Then he stretched, his back letting him know that even in good shape, there was such a thing as too long in one position. In this case, bent over for the lower branches. Not to mention he had debris all over him. And he'd quickly worked up a sweat here in the direct California sun. Even spring could be a baker here, and this sunny Saturday was proving that.

For the first time, he had the thought that maybe he'd bitten off too much here. Not that Shan Kelleher's garden—which consisted of a couple of acres around the house—wasn't turning out exactly as he'd envisioned it. It was, and he was pleased with it. Especially now that spring was here and it was blossoming into exactly what he'd envisioned.

More importantly, Shan really liked it, as did Juliette—

which Flynn had the feeling was even more important these days.

No, it was more that he was starting to wonder if he could keep up with it alone. He was sure Shan would hire help if he asked In fact, he'd suggested it a couple of times as things had started to truly take shape. But Flynn knew he'd gotten spoiled here. He had this little paradise of his own making pretty much to himself, and he didn't really want to share either the garden or the peace he'd found here.

But now it was full-on spring and the whimsical, mystical place he'd created for the dragon of Dragon Hill was going a little bit too wild. It looked great today, but by tomorrow there would be more to do. Shan had wanted it to look untamed, in rebellion against the rigid, geometric formal garden that had been here before. But there was a fine line between untamed and out of control, and Flynn wasn't sure one man could hold that line. Maybe if he quit his other jobs, but if he did that, quit working for John and Jake and Matt, he could all too easily slide into full on hermit-hood, a place he'd very nearly been when John had called him to ask for help keeping Jen safe while he dealt with some leftover business from their time in the Rangers. He would—

The sound of a car approaching cut off his rambling thoughts. A split second later he realized it wasn't just any car, but one he'd heard—and driven—just yesterday. He turned, and sure enough, the worse-for-wear blue compact was headed toward him. From here, he could see two people inside, one much shorter than the other. So Gracie's mom must be feeling better.

He saw Gracie point as she spotted him. The car, still with that semi-rhythmic knock that told him there was a fuel burn problem, slowed, then stopped. Gracie was out immediately and running toward him. There was something about her happiness in seeing him that did crazy things to his insides.

"Hi!" It ended in a yelp as she skidding a little in the loose dirt. He instantly reached out to steady her.

"Hello, Gracie. Did you come to see your new acquaintance? I think he takes offense if you don't, once you've been introduced."

The girl laughed delightedly. "Can I? Later—my mom wants to thank you first." She gestured back toward the car. Flynn looked instinctively. And stared.

This couldn't be the same woman he'd seen just yesterday. She must have been really, seriously sick. Because the woman walking toward them now, tall and lithe and graceful, bore no resemblance to the almost gaunt, hollow-eyed woman he'd carried down this same road just twenty-four hours ago.

He'd known from doing that she was tall, but the dark hair that had been a dull tangle then was a silky, shiny mass that fell well past her shoulders now. And the bloodshot eyes surrounded by dark circles were now clear and bright and vividly blue, just like her daughter's. The other features he'd barely noticed then because he'd been concerned about how feverish she was he noticed now; delicate jaw, lovely, slightly upturned nose, and...a soft mouth now curved into a smile.

She was beautiful.

Damn.

She was looking at him rather assessingly, and he wondered how much she remembered. She came to halt next to Gracie.

"I understand thanks, times two, are in order, Mr. Flynn. For the rescue, and some delicious soup."

"Not necessary," he said, barely managing to get the words out.

"But it is. For me." She sighed audibly. "I haven't been that sick in a long time. Maybe ever."

"You should probably still be resting." *And not here, making me...whatever the hell I am at the moment.*

"I'm fine, truly. And it appears this might be welcome."

She held something out to him, and he only now realized she was holding the insulated thermos he'd put the soup in. Returning it. He took it, realized it was full. He couldn't imagine wanting anything hot at the moment. Looked at her, realized she was smiling. God, that smile...

"I promise, it's not hot."

He blinked. How had she known what he was thinking? He opened the lid, saw a yellowish liquid. Lemonade? He took a sip, and a carnival of flavors—lemon, lime, orange something he couldn't name— danced over his tongue.

"Wow," he said.

"Isn't it good?" Gracie exclaimed. "It's Mom's special punch, and it's got all sorts of stuff in it."

"It is good. Very good." And it was hitting the spot. He took another, much longer drink. "Thank you...sorry, I don't know your name."

She smiled again. And again, it was like a jolt of electricity. "I'm Riley, Riley West."

She held out a hand. He didn't take it, just turned his own hand over so she could see how dirty it was. "You don't want to do that, Ms. West."

"Riley, please. So let's not and say we did?" she suggested.

Let's not because I don't dare. Not when just a smile makes me want to run.

"Something like that," he muttered.

"Do you always work this hard on the weekend?"

He shrugged. "It's just another day. And in spring, keeping up with all this is..."

"An adventure?" she suggested, smiling again. He lowered his gaze because he had to, and merely nodded.

"Gracie says you work for Matt McLane, too."

His head came up. "Yes."

She let out a breath visibly. "Obviously, I'm interrupting you, Mr. Flynn. Sorry. I just wanted to return your thermos, and say thank you. So, thank you."

He watched her turn and start back toward the car. Yanked his gaze away from her when he realized he was enjoying watching her walk from behind a little too much.

"Are you mad at us?"

His head snapped around to Gracie, who was looking up at him with a troubled expression. Something knotted up inside him. "I...no. Of course not."

"You sound like you are."

Sound. Not look. Sound.

Riley had stopped, and come back a few steps, as if she'd reached the end of that maternal tether good mothers seemed to be always on. And she was looking at him as if she'd been thinking the same thing as her daughter. He only realized he'd tightened his jaw when he had to relax it to say, "Sorry. I'm...not used to..."

He gave it up with a disgusted sigh.

"Not used to what?" Riley asked, her voice oddly gentle.

He didn't want to do this. He could feel words bubbling up, wanting to escape, but he did not want to start this. Not with this woman.

"Don't you talk to people?" Gracie asked bluntly

He switched his gaze to the child, who was looking at him

with a simple, open curiosity. And he found he couldn't dissemble or brush her off. "It's more they don't talk to me."

"Why?" the child asked innocently. Honestly.

He found himself unable to answer any other way but the truth. All he could do was try to keep the bitter edge out of the words.

"Because usually that involves looking at me."

CHAPTER FIVE

"Well, that's silly," Gracie pronounced with a disgusted look.

Riley saw him let out a breath, as if he were relieved. She couldn't remember a time when she'd felt worse for another human being. Yet she also knew, somehow, that the very, very last thing this man would tolerate was pity. That was not what she was feeling, but she wasn't sure she could convince him of that.

She had supposed it was a sign of how ill she'd been that she hadn't noticed the scars that day. But now that she was well again and seeing him with clear eyes, she wasn't so sure. Because while shocking at first, especially the missing portion of the top of his left ear, they could hardly overpower the impact of the man himself. How could anybody focus on that small area marred by one of life's cruelties and miss the rest of him, the tall, strong, beautiful rest of him?

And then, belatedly, something struck her. Something Gracie had said.

...he used to be in the Army...

Was that the source of the scars? Had he earned them while serving his country, the country with far too many people, in her view, who took that service for granted and dared to recoil at the evidence that sometimes that service came at a very high cost?

While his attention was on her daughter, she took the chance to really study the left side of his face. Not out of any morbid interest, but because she never wanted to do it to him again. She wanted it to be less noticeable, to matter much less than the fascinating green and gold of his hazel eyes, the way his hair fell forward over his forehead, the breadth of his chest and shoulders...all those things that made him, in her eyes, the most appealing man she'd encountered in a long time. And given what a hard sell she was, that was saying something.

One raised ridge of scar tissue ran from his temple back toward his left ear, or rather what was left of it; the top half-inch or so had been sheared off. The other ran vertically from halfway up his forehead down over his left eye—it was a wonder he hadn't lost it—to his cheek. There it then divided into two paths, one down to his jaw and the side of his neck, the other to the corner of his lips, where it seemed to tweak his mouth into a rather lopsided, wry expression. A rather endearing expression, actually. Or was that just her reaction to the rest of that mouth?

"Sometimes," he was saying to Gracie, "my scars are all people see."

"I'm sorry that some people can be so very shallow," Riley said, meaning it rather fiercely.

At her words—or perhaps her tone—he looked up at her. He didn't say anything more, only shrugged, but she saw that muscle in his jaw jump. He might brush it off, but it had to get to him. How could it not? But his expression was hard to read, because of the pull of the scar. It didn't seem possible he could be at all amused, and yet...

On impulse she said, "So, do people always think you're joking, or not serious?" He drew back sharply. Stared at her. And something in his expression answered her. And she couldn't stop herself from smiling at him. "You use it, don't you? Heck, you'd be crazy not to." His eyes widened, and she knew she'd struck gold. "I almost envy you. People seem to be able to read me like a road map."

"Wanna trade?" He said it so dryly she wasn't sure how to take it. So she went with honesty.

"Sometimes I would. When I get to wishing people would just leave us alone." His gaze narrowed. "But then I realize life is hard enough, and that there's a big difference between being alone and being lonely."

"We're not lonely," Gracie declared. "Because we've always got each other."

And that simply, her little girl nearly put her on her knees. "That we do, sweetie." She didn't even care that her voice had gotten suddenly thick.

"Now that," Flynn said softly, "is something to envy."

Gracie turned back to him, her brow furrowed. "Are you lonely?"

"Sometimes," he said.

Most of the time, was what Riley read in his expression now. And the quirk of the scar couldn't hide it.

"Well now you don't have to be," Gracie said simply. "You've got us."

Flynn went very still. Riley didn't think he was even breathing for a long moment. And she had the distinct impression her baby girl had done to Flynn exactly what she'd done to her a moment ago.

She'd nearly put him on his knees.

You've got us.

Three simple words, uttered with complete honesty and innocence. Gracie couldn't possibly have any idea what they'd done to him.

He didn't dare look at her mother, to see how she had reacted to her daughter's declaration that they were now part of his life. He was still stunned when it hit him at odd moments that he had the Wild Oak Bunch in his life. And it had taken him nearly a year to finally admit that, even to himself.

Now this child was cavalierly announcing it in shy of forty-eight hours.

"Thanks for the cold drink. I...should get back to work."

"But it's Saturday," Gracie explained in a very patient tone.

For a moment that seemed far too long, he couldn't think of anything to say. Could barely remember how to breathe, let alone carry on a conversation. Then, quietly, Riley spoke.

"I don't think the plants know that, Gracie."

The girl's brow furrowed, then cleared. "Oh." As if the whimsical thought had made perfect sense to her. And suddenly he could breathe again.

"Neither does the guardian at the gate," he said.

"Oh!" The girl smiled then.

"And I wouldn't want him mad at me," Flynn added.

The smile became a grin then, and he felt absurdly pleased that he'd managed that.

"Let's let him do what he needs to do, honey," Riley said, and held out a hand to her daughter.

He watched them walk away, back to the car. And wished he could somehow change himself, so that his first instinct wasn't always to get away from people. But he'd always been that way, a little bit, and what had happened to him had only strengthened the urge toward isolation.

He turned back to the hedge and tried to focus, decide if he needed to take a little more off the top. He heard the car start, heard the telltale knocking of the engine. Then a sputter. And silence. He went still. Listened to her try to crank it over a couple more times, until it wouldn't even try.

He closed his eyes for a moment. And had the thought that the universe had a rotten since of humor; when he'd wished he could change himself, this wasn't what he'd had in mind. But he couldn't just leave her sitting there in the car that probably should have died a thousand miles ago.

He walked down the drive toward them. Saw before he'd covered a yard that her forehead was resting against the steering wheel as if the car's failure had been the last straw.

Should we call someone? Your dad?

Don't have one.

Maybe it was the last straw; single motherhood had to be the pits. Gracie had been pretty blasé about it, though. Or maybe you didn't miss what you'd never had. He didn't miss his own dad, who'd been drunk more than he'd been sober most of Flynn's life. But then, he'd been married to his mother, which might drive anyone to drink.…

He tapped on the driver's window and her head came up. His stomach knotted a little at the obvious sign of tears in her eyes. She looked away, as if she had to search for the window control, but he noticed she also took a quick swipe at her eyes as the window went down.

"Pop the hood," he said.

"You don't have to—"

"Just open it, Riley."

She sighed, but she pulled a lever under the dash and the hood popped loose. He poked around, and before he'd been looking a full minute, he had a list of five things that needed to be done.

He heard a car door open and then Gracie was there, stretching up to peer into the engine compartment. "Do you know what's wrong?"

"I know several things that are wrong," he muttered.

Just as he said it, he heard the driver's door open. He wondered if Riley had taken the extra few moments to regain control. She had to know the vehicle had problems. It didn't take much to put the old, tired car together with the least expensive apartment house in town and gather she didn't have the money to spend on costly repairs. He didn't look at her when she came up to the front of the car and stopped beside him.

"How old is the battery?" he asked.

"Too old." He heard the faintest of sighs. "Everything on it is too old."

"It even has a thing in it that plays music on little tape things," Gracie said, obviously amused at the idea.

He looked over at her. "And when you're as old as this car, people will laugh at you when you talk about streaming, because by then people will probably have chips to play music implanted in their heads," he said wryly.

Gracie's eyes widened as she considered this. But Flynn barely noticed because Riley had laughed. A short, startled laugh that sounded as if it were the last thing she'd expected to do right now. He took the feeling that gave him, that he'd been able to make her laugh just now, and tucked it away somewhere deep, thinking it had made getting up this morning worth it.

He checked a few more things, including tilting out the battery so he could read a date sticker on it. Then he ducked out from under the hood and straightened up. "I can give you a jump to get it started now, but I'd say your chances of it starting again on its own are slim. That battery's expiration date was a long time ago."

Any sign of her moments-ago laughter had vanished. And when she spoke, her voice had a stiff, formal edge he didn't like. At all.

"If you could do that, I would greatly appreciate it. I just need to get home."

"But Mom, how will you get to work on Monday?"

"I'll walk."

Her daughter gaped at her. "But that's a long way!"

"So I'll have to start early."

"Where do you work?" Flynn asked.

"It doesn't matter. We've already been too much of a problem for you." Her voice was taking on a frozen tinge now.

He looked at Gracie. "Where does she work?"

"At the Oak Tree Restaurant," the girl answered.

His gaze snapped back to Riley, who was giving her daughter a glare the child seemed to be ignoring. "That's downtown." And the distance was fresh in his mind, having just stopped there for the gift card for Kevin. "Over three miles from your apartment."

She looked back at him then, and he wondered if the color in her cheeks meant she was embarrassed, or angry. But she didn't speak. And he wondered if she might have even been there, when he'd stopped in. If she hadn't already been sick.

"So," he said slowly, and very evenly, "you plan on walking three miles to work a day after being so sick you passed out?"

She grimaced. "Well, when you put it that way..."

"What other way should I put it?"

"Maybe that I have no choice?"

That came out with a little snap. He studied her for a moment. Resisted the urge that prodded at him. Or tried to, because within less than a minute he was giving in.

"I'll get it started. Then follow me."

She blinked. "What?"

"Just follow me around to the other gate, and we'll figure out what the car needs and—"

"I know what it needs, just like I know I can't afford it. Happy now?"

Embarrassed, then. He reached deep for some tact, something he rarely worried about because he rarely spoke to people who didn't already know him.

"No," he said. "I'm not happy. I'm just trying to help. I've got a lot of tools and parts for various vehicles. There might be a thing or two that would work or could be adapted."

"So I'm just supposed to accept that and follow you?"

He sighed. "I'd offer to trade you vehicles, but that thing—" he jerked a thumb toward his tool-laden truck "—is pretty big if you're not used to driving one."

Her eyes widened at his words, and she mutely shook her head. Gracie turned to look at her mother rather mutinously. "Mom, seriously? He offered you his truck. He's trying to help."

"Gracelyn," she retorted in the same tone, "we don't even know him. What have I told you about strangers?"

"He works for Jimmy's dad, and Mr. K. He's not one of *those*, Mother."

Flynn didn't know whether to be amused by her tone, wary of the way she said "mother," or bothered that she knew what one of "those" apparently meant. And somehow that she used the local nickname for Wild Oak's resident billionaire seemed significant. She was a smart, smart girl. But he already knew that from how she spoke.

"She's right to be careful, Gracie. People aren't always what they seem."

Riley went rigid, and his gaze shifted to her in time to see something flash in those blue eyes. Something dark and painful. Sometime, somewhere, she'd learned that the hard way. And that bothered him more than it should.

"But you are," Gracie insisted. "You really do want to help."

He wasn't sure he really did, only that he'd felt compelled. But he didn't say that. "Yes. But it's up to your mother."

"And me," Gracie said stubbornly. She shifted her gaze back to her mother. "I don't want you to get sick again. Remember when I had that flu? How you made me stay home an extra day after I was feeling good again?"

Riley looked at the girl wryly. "You never forget anything, do you?"

Gracie grinned at her then. "Nope."

Flynn smothered a smile. This kid was something else. "Since it has to be done either way, why don't I get you started, while you decide?"

He was just coming back from his truck with the jumper cables he'd dug out when he heard Gracie exclaim, "I know! Call Jimmy's dad. He'll tell you it's okay."

"Gracie, I don't want to bother—"

"He's not working today, I know, 'cuz Jimmy said they were going out to the stables with Kelly."

"I don't even have his number, honey."

"But Mr. Flynn does—" her gaze switched to him "—don't you?"

"Uh...yes. I do."

The idea of her calling Matt and asking if he was trustworthy unsettled him a bit. Not to mention what Matt would think. But under the child's steady stare he surrendered, pulled out his phone and called up the number.

CHAPTER SIX

A bit to Riley's surprise, Matt McLane knew who she was before she even explained that her daughter went to school with his son.

"You're Riley, from the Wild Oak Restaurant, right?"

"I...yes." She had, in fact, waited on him a couple of times, and later he and his fiancée, Kelly, who she knew was a nationally famous rider from the nearby stables, but she hadn't expected him to remember that.

"Flynn?" he asked when she explained why she'd called. "Absolutely you can trust him, with anything. He's the kind of guy you want on your side. He was a hero, Riley. He got those scars fighting for us."

"I...guessed that."

"Another friend of ours was the commander of his team in the Rangers." She noted both that he said "ours"—clearly he, Jimmy, and Kelly were already an inseparable unit in his mind —and the identification of what Flynn had done in the military. Weren't the Rangers the guys who had been in front on D-

Day? "John says he was the toughest, fiercest guy in their unit. But that he was always meant for something else. He said he grew things even in the middle of the desert."

"So now he grows things here," she said slowly.

"Yes. And fixes things. You—and your little girl—couldn't be in better hands."

Riley found herself smiling when she heard Jimmy's voice in the background complaining that he and Gracie were almost the same age, and he wasn't "little."

"Good to know," she said, meaning it.

"But," he added almost sternly, "if you needed help, you could have called us. Gracie knows our number from Jimmy."

She felt her cheeks heat. Again. It seemed to be her lot today. "I...thank you, Matt."

When he went on, his voice was back to its normal, cheerful tone. "But I'll gladly hand this one off to Flynn. He's a lot better mechanic than I am."

She was still smiling when she ended the call. She barely knew Jimmy's dad, yet he'd made her feel so much better. She handed the phone back to the man beside her, wondering if there had been more to his suggestion she use it than just that he already had the number called up. If perhaps he'd guessed her phone time was limited by how much she could afford, which wasn't much.

Flynn's face was unreadable as he took the phone. Well, except for that slightly amused tweak the scar gave his mouth.

"That was...quite a recommendation, Mr. Flynn."

"Just Flynn. Matt's a good guy. One of the best. He went through hell and came out the better for it."

She gave him a curious look. "And you? How did you come out after your hell?"

He didn't answer her, just went very still. She didn't blame him; it was a very presumptuous question. But something in those gold-flecked eyes told her he might still be in that hell. Something she could relate to.

IDIOT.

The word kept repeating in Flynn's mind as he drove back down to Oak Tree Road, then made the right turn.

He doubted Shan would be upset if they'd gone through the main gate, by the dragon, and he wasn't here to see anyway, but Flynn still wasn't quite comfortable treating the entrance to the easy-going—at least with the Wild Oak Bunch —billionaire's estate like his own personal property. Besides, his place was much closer to the west fence; going through the back gate, they'd be there in thirty seconds instead of the meandering couple of minutes it took coming from the main gate.

"Don't shut it off yet," he called out to Riley as he stopped his truck out of the way. He'd already hit the opener so the main garage door was lifting. Gracie was apparently in no mood to wait, and hopped out of the car to run and look before he even got over there.

Her eyes widened at the array of machines. "Wow! Is all that yours?"

"Mr. Kelleher's, actually. I just run them for him."

"What do you do with them?"

"Generally mow, dig, build, and tow."

She looked at the machines thoughtfully for a moment. Then, correctly, she pointed at the mower and said "Mow," the backhoe, "Dig," the moveable scaffold, "Build," and the tractor, "Tow."

He couldn't help it, he grinned at her. She grinned proudly back.

Riley had gotten out now, leaving her car running—such as it was, with that knocking—and came over in time to hear the exchange. He glanced at her—quickly, since if he really looked at her he seemed to forget whatever he'd been about to say— and said, "Let me move a couple of things to make room, then you can pull it in and shut it down."

"All right."

Once he had that done, she pulled it into the emptied space. And hesitated. He didn't blame her.

"You'll get home, one way or another," he promised, and couldn't help noticing her rueful smile as she reached for the key and turned the ignition off.

"You sure you remember about cars this old?" she said as she got out. Her tone was half as rueful as that smile, half-teasing.

"I've worked on vehicles old enough to be this one's grand-parents." Gracie laughed, but Riley went still. Again, he barely glanced at her. But it was enough to see that look flash in her eyes again, that dark, painful...something.

"Cars don't have grandparents, silly," Gracie said.

"Maybe that's why they keep breaking down," Flynn joked, trying to push back the feeling that look of pain had given him.

Riley turned away this time, and he wondered what it was in what he'd said that had made it worse.

As he opened the hood, Gracie looked around the garage again. Then she darted over and grabbed the stool from under the main workbench and brought it back to stand on so she could see better. Flynn looked at her. "There's a TV and computer upstairs in my place. Wouldn't you rather be doing that?"

Gracie shook her head firmly. "No. I want to watch."

Riley turned back then. "You live upstairs here?"

He glanced at her. Nodded. "Shan's idea. It's handy. And a lot nicer than the place I was in before this."

"It's...good of Mr. Kelleher to do that."

"He's a good guy."

"So I hear."

"His little boy wasn't as lucky as Jimmy," Gracie said. "He must have been very sad."

"Very, very sad," Flynn agreed as he started checking hoses, knowing his boss had almost broken under the loss.

"Is he happier now?" the girl asked, and the hopefulness in her voice, for a man she'd never met, tugged at Flynn.

"He is. He...found someone who makes him feel a lot better."

"Good," Gracie said with a nod and a smile. *Oh to be young again, and have your world righted so easily...* "What's that?" she asked, pointing.

"A distributor." He thought for a second. "Its job is to send electricity from the ignition to the spark plugs." He decided to leave it there for now; she didn't want a course on the internal combustion engine.

"Do spark plugs spark?"

He couldn't help smiling again. Maybe she did want it. "It's more like...a tiny bolt of lightning."

The girl's eyes widened. "Really?"

"That's what they're supposed to do. Some of these are suspect, though."

"Is that what's wrong with it?"

"Maybe partly. I won't know until I take them out."

"This is starting to sound really complicated," Riley said, sounding worried. "And I don't want—"

A rather loud, oddly rhythmic drumming sound stopped her. He wiped his hands off on the rag he'd grabbed and pulled out his phone. He glanced at her and half-shrugged. "It's a ring I can hear over whatever machine is running," he explained, wondering why. Then he looked at the screen. And blinked.

"My boss," he said.

"Mr. K?" Gracie said with a grin. "Maybe he heard us talking about him."

"He's got good ears, but Idaho's a bit far even for him," Flynn said, deadpan. Gracie laughed once more, and Flynn felt that crazy tightening in his throat again as he tapped to answer the call.

"Hey, Flynn." He wasn't quite used to the lighter, easier tone of Shan's voice yet. He was beyond happy for the guy, but it still brought on a tinge of wistfulness for something he himself would never have.

"Hey, boss," he said, even though Shan had told him repeatedly to use his first name. "How's Idaho?"

"Gorgeous. And friendly, and nice. Wish I could transport the whole Wild Oak Bunch here. Except then we'd have to change the name." Shan sounded like he was half serious, but before Flynn could ponder that he got to the point of the call. "I've got a delivery coming that's apparently going to arrive earlier than I expected. Probably this afternoon. Can you keep an eye out and get it inside in case that rain really shows up?"

"Of course."

"Thanks. So who was laughing?"

Well, he hadn't expected that. "I...it's a neighbor kid. Her mom's car broke down out front."

"So you're helping out?"

He didn't sound upset, although Flynn hadn't really thought he'd be. "Trying to. I'll get back to the hedge—"

"Don't worry about it," Shan said, cutting him off. "You already give me twelve-hour days, plus weekends, for crying out loud. So, the car's in bad shape, huh?"

"Very."

"And a new one isn't in the picture?"

"Along with a lot of other things, no," he said, carefully not looking at either Riley or Gracie.

"Good that you're helping, then. Hang on a sec." Flynn heard him talking to someone else—Juliette, he guessed, since they were never far apart these days—and then he was proved right when he heard Juliette's voice next.

"She's a neighbor?"

"Yes. Her daughter goes to school with Jimmy."

"Oh! Then loan her my car, until hers is fixed."

He blinked. "What?"

"You know, that lovely little blue thing Shan insisted I get?"

"I know, but—"

"We're not there, so obviously I don't need it. Tell her I remember too well what it's like to drive a junker. The keys are on the rack by the door into the garage."

"I'll...suggest it."

"She's got some pride left, huh?"

"Barely, I think."

"Take care of her, Flynn. That's what neighbors do, right?"

He had to swallow again, wondering what the hell was wrong with him today. "Shan is a lucky man, Juliette."

"Yes, I am," Shan said, obviously having taken the phone back. "You see why I love her."

"Yes."

"Okay, do whatever you need to, buddy. Help however you can. If you need parts, put it on the grounds account. See you when we get back. "

"Yes," he said, barely managing not to add "sir", which genuinely irritated the man.

He ended the call, and looked at Riley. He didn't have the slightest clue about how to do this without her pride getting in the way. He had his marching orders, but he needed time to think.

Marching.

"Let's take a walk up to the house," he said.

Riley's eyes widened. "Mr. Kelleher's house?"

He nodded. "I need to check on something, and then I'll get started on doing what I can on the car."

"You don't have to—"

"Yes, I do. Even if I didn't want to," he said with a smile, "my boss made it clear."

She blinked. "Mr. Kelleher said you should work on my car?"

"Among other things. Come on, it's a nice walk."

"Let's go, Mom! I want to see the garden. You can only see a little of it from the gate, but it looks so cool!"

Still, Riley hesitated, so he said carefully, "Or we can drive up in my truck, so you don't get tired." She drew herself up straight and frowned at him. Somehow he'd known she wouldn't like that. "I mean, after you being sick."

"No. That would be silly. And wasteful."

He winced a little inwardly at this further evidence that she was quite used to doing without.

"Come *on*, Mom!" Gracie said.

She gave in finally, and they started walking.

And Flynn started thinking about how on earth he was going to sell her on taking Juliette's generous offer of driving her nearly brand-new car.

CHAPTER SEVEN

"Wow. Wow."

Gracie just kept saying it as they went, and she spotted a little hidden recess here, a niche there, each with a different array of plants and blooms, as if each had its own theme. Riley could see the house from here, could see that they were walking around the corner of it. But it was the garden that captured the eye and almost all her attention with an explosion that screamed spring. It seemed to run through every possible color both in flower and foliage. It was, in a word, enchanting.

And Gracie was clearly enchanted.

They came even with the back of the house and the girl slowed to a snail's pace. Riley watched her girl turn slowly three hundred and sixty degrees, staring at the little haven he'd built here. "This is...this is so cool!"

Riley couldn't argue with her daughter's assessment. Just outside the back of the house, where the bank of three sets of glass French doors must make it both visible and easily accessible from inside, was a cool, shady haven that was so calming it amazed her.

There was a theme here, too, she noticed. Reds, all shades, contrasting with deep green leaves. A gracefully curving line of shrubs exploding with bloom, enclosing a room-sized space that was carpeted with rich green grass, neatly trimmed up to the edge of a small, amazingly natural-looking water feature, that looked for all the world as if a stream had been hidden behind the plants all along, and had chosen here to flow into view and down three rocky stair steps.

Above it all was an arbor, with all sorts of trailing plants, including several thin, frothy looking things with long, trumpet-shaped blooms in a brilliant shade of red orange. The feel, the shape, overall and of the blossoms and leaves, of the occasional pot, and the placement of the plants, and over there the nook that held a porch-style swing under the most riotous burst of color yet, it was all...perfect.

"You did this?" Gracie demanded, before Riley could ask—hopefully with more politeness—the same thing.

Flynn nodded. "There was a formal garden here before. All straight lines and precision. My boss didn't like it, said it was too perfect."

"No," Gracie said firmly. Her daughter was nothing if not certain of her opinions. "*This* is perfect."

He looked pleased, and that pleased Riley. She liked that a child's compliment meant something to him.

"Rumor has it," he said to Gracie in a mock whisper, "that that guy at the gate likes it too, and comes up here to sleep at night."

Her daughter's eyes widened. "Is that why the grass is here, so it's soft?"

"Yep," Flynn said. "Good guess."

Riley had no idea what they were talking about, but she'd never seen Gracie like this before, so utterly entranced.

"What are those plants?" the child asked, pointing up at the frothy-looking things, thin strands of green holding the explosion of tubular flowers.

"Those are *russelia equisetiformis.*" When Gracie's brow furrowed he laughed. "The more friendly name is the firecracker plant."

"Oh!" Gracie's grin was back.

Riley found herself smiling as well. "They do look like fireworks."

"And those are for him, too," he said, pointing at the meandering, lush border plants with the oddly shaped leaves and the overflowing red blooms. "They're begonias."

"That's a funny name," Gracie said.

"Yes, but they're a special kind. They're dragon wing begonias."

Gracie's eyes widened. "Really?"

Flynn nodded. It was amazing, how patient he was with her. But perhaps he just enjoyed showing off his clearly brilliant work.

"Can you figure out why they call them that?" he asked the girl.

Gracie walked quickly over to look at the plants that came up past her knees. Riley truly liked the way he asked her questions, guided her toward figuring things out on her own. As if he knew how smart the child was, and wanted to nurture that.

Which was a ridiculous thought about a man she'd just met.

But also the man who had literally carried her to bed when she'd been half-unconscious.

"Thank you," Riley whispered to him.

He looked at her as if puzzled. "For what?"

"Showing her this. Being so kind to her." She gestured back the way they had come, toward where her dead vehicle sat. "For everything."

He merely shrugged as if it were nothing, when in fact it had been a long time since anyone had helped her this much.

Well, maybe more accurately, a long time since she'd been cornered into accepting this much help.

"Is it okay to touch them?" Gracie asked from a few feet away as she studied the plants.

"It's fine," Flynn called out to her. "For both of you."

Riley smiled at that, and glanced at him. And her breath caught in her throat. He was on her left, so as he watched her daughter the unscarred side of his face was toward her. And he was...stunning. Way beyond merely handsome or good-looking. This, this was the face she remembered from the moments before she'd fallen into that fevered sleep. And she couldn't help wondering if that had made it even harder to accept what had happened to him.

"It's the leaves!" Gracie yelped it with excitement as she whirled to look back at Flynn. "It's the leaves, isn't it, the two of them together, they look like a pair of wings!"

He looked pleased but not at all surprised. "Exactly. You're as smart as I thought you were."

Gracie looked as if she'd been given an unexpected but much-wanted gift. The expression on her little girl's face squeezed at something inside Riley; she didn't see this look often enough. Gifts were few and far between in their lives. But by the same token, she was proud that Gracie felt that way about something as ethereal as a compliment from a near stranger.

Although it was quite clear already that she didn't consider Flynn a stranger at all.

"There's another plant that looks like these, but the leaves are rougher around the edges. Sort of feathery. That's why they call those angel wing begonias."

"I'll bet they're pretty," Gracie said. "But he wouldn't want them in here."

Flynn laughed. It was a great laugh, even if it did sound a bit rusty. "No, he wouldn't."

"You picked the right ones."

"Thank you," he said with a bow of his head that was almost courtly. And Riley had the strangest feeling he felt the same way about this compliment from a child. And to her, that said a great deal.

And the two things together made her feel ridiculously light, given she had a dead car parked over the hill.

"Okay, you two," she said, "I give. Who is this 'he' you keep talking about?"

Flynn blinked. Gracie ran back from the plant border of the cozy, welcoming space. "She hasn't seen him, Flynn! Can we show her?"

He looked a little taken aback at Gracie's casual utterance of that "we." He seemed to hesitate for a moment, then nodded. "Sure."

"Come on, Mom!" her daughter exclaimed excitedly, grabbing her hand. Then she stopped, and rather sheepishly looked at Flynn. "Oops. I don't know which way from here."

Flynn wasn't sure why he didn't just point, but the next thing he knew he was saying, "There's a map to a shortcut, if you look carefully."

Gracie's eyes widened. "A map?"

"If you can figure out what to look for."

The girl instantly started looking. And a little to his surprise, so did her mother. And it was her mother who realized it first.

"The firecrackers," she said. And Flynn caught himself smiling yet again.

Gracie looked up at her mother's words. Looked at him. Then looked around again. And suddenly lit up. "It's a trail! The firecrackers mark the trail!"

"They do."

She was off in a flash. Riley went rigidly still. "Gracie!"

"She'll never be off the property. She'll be fine." Then he grimaced and started after the girl. "Unless she doesn't watch the ground and trips and falls."

He was two steps away before Riley moved. They were walking quickly, although he shortened his stride a bit so she didn't have to work quite so hard to keep up.

"I suppose you think I'm a helicopter parent," she muttered as they went.

"I don't give opinions on parenting."

She gave him a sideways look. "Because you're not one?"

He nodded. "Closest I've ever been was when I watched a baby being born last year."

"That doesn't stop most people," she said dryly.

"That's the other reason I don't."

"I wish more people would see it that— Oh, my gosh."

She sounded more than a little breathless, and he smiled. She'd spotted the dragon. An instant later, Gracie called out, "Hurry up, Mom! You've got to see him up close!"

"She's right about that," Flynn said. "He's even more impressive up close."

She didn't even look at him, just kept heading for the massive sculpture. And when she got there, he saw her tentatively reach out to touch it with a delicate forefinger. As if she hadn't believed it was real.

Gracie spun around and he could almost see the words about to spill out. But he shook his head, put a finger to his lips, and somewhat to his surprise, the girl stayed silent. But she came over to him, while Riley slowly, very slowly, walked around the dragon, looking up and down, taking in every detail. The child looked up at him questioningly.

"We shouldn't interrupt them getting acquainted," he whispered.

"Oh," Gracie whispered back, then nodded as if that made perfect sense and turned back to watch her mother. And Flynn wondered what it must be like to have a mother like that, one who allowed herself to get caught up in her child's fantasy so completely.

Especially when she was the kind of woman men had fantasies about.

CHAPTER EIGHT

"Who?" Riley asked, barely aware of how breathless she sounded. She wouldn't have cared anyway; nothing mattered in this moment but this magnificent piece of work. If the creature who towered over her had let out a breath of fire and smoke, she would not have been in the least surprised.

"Local guy. Jake Stone."

She blinked. "Jake Stone. *The* Jake Stone?" She'd read an article about him just last week, in a national magazine.

"The horses!" Gracie exclaimed. "Isn't that the name on the horses?"

"At the Atrium," Riley said, remembering the metal plaque on the amazing sculpture of three horses swirling up out of a block of wood in the lobby of the building that housed Gracie's pediatrician. Then she looked back at Flynn. "He did this?"

Flynn nodded.

"And he's local?"

"That baby I mentioned? It was his."

She blinked. "You mean the one you saw being born?"

He nodded, gave her a smile that had a wry twist to it. "Delivered by my former team leader, in the Rangers. In Jake's house, after his wife slipped and fell."

She was staring at him now. "He actually delivered the baby?"

"He did. We all had some basic medical training, but John…well, he'd done it before, under less than optimum conditions. So I bailed and made him do it."

Riley shook her head slowly in wonder; what they taught our guys—and the uses they put it to—was amazing.

"Babies are yucky," Gracie announced. "They make a lot of noise."

He smiled at her. "Cammie can make noise, all right. But nobody minds because she was early, and we were all just glad she's all right."

"We?" Riley asked.

"The Wild Oak Bunch."

She blinked again, startled. "Now that's a name with a story attached."

He looked as if he regretted having said it, and gave her a one-shouldered shrug. "It's just some people who…connected. And clicked. Get together every month, at least."

"And Jake Stone is one of them?"

He nodded. " And Rachel, Jake's wife, works with my boss's clinic. And Jake's sister is married to John."

"Your Army buddy?"

"He's a lot more than that, but yes." He glanced at Gracie, who was on the other side of the dragon, inspecting the wing Jake had somehow managed to make look real, with bones and veins. "Jimmy's dad and his fiancée, too."

"And what about you, Mr. Flynn?"

He lowered his gaze, as if embarrassed. "Sometimes," he said.

"Only sometimes by your choice?" she guessed.

He let out an audible breath. "Yeah. It's...harder these days."

"For me, it would be hard to be around all that together when I'm...not," she said quietly.

"Exactly," he said, sounding a little grim. Yet at the same time, some tiny part of his mind was leaping at the fact that she, too, was apparently unattached.

"And thus endeth the third degree," she said, trying to lighten it up. "That is, except for one question."

His mouth quirked. "I'm almost afraid to ask. What?"

"Who made the soup?"

She'd startled him then. "Uh...Juliette. Shan's lady."

"Whew." She let out an exaggerated sigh of relief. He gave her a questioning look. "If you'd said you'd made it, I was going to have to kidnap you and hold you for a soup ransom. That was the best I've ever had."

He burst out laughing, whether at the silliness of the words themselves or merely at the idea she could even make him breathe hard, let alone kidnap him, she didn't know. And then he looked so startled, as if stunned at his own laughter, that her chest tightened in response.

And she quickly and completely denied that anything else had popped into her mind at the thought of making him breathe hard.

"Speaking of Juliette," he said when he'd recovered, "she pretty much gave me an order. We need to head back to the house."

She'd already taken him away from his work and didn't want to make it any worse, so she called Gracie to come with them. But when they arrived back at the large, timber-frame style house he went around to the expansive garage. He unlocked a small side door, and flipped on a light inside.

Riley didn't know what she'd expected. Some billionaire's collection of expensive, luxurious vehicles, she supposed. But that wasn't what she saw. There was one under a cover that she suspected might fit that bill, but next to it was a blue pickup truck that was probably older than Gracie. And next to it a much newer vehicle, also blue, but it wasn't some top of the line European import either, but rather a compact SUV that ran more to utility than bells and whistles.

She had the feeling this garage probably said more about Shan Kelleher than just about anything.

"Gracelyn," she said warningly when it appeared the ever-curious child was going to go tug at that car cover. With a sigh, the girl came back as Flynn walked over to another door that she guessed led into the house. She held back her own curiosity; she'd never set foot in a billionaire's house, but she wasn't going to start with Flynn's boss. He reached inside the door without actually going inside, and came back with a set of keys on a ring with a fob that matched the SUV.

"I said she gave me an order," he said, sounding a bit doubtful. He held out the keys. "Take these."

Her brow furrowed, but she took them. She wondered what he needed her to do. She'd do it, if she could, he'd already helped her more than she had any right to expect.

"I'll open the door for you, and you can back it out."

Her gut immediately curled up in protest. Drive one of Shan Kelleher's cars, even just backing it out of the garage?

"Please, Riley," he said, sounding a bit wary. Or maybe weary. Either way, she needed to conquer her qualms.

So a couple of minutes later, she was sitting in the new

vehicle and easing it out into the driveway. She could see now it was indeed nearly brand-new; the odometer read less than five hundred miles, and it still had that new car smell. She recognized it because she'd had a new one once. In that other life.

"Now what?" she asked, and was startled when, in answer, he directed Gracie into the back seat while he got into the passenger seat.

"Drive us back to my place," he said, pointing at a narrow gravel track headed back that way.

Before she could ask anything more, he was pointing out the various controls: parking brake, hatch release, sound system, and advised her the headlights were on automatic, but a push forward on the lever would bring on the high beams.

"The windshield wipers are rain-sensing, but if for some reason it doesn't work, and that rain they're predicting actually arrives, the control is there," he said, indicating the lever opposite the headlight control. "And that button," he said, gesturing upward, "opens the main gate."

She was about to ask why on earth she needed to know all this for a drive of maybe a quarter mile, but then they were there.

"Move over anything you need out of your car," he said. Then, to Gracie, "You, too."

The girl's eyes widened. "We're taking this car?"

"No, Gracie, don't be…" Her voice trailed off when she saw Flynn's expression. "No," she said. "No, no, no."

"That was the order," Flynn said. "Give you her car until yours is fixed."

"That's crazy. She doesn't know me, she's never even met me."

"True. But she knows you're a neighbor."

"I don't want the responsibility of her brand-new car."

"She said to tell you she remembers too well what it's like driving a junker."

She blinked. Shan Kelleher's girlfriend drove a piece of junk car? "She does?"

"It's a long story, but yes, she does." The unscarred corner of his mouth quirked upward. She wondered, inanely, if the injury had damaged the nerves on the other side. "And if you don't take it, she'll be upset. She's only just found level, so I don't want her upset."

He was worried about his boss's girlfriend? Sure, a certain amount of that made sense, but there was something in his voice when he said it.

"You…care about her?"

He gave her a quizzical look. "More worry. She worked incredibly hard to make up for an understandable mistake she made once. She's a good person."

She was sure then, that he'd meant just that. There was no romantic interest there. And why that had even occurred to her she didn't want to think about just now.

"So are you," she said quietly, as certain as she could be about it. Which meant only she would be more surprised than usual if or when she found out she was wrong.

He looked a bit startled at her words, and only shrugged before adding, "She makes my boss very happy, and that's worth a lot to me."

She could only imagine keeping a boss the likes of Shan Kelleher would be worth a lot. She'd always heard he took care of his people, and it seemed it was true.

Then, in an obvious change of subject, he gestured toward her car. " Give me your number, and I can call you when it's done. Unless I find something deeper than I expect wrong, like a damage to a piston or cylinder, you can have it back in a couple of days."

"Darn," Gracie said, eying the pretty new vehicle. "I wish we could have a car like this."

"Well, we can't," Riley said briskly. She didn't dwell on that fact, not when she was trying to focus on the fact that this was apparently happening no matter what she thought about it.

"I know, I know," Gracie said, "we're poor."

That snapped her out of her thoughts. "Gracelyn West, we are not poor," she said sternly. "We're lucky to be living here. Compared to a lot of the world, we're richer than they can ever hope to be."

The girl grimaced. And then Flynn spoke, softly. "She's absolutely right, Gracie. I've seen some of those places, and they'd think that car of yours luxurious compared to walking miles just to get water."

Gracie's eyes widened. "They have to walk to get water?"

"Some do. And there are places where rat meat is as close as they come to food."

The child's face screwed up and she let out a long "Eww!"

Riley studied him while he watched the child, grateful for the way he had of making the point in ways the girl clearly understood. Gracie ran over to gather what things she had in their car to move them over to this temporary bit of luxury, while Riley gave Flynn the number to her bare-bones cell phone.

"I'll move your purse and stuff, too, Mom," she called out.

"Thanks, honey."

Flynn was still watching Gracie with that bemused expression. This time, Riley was on his left, so the scarred side of his face was toward her. She felt an odd sort of ache inside, thinking of what he'd gone through, how close he must have come to dying.

"Pretty, isn't it?" he said. Clearly he'd known perfectly well she was staring at him.

She went with what was in her heart. "As badges of honor go, it's beautiful."

His head snapped around. His gaze was suddenly intense, and she had the feeling she was getting a glimpse of the man who'd earned that badge of honor, and probably more.

"I'd prefer honesty," he said flatly.

"That's what you got," she said sweetly. "Did it affect your hearing?"

He blinked. Drew back slightly. And again she thought she saw the undamaged corner of his mouth twitch. "No," he said.

"Just your vision, then. Made you see everything in the worst way."

She was sure about the mouth twitch this time. "Ouch. I heard that fine."

"Just wondered, with the piece missing." If he wanted blunt honesty, he'd get it.

He shrugged, flicked a finger at the top of the ear in question. "They left enough to keep my sunglasses on. That's all that matters."

She couldn't help it, she laughed. And after a moment, he smiled.

And that might seem a small victory to some, but to her, it had somehow become amazingly important.

CHAPTER NINE

F lynn started the motor and let it run. He listened closely —smothering a smile as the memory of Riley asking him in that overly sweet voice if his hearing had been damaged— for any sign of the knocking, but heard nothing. He'd added some octane booster, and figured he'd leave her some in the trunk, guessing that buying high-octane fuel wasn't on her list of things she could spend money on. A complete new set of plugs, carefully gapped, a little work on the distributor, and some work on the timing, and it seemed to be running smoothly. With the new battery he'd picked up and installed this morning, and the multiple hoses he'd replaced, she should be okay for a while. As long as that radiator didn't go on her; it was on the edge. He'd done what he could, but eventually the thing was going to require some major work. More than the vehicle was worth.

Some would say what he'd done yesterday and today was more than it was worth. But when it was all you had, it was worth a lot more.

He wondered how they'd ended up in such tightened

circumstances. Why Gracie's father wasn't in the picture, at least financially. How could a man have a daughter like that, clever, quick, smart, and beautiful, and not want to see her taken care of? He might not be father material himself—hell, no might about it—but he knew enough to know you saw to your own. As Jake did. As John would.

His mind wanted to career down a path he'd been avoiding for weeks now. Down the path laid out by that man he respected more than anyone, his former team leader, the man who had asked such a simple thing of him. A simple thing, and yet he recoiled from it as if it had been a live grenade with the pin already pulled.

We want you to be the baby's godfather, Flynn.

He knew he'd stared in shock, able only to shake his head. *No. No, no, no, you don't.*

We do.

I can't.

And then John had pulled out the big gun and sicced Jen on him.

You're the one we want, Flynn. The only one we trust to help keep him safe if anything should happen to us, to teach him how to be the kind of man his father is.

He couldn't. He just couldn't. Because if he said yes, if he committed to that, then he was committing to being around for the long haul. And he hadn't completely settled that in his mind. Not that he was going to eat a bullet, as he'd once come so close to doing, but...sometimes, being around people was just too much. Sometimes, he just wanted to go hide somewhere, maybe up in the mountains, where he didn't have to see anyone. Or rather, where they didn't have to see him.

He slammed the hood down hard, then regretted it; on a

car held together with a wish and prayer, it didn't do to bang it around like that.

Think about something else. Anything else.

Even as he thought it, he called himself a coward; there were vets much worse off than him, he had no right to whine. He had a decent life here. Work to do, work that he actually liked. And he had somehow acquired some good people around him. He had all his limbs, his brain still functioned— except for the occasional blip the docs had told him would fade in time—and he could see and hear.

And his mind landed, as it had many times since they'd left on Saturday, about the way Riley had actually teased him about his ear. No one ever did that, not even John. He hadn't realized how much easier it made things.

And what she'd said, about the scars being a badge of honor...it had had the ring of heartfelt truth. And over the years since it had happened, he'd learned to tell the difference between that and platitudes uttered because the person couldn't think of anything else to say.

He found himself smiling even now, and some of the tension in him eased. Satisfied with the way the car was running now, he went to shut it off. Remembered that it was down to a quarter tank now, and decided to go fill it up. And maybe when he got back here he'd wash the thing; it was pretty bad. There was no place she could do it herself at the apartment, and obviously paying for a wash wasn't in the budget either. He could vacuum it out, too, although the inside wasn't too bad. Hell, he had the stuff, he could throw a coat of wax on it, too. If he put enough into it, it might look halfway decent by the time he was done.

Now that he had a plan, he went after it with full intent. He drove the long way around to the gas station he preferred, because it took him on the winding, hilly road Shan liked to roar down on his bike. He wanted to see how the car did under some pressure, see if he could find anything else he could deal with. It needed new shocks, but that seemed a bit too much to put into the old thing, at least for now. It seemed to run well enough, and with luck it should hold for a while.

Once the tank was full and he'd started back, on impulse he stopped by the auto supply where he'd picked up the plugs, oil and filter, hoses, and the new battery. He discovered that, amazingly, they had touchup paint for the year and model. And suddenly his afternoon was full. He didn't mind; it was Sunday anyway, and it would keep him busy. And it felt good to help out somebody who was trying so hard. Somebody capable of raising a kid like Gracie.

When he'd finished hours later, it was after seven. The lights in the garage reflected off the car, and he was pleased with the results. There had been some decent paint left under the oxidation, and the cleanup and touchup had taken at least five years off the appearance of the thing. And it had run well out on the road, so all in all she was in a lot better shape.

He glanced at the time, wondering what time Gracie went to bed on a school night, or if she'd still be up and Riley would want to come get it even though it was getting late. But what did he know about what was late for a kid her age?

He pondered calling. He'd said he would, when it was done. And if she got it tonight she could drive it to work in the morning. She hadn't been comfortable driving Juliette's car, no matter how excited Gracie had been. But it was Sunday night. Maybe she had other plans. A date, maybe.

When he realized he was frowning at that thought, it brought him up short. If she'd been a guy, he would have called by now, it wouldn't have mattered. So why did it just because it was Gracie's mother, not her apparently not-in-the-picture father? It wasn't like he was thinking of her in some kind of…male to female way. He'd given that up a long time ago. The days when woman threw themselves at him—and they had, he'd realized that shortly after it had stopped, after he'd gotten out of the hospital and begun what he called the after life. Not in the sense of being dead, but being what was left of him after that boat propeller had tried to slice him to pieces, and had almost succeeded. Would have, if not for John.

But he'd learned an important lesson out of it. And he counted that as the one blessing to come out of his disfigurement; he knew now just how much of those women being after him was strictly because of his looks. They hadn't cared what he thought, what he believed or didn't believe. They'd only cared that he had, as one of them had put it, looked like he'd come out of central casting for hunks.

Only John and their team hadn't changed how they interacted with him. And the rest of the Wild Oak Bunch didn't seem to care, since they hadn't known him before.

But only Riley West had ever teased him about it. And he wasn't quite sure how that made him feel.

"Make the damned call, Flynn," he muttered to himself.

He called up the number and tapped the screen. Was relieved—which irritated him all over again—when it went to voice mail. He left a message, hung up, and stood there for a long moment. Too long. And had some choice words for himself as he closed up the garage and headed upstairs to clean up. Something he would do anyway, and had nothing to do with the possibility the two females who had barreled into his life would be back tonight. Nothing at all.

CHAPTER TEN

"**K**nock again, Mom."

Riley looked at her daughter, who was balancing the big plate carefully. "Let's give him a minute, all right? He might be—"

—half naked right in front of me.

"That was fast," he said.

It was a good thing Gracie could talk, because she couldn't.

"We were already coming over with these. I made them for you myself. They're chocolate chip."

Riley knew she was staring, probably gaping, but what else was she supposed to do when the door opened and she was confronted with...this? Judging by the slicked back, wet hair and the damp towel around his neck, he must have been in the shower when she'd knocked. He was barefoot, but had pulled on some jeans. And if he'd intended to zip them all the way, he hadn't quite made it. She hadn't seen so much pure maleness in a long time. The broad, strong chest and shoulders, the ridged abs, the narrow hips, with that tempting V exposed by the half-zipped zipper arrowing downward...

There was another scar or two here and there, but smaller ones; whatever had damaged his face and neck had clearly been limited to that area. And...and she was standing here assessing as if she were taking inventory.

It could have been worse. He could have answered the door in just the towel. *Worse? Better, you mean, don't you?*

She nearly gasped aloud. She hadn't reacted like this in so long, it felt almost alien, as if she'd been seized by a sudden fever. She had sworn this off long ago. Years ago, ever since the first and only time since Gracie's birth had been a disaster.

Riley tuned back into Gracie's excited chatter with a snap she thought must have almost been audible. And she was immensely grateful to realize Flynn was looking at Gracie, and not at her. Since she was staring at him.

"They smell great," he said, sounding utterly disconcerted.

"They taste better," Gracie promised. "I snuck one on the way over," she added with that very Gracie grin.

"I don't think it's really sneaking if you confess at the first opportunity." He said it seriously, but once more, Riley saw that corner of his mouth twitch.

Gracie's grin widened. "Guess not, huh? I figured the dragon would tell on me anyway."

"He does see all," Flynn said gravely.

Riley loved the way he played along with her fantasy, as if he didn't see anything strange in such a bright child indulging in flights of fancy.

"So," Gracie said, "Can we come in?"

Flynn's gaze shot to her face. "That wasn't the plan, Gracie," she said hastily. "We're just going to drop these off, remember? Mr. Flynn's already done too much for us."

He shrugged. Those broad, naked shoulders. "The car was Juliette's idea."

"And getting mine running again was yours." There, that was steady enough. *Just stop staring at him!*

"I can make her some cookies too," Gracie suggested.

Riley could only imagine giving the girlfriend of billionaire Shan Kelleher a plate of Gracie's slightly lopsided cookies. Then again, if she was kind enough to do what she'd done, she probably wouldn't laugh at the child's efforts.

"She would like that. If there were any left after Shan spotted them."

Riley tilted her head slightly; he was speaking of his billionaire boss as if he were any other guy. But then, the man had a dragon guarding his gate, so he had to have a sense of humor.

Flynn seemed to suddenly realize they were still standing on the small landing at the top of the outside stairs. "Sorry. Come in. I'll get some shoes on and we'll go get your car."

Riley didn't know whether to hope he meant a shirt too, or not.

You'd better pray he puts on a shirt, girl. So you're not fanta-sizing about licking from the low end of those abs all the way up to that neck....

He stepped back so they could come in. And Riley stopped in her tracks, staring again, but this time at the unexpectedly expansive, modern space. She hadn't realized how big that garage downstairs was with all the equipment in it, but it was obvious now from the spaciousness of the living area above it. The far wall was all windows, looking out over rolling hills, without another building in sight. There was a sizeable flat screen on the wall to the left, over what looked like a gas fire-place. On the opposite wall was a desk, holding a laptop and where his phone appeared to be charging. To her right was a compact but fully equipped kitchen with gorgeous granite counters and sleek new appliances, open to the large space, giving a great room effect.

To the left she saw the bathroom he'd come out of, which looked just as sleek and modern as the kitchen. Behind that was a walled-off section that she guessed must serve as the bedroom. And when he disappeared into that space, she set herself to not thinking about him in either of those two places.

"This is so cool!" Gracie exclaimed, setting the plate of cookies down on the counter and running over to look out the wall of windows.

It was interesting, Riley thought, that the soft leather couch was arranged more toward those windows than the television. Telling, somehow. And the room was tidy for the most part. There was a half-full glass of water on the table next to the couch, and a stack of books next to that. On top of the stack was an e-reader. He was obviously a serious reader. She liked that.

She walked over to look at the books. A hardcover on the bottom, two paperbacks on top of that. The hardcover, to her surprise, was a book on Aristotle. The one in the middle was a biography of Churchill. The top one was a military memoir about a dramatic rescue of a downed pilot, apparently written by that pilot. That almost surprised her more than the one about the great philosopher; she would have thought a man who'd been through what he had would want to avoid reading about it now that he was safely out of it. Being careful of the e-reader, she picked up the memoir, saw a business card from the author marking a spot, and looked to find the author had signed the book. And suddenly, as she read the inscription, the book's presence made sense.

To Flynn—

It's true what they say about Rangers, and I don't just mean they lead the way. Small numbers, big impact. Thanks for my life.

Her eyes wide now, she set the book back on the stack with great care. And fought off a shiver as she thought of what the people who protected the country risked.

There was a framed photograph on the desk, and now she couldn't stop herself from walking over to look at it. It was of a group of men in camouflage, wearing what she guessed were bulletproof vests, with pockets loaded with gear. They were all carrying weaponry but casually, if such a thing was possible. And they all had on very dark sunglasses, the kind that would cut down desert sun, she supposed. They also masked their faces, but she had no trouble picking Flynn out, second from the right. He was looking to the left in the shot, so she couldn't tell if this was before or after he'd been hurt. But it had to be before; surely he wouldn't have gone back after that.

She didn't want to be caught snooping, although with the photo out in plain sight that wouldn't really apply, but still she walked over toward Gracie and joined her in looking out the big windows. A moment later, she heard a sound behind her and braced herself to turn around.

He had, thankfully for her nerves, pulled on a shirt along with the running shoes that looked as if they were actually used for the intended purpose. He'd apparently toweled his hair, because while it wasn't dry, it was no longer dripping. It looked like the closest it had gotten to a comb was his fingers. She liked the tousled effect, liked even more that he was probably totally unaware of it.

"This is a great place," she said.

"I like it. It's quiet, peaceful."

Did he feel the need for that, for a certain amount of peace? She could certainly understand.

Gracie had torn herself away from the windows and come back. "It must be nice to have no neighbors."

"I like that, too," he said. And thinking of how crowded her apartment building seemed sometimes, Riley wondered if he craved isolation the way she sometimes did, a place to simply...be. But that was not a conversation to have with a man you'd barely met.

"You have a beautiful view," she said instead.

"Yes. The sunsets are pretty spectacular."

That seemed to spark a renewed interest for Gracie, and she went back over to look out the windows.

"This all looks new," Riley said. "And very nice."

"It is fairly new. And it's nice because Shan lived here when he first bought the place, while the house was being redone."

She blinked. "Shan Kelleher, billionaire extraordinaire, lived over a garage?"

"He didn't mind. He started out over a garage, years ago."

"I had no idea."

"Most people don't."

She studied him for a moment. "You really like the man."

"Yes. He's taken the hell life dished him and turned it into something remarkable, just to save others from going through what he went through."

"His little boy died, didn't he?"

"He did."

Gracie came back to them. "That's sad," she said. Riley noticed Flynn didn't seem at all surprised that Gracie had heard them from across the room, and he shifted his gaze to the child.

"Yes. Very sad. He was younger than you, even." Flynn frowned. "I think. You're what, six? Seven?"

Gracie glared at him, obviously completely distracted from

the sad topic. "I'm almost nine!" Then her brow furrowed. "Wait. You already knew that, from when we talked about Jimmy. You were just teasing, weren't you?"

That twitch of his mouth again as he held up his hands. "Guilty. I'll have to remember you…remember things."

"I do," Gracie said firmly.

Riley felt her eyes stinging again, as they had before as she'd watched her little girl interact with this man. Since she didn't date, there hadn't been much opportunity for this other than teachers and their landlord, who was a gruff old man who would never take the time. Probably never had the time, she amended her unkind thought, given the age of the apartment building.

"You really fixed the car?" Gracie asked.

"Fixed might be going a little far," he said with a grimace.

"But it runs now?"

"It does. And more quietly."

Gracie's eyes widened. "It doesn't bang anymore?"

"Nope."

Before she could descend into thought about how the car wasn't alone in that, Riley said to the child, "Let's get it out of his way, then."

"I need some sustenance first," Flynn said.

"What's…sus…ta..nence?" Gracie said carefully.

Flynn grabbed two cookies from the plate, stuffed them in his mouth and chewed with exaggerated gusto. Gracie laughed.

"That," he said with emphasis after he'd swallowed, "is sustenance. And those are really good."

Gracie beamed. He walked over to a door she'd thought was a closet, but it turned out to be to the inside stairway down to the garage. He flipped on the lights below, and Gracie raced down. Or at least, almost down; she stopped dead on the last step, staring.

"Is that...our car?" she asked, sounding astonished.

"What do you mean, honey?" Riley asked as she followed. "I—"

Riley stopped dead as she came even with Gracie and saw what she'd seen. No. It couldn't possibly be. She leaned back to where she could see the license plate. It was.

She turned to look at Flynn, not caring this time about staring at him. "What did you do?" she asked, still unable to quite believe it.

Again the shrug. "Amazing what a wash and a little wax will do."

"I can't afford taking it through a fancy car wash," she said, feeling a bit of panic.

"No fancy car wash, just me."

Gracie shifted her gaze back to him. "You made it look like that? Shiny?"

"Well, it was the wax mostly. I just supplied the elbow grease."

Gracie frowned. "The what?"

"It means hard work," Riley said, not even wanting to imagine the effort that had gone into taking her old, battered car and making it look like this.

"Some say," Flynn said to Gracie, "the term originally came out of doing that exact kind of work, because to polish something like a car—or in the old days, a carriage—you have to bend your elbow a lot."

"Oh. I guess that makes sense," Gracie said. "But sometimes English is silly."

"You mean the language where saying 'fair' can mean being treated justly, or a weather condition, or a place to go ride a roller coaster? That," Flynn said with a lopsided grin that took Riley's breath away, "I cannot argue with."

Gracie burst into peals of laughter. A kind of laughter Riley had never heard from her daughter before. How had he known she loved word play? Or was it simply that he did, too?

"Hey, wait," Gracie said when the laughter finally faded. "What happened to the scrape?"

Riley frowned, and looked back at the car. The car that had had, ever since she'd bought it, a thin scrape through the paint almost to metal on the side panel above the right rear tire. But now it was gone. As, she realized, was the scrape on the back of the passenger side rear view mirror; that one had been her fault, trying to slide into her parking slot when her neighbor had been over the line, she'd rubbed up against the post between them.

She was utterly confused now. It had to be her car, but...

She turned to look at Flynn. And again got the shrug. "I saw they had the right touch-up paint at the auto supply store. I'm no painter, so it shows if you know where to look—"

"I knew where to look, and I couldn't tell," she pointed out.

"Well, from here maybe."

She simply looked at him for a moment, wondering why he was disparaging what he'd done. But also finding it dispiriting that he'd put money—she sighed inwardly; paint was the last thing she could afford to spend money on—into that with everything else that was wrong. Sure, it looked great, almost unrecognizable as her tired old car, but what good was that if it couldn't get her to work and back, and Gracie to school?

"Mom!" Gracie had run the rest of the way and had the car door open now. "It's so clean inside!"

She walked to her daughter and looked; it was clean. Everything that could gleam did, and the bits of debris and leaves and mud that seemed to inevitably get tracked in every winter were gone. He'd done that, too? This was not what she'd expected at all. He didn't seem like a man who'd go for the cosmetic over the practical.

But then it struck her; he'd created that magical garden. In essence, he was an artist, different than the man who'd created that magnificent creature at the gate, but no less. Maybe the appearance did matter more to him.

"I'm not really a slob," she began awkwardly.

Again the shrug. "Hard to keep it clean when you don't have the gear, or any place to use it." Okay, so the shrug wasn't so bad. And the understanding was...heart-easing. "Biggest concern is the radiator. Don't know how much longer it will hold out. You probably need to check the level regularly, and make sure you keep up on the antifreeze. And don't try any really long drives in the summer heat around here."

"I don't. Won't."

"How come you need antifreeze if it's hot?" Gracie asked.

Well, that was a logical question. Curious, she waited to see how Flynn would answer this one.

He did it very seriously. "Because it's kind of misnamed. Actually, it doesn't just make it harder to freeze. You know what the radiator does?"

"Mom says it keeps the engine from getting too hot."

He nodded. "She's right. Originally, they used just water, but there's not much temperature range between freezing and boiling with pure water. Antifreeze increases that."

Gracie's brow furrowed. And Riley loved the way he just waited, let her work through it. Clearly, he got how smart her girl was, and understood that she could grasp more than most people would expect.

"So...antifreeze doesn't just stop it from freezing, it stops it from boiling, too?"

"Not stop, but with antifreeze, it has to get a lot colder and a lot hotter before either of those happens."

"Cool," Gracie said.

"Literally," Flynn said, still serious. But again, that corner of his mouth twitched.

Gracie blinked, thought, then laughed out loud again. It washed over Riley, warmed her in ways that were all too rare these days. She often feared her little girl was too mature for her age because she sensed how worried her mother was, about so many things. Hearing her laughter eased that fear, that ache.

And for that, she would do a lot more than pay for some paint.

CHAPTER ELEVEN

The moment she turned the key and the motor fired up instantly, Riley turned her head to stare at him. Flynn guessed she was remembering the hesitation that had come from the weakness of the battery.

"You charged the battery?" she asked.

He hesitated, then shrugged. "Pointless. It would have been dead again in a couple of days. So I picked up a new one."

Her gaze skated away from him, but he saw her wince. He frowned.

"It's not making that noise, Mom!" Gracie exclaimed. Then the girl looked at him. "Why? What made it do that?"

He'd never encountered a child with such voracious curiosity about...everything. Of course, he hadn't encountered that many children at all, at least not on this personal a level.

Which is why John and Jen were completely crazy, asking him, of all people, to be the godfather to their son when he arrived. Which could be any damned minute now.

He shook off the persistent thought yet again, and tried to

focus on an explanation for Gracie. She was smart, and wanted to know, but she was still a kid.

"Do you ride a bike?"

"I don't have one now, it got stolen, but I know how."

He felt a jab of anger; steal a bike from a kid? That was low. Especially when it was a kid who obviously wouldn't be getting a new one any time soon. But he just went on with what he'd been going to say, hoping it would make sense to her.

"You know how you pedal and it transfers to the back wheel and you move?" She nodded, looking puzzled but waiting for him to make sense of it. And that realization made him feel a jab of something altogether different. It was a moment before he could get past the feeling and go on. "The mechanics in between are different, but the idea is the same in a car. You have a set of tubes, cylinders, in an engine. And pistons, a solid piece that fits inside each tube. The fuel, gasoline, comes in, the first spark—remember those spark plugs?— lights it, and because there's air too, it burns and pushes the piston away like you push the pedal away."

"Oh!" Gracie's expression cleared. "So that's what makes the wheels go, the pushing?" He nodded. "But what made it make that noise?"

"That happens when the fuel burns unevenly, because the mix of air and fuel is wrong, or the spark plugs are faulty or worn out."

"So...it's the car telling you what's wrong?"

He had to smile at that. "Exactly that."

"So it's car language."

And that made him laugh. "Yes."

"How'd you learn to speak it?"

"We had a lot of equipment to keep running when I was in

the Army. And there wasn't always a mechanic around to do it."

"So now you keep all that stuff here—" she gestured at all the machinery "—running?"

"Try to."

"Would you teach me? So I can help my mom?"

He heard a tiny sound from Riley, and when he glanced at her, she was biting her lip. And as she looked at Gracie, he didn't think he was mistaken about the suddenly increased sheen in her eyes, that same shade of cornflower blue as her daughter's.

"I think," he said slowly, "you help your mom just by being here."

Riley's gaze shifted, and for the look she gave him then, he would have done a hell of a lot more than just a little car maintenance.

Riley listened to the engine, running smoothly without the knocking, remembered how it had started instantly, minus the hesitation from the old, tired battery he'd replaced, noticed that the gas tank that had been down to under a quarter was now registering full.

She thoroughly castigated herself, not just for suspecting him of ulterior motives, but for the places her mind had gone when he'd been talking about pistons and cylinders...

"Your A/C should work now, too. How long have you been doing without?"

She swallowed tightly. "Always."

"A/C?" asked Gracie.

"Air conditioning," Riley explained.

Gracie's eyes widened. "This car has air conditioning? You mean we won't melt any more in the summer?"

That crooked—endearing—smile came again. Riley looked up at him, and gave a slow, wondering shake of her head. "I don't know what to say to you. How to thank—"

He held up a hand, shaking his head in turn but more definitely. "Not necessary."

"It is to me."

"Look, Shan said do it, so I did it."

"I get that. But," she pointed out, "he only did that after you told him. So thank you. If you'll give me the bills for the battery and whatever else you used or had to buy—" she cringed inwardly at what the battery had to have cost "—I'll see that you're paid back." Somehow.

Again he held up a hand. "It's covered."

She went very still. And drew herself up straight. "No."

"Look, I—"

"I may not be rich like your boss, but I'm not a charity case, Mr. Flynn."

"Just Flynn," he insisted. "And that's my boss's orders. He said to cover it with the grounds account."

"I can't accept that."

"Trying to get me fired?"

She blinked. "What?"

"When Shan makes up his mind, he's pretty much an immoveable object. And I don't want to cross him."

"But why would he—or his girlfriend—want to do this?"

"Because they're good people."

"But they don't even know us."

"Juliette really did drive a car in worse shape than this. She literally coasted into Wild Oak as it was breaking down. And

Shan," he said, glancing at Gracie, "will forever look out for kids, even ones he doesn't know."

"Because he lost his," she said softly. Flynn nodded. "I...saw a photo of him once. At his little boy's funeral. It was wrenching."

To her shock, Flynn let out a short laugh. She stared at him. She knew now how he felt about his boss, so there had to be a reason for what seemed like a very inappropriate reaction to that photograph. Taking a page from Gracie's book, she simply waited. And after a moment, he explained.

"He hated that picture. With a passion. For several reasons. More than once, he wanted to track down the photographer and do damage."

Apparently she didn't have her daughter's patience. "And this is funny because...?"

"Fate made it funny. That photographer was Juliette."

She blinked. "His girlfriend?"

"Now. And that's a long story that's not mine to tell." He sounded as if he regretted telling her as much as he had. She supposed the billionaire had reason to be wary about being talked about by his employees, even his...gardener? Groundskeeper?

Artist. That's the word that really fits. And I'll bet that's how Mr. Kelleher sees it.

Although it seemed as if their relationship was as much friends as anything else. Which made her ask, "Is your boss the billionaire part of this group you told me about?"

For a moment, she thought he wouldn't answer, and she again had the thought he regretted telling her as much as he had.

It must be nice to have no neighbors.
I like that, too.

His exchange with Gracie popped into her head, and she wondered if perhaps he simply wasn't used to talking to people at all.

"He is," he finally said. "He likes it because there, he's just Shan from over the hill."

"I...that's nice." She wanted to ask where "there" was, where this group that made her miss things she hadn't thought about in a long time, gathered, but she knew it was none of her business and did not. But the thought of that group, including a billionaire and a famous artist, made her feel her own status—or lack thereof—more fiercely than usual.

There was nothing she could do about repaying him right now, but she'd think of something. Somehow. Sometime. She hated this feeling of indebtedness, of being a charity case. She'd hated it for years, ever since a cruel fate had forced it on her.

But fate had evened the score in a huge way by giving her Gracie. And for Gracie's sake, she would do much more than swallow her pride.

CHAPTER TWELVE

Flynn did something he rarely ever did that Sunday night. He dug back in a cupboard and brought out a bottle of smooth Kentucky whiskey. This—or rather the cheaper imitations—had been his father's downfall, so he'd always been wary, but if ever there was a night for it, it was tonight.

All day, he'd been able to focus, to concentrate on the literal mechanics of what he was doing, from checking the gap on the new spark plugs to tightening the hose clamps on the new hoses. And he'd thought himself prepared, when he'd left the message that she could pick up the car. But then, he'd thought it would be a quick handoff. She'd be eager to give back Juliette's car; he didn't doubt she'd meant it when she said she didn't want the responsibility. He'd been a little worried himself, not about her, but where she lived. Open parking like that was an invitation to damage of one sort or another.

So he'd expected to trade keys, endure a probably too effusive thank you—he knew that much about her—and it would be done. Instead, he'd turned into a motor-mouth. Telling her things he had no business talking about, about Shan, Juliette.

And Gracie...what was it about that kid that had him talking like he was some kind of instructor or something? Her obvious intelligence? The intense and varied curiosity?

Or was it the way she looked at him, as if she trusted him to always have the answer to her questions—and to want to answer them?

Even as he sat there pondering the wonder that was Gracie West, he was aware of what he was avoiding. Avoiding because going there wouldn't just be unwise, it would be downright stupid. Beyond stupid, to think Riley West had been anything other than embarrassed when he'd answered the door half dressed, no matter how she had looked him up and down.

He hadn't expected them so quickly, had figured he'd have plenty of time. So when the knock came, he'd thought it must be one of the Wild Oak Bunch—Matt maybe, or his Uncle Lew, out on patrol. They stopped by sometimes when things were slow. They passed it off as this being on their beat, but Flynn had the feeling they were also checking on him. He'd wondered what John had told them about his state of mind.

A knock on the door jolted him out of the thought. And brought him instantly back to the moment when the last knock had come and he'd opened it to Gracie and her mother. The mother who had, for an instant, looked at him almost avidly.

That was your imagination. No woman who looks like her would look at a man who looks like you that way.

When he opened the door, he found himself jolted again. As if his last thought had conjured him up, John Reese stood on the landing.

"Hey," his former commander said, sounding half sheepish, half harassed.

"What the hell are you doing here?" he asked as he stepped aside to let him in.

"Thanks for the warm welcome, buddy."

"You're the one with the nine-months-pregnant wife at home." *Not me. Never me.*

"Who do you think kicked me out?" John said dryly.

He blinked at that. Then, slowly, smiled. "Hovering a bit, were you?"

John grimaced. But his eyes held more worry than Flynn had ever seen even under fire. "I'm just...I know she's not due for a couple of weeks, but..."

"John, you freaking delivered Rachel's baby practically on the floor of their cabin."

"Different," John said. Then he let out a long breath. "I like Rachel—hell, I love Rachel. But she's not my soul."

"Maybe it's her you should be talking to. She could talk you down."

That got a smile out of the man. "My sister-in-law could talk the birds out of the trees."

Flynn shrugged. "Then she should be able to handle a guy who's being bird-brained at the moment."

John gave him an icy look. "You didn't just say that."

"I did."

John's gaze narrowed. "Are you...you are spoiling for a fight."

"Maybe," Flynn admitted. "But you're not going to really throw that punch you just thought about."

"And you sound almost sorry about that."

He let out a long breath. "Maybe," he said again.

"What's got you all revved up? Not that I'm not glad to see it, mind you."

Flynn blinked. "You're glad I was half-hoping you'd throw that punch?"

"I'm glad you care enough about something to be that wound up," John said, rather flatly. Then, his gaze landing on the table beside the chair Flynn had been sitting in, and the bottle and glass that sat there, he added, "Enough to break out the good stuff?"

"Afraid I'll go on a bender? Wind up dead drunk?" Flynn asked, his voice tight now. There were things only John knew, and they gave him a certain power, as knowledge does.

"No." The man he'd followed into hell on earth turned back to look at him levelly. "You won't drink yourself to death, like your old man probably did. You'll eat a damned bullet."

"Well, you got that right," Flynn said.

He'd always known if he ever gave up, that would be how he would go. One little tug on the hair trigger of his M9, and it would be over. It was why he kept the Beretta he'd brought home from his service unloaded despite knowing that if he ever needed it for protection, it was now useless. But he had some dim hope that in the time it took to jam in a full magazine and get one in the chamber, he might change his mind about blowing his brains out.

But now he saw in the man he admired more than anyone the pain behind the flat words. As he had downrange, he took any loss hard, but Flynn knew well enough what it would cost this man if he ever took that final road. Because he knew what it would do to him if John ever did.

Not that there was any chance of that, not now, when he had the life he'd thought lost forever back.

Not when he's a stronger man than you ever were.

"Flynn," John began, and the pain sparked into fear in those cool gray eyes he'd never seen fear in before.

"Not tonight," he said quietly. "It was just an...unsettling day. Want some of that good stuff?"

John let out a visible breath of relief. "Yes. And not any night, damn it. My son's counting on you."

Flynn blinked. "The son who's not here yet?"

"Yes." John stared him down. "*I'm* counting on you. Just as I always did." Flynn suddenly found it a little hard to get enough air past the tightness in his throat. John nodded as if in satisfaction before he said, "I'll get my own glass."

RILEY ONLY KNEW how much the unreliability of her car had been weighing on her now that the weight had been lifted. It was going to take a while to unlearn the coping habits she'd developed. She was down in the car with Gracie at her usual time Monday morning before, when it started immediately, she realized she didn't need the extra time built into her schedule to compensate for possible breakdowns. She'd rushed around as usual, hustling Gracie along, grabbing her work shirt—the last clean one, she'd have to do laundry tonight—with the logo for the Wild Oak Restaurant, and pulling it on as she went out to the kitchen to grab the girl's lunch out of the fridge. Prepared last night, because of course she wouldn't have time this morning.

Except she would have, now.

She felt tears welling up again, at the sheer relief of it.

She took the extra time and a small amount of the fund she'd been trying to build for the car repairs to buy Gracie her favorite breakfast at the local drive-through, and they went to the park near the school to sit and eat. And talk. Gracie chattered away, delighted at the change in routine.

And Riley soaked it up, the wonder of this child she'd been gifted with.

"You seem happy, Mom," Gracie said as she wiped her fingers after finishing her treat.

"I'm...yes, I guess I am."

"Because you don't have to worry about the car anymore?"

Riley turned her head to look at this wonder she'd birthed, to look into the eyes that were a duplicate of her own. "Sometimes I forget just how smart you are."

Gracie grinned, but when she spoke again, it was quiet and obviously genuine. "I'm glad you don't have to worry. I don't like it."

"Well," Riley said, reaching out to put an arm around the girl she loved more than anything in the world, "you'd better get used to it, because I will always, always worry about you."

Gracie hugged her back but then, looking up at her with that same genuine concern. "But who worries about you?"

Riley smothered a sigh at her daughter's seemingly built-in understanding and empathy, far beyond her years. Because the only people who had ever truly worried about her, her father and her grandmother, whom Gracie had been named for, were gone now. "I've got you," she said with her best effort at cheer, "I don't need anyone else to worry about me."

They'd run through the spare time granted them by whatever fate had sent her tumbling into Flynn's orbit, and they walked back toward the school. Automatically, she smoothed her daughter's hair as they stopped near the school's entrance, then watched as the girl ran happily inside. By rights, Gracie should be in some advanced, gifted school somewhere, but that wasn't in the financial cards any time soon, so Riley simply grateful that this elementary school, along with every school in town, was ranked one of the best in the state, in fact, in the country. It was, after all, why she'd decided to stay here.

And a connection belatedly hit her. The reason the Wild Oak school system was among the best was that Shan Kelleher saw to it. Flynn's boss. Whose girlfriend had practically demanded that a total stranger drive off in her new car, simply because Flynn had in essence vouched for her, and she herself knew what it was like to have an unreliable vehicle.

There had to be a way she could thank the man. He'd said repeatedly it wasn't necessary, and maybe it wasn't, for him. But it was for her.

She was still pondering this as she worked. Mornings at the Wild Oak weren't that busy, so she wiped tables, straightened menus, and did a few of the other little chores that piled up. The manager, an astute woman named Melanie, always noticed and thanked her, and Riley wasn't above currying that favor; the only thing worse than the car dying on her for good would be losing her job.

And yet again, she caught herself. She didn't have to worry every moment about the car anymore. Flynn had warned her the radiator could still go, so she wasn't completely safe on that score, but so much more than she had been it was almost dizzying.

They were well into the lunch rush when she noticed her shift supervisor, Marny, seating a solo at the back table. A tall, handsome man in uniform, with a distinctive streak of gray in his dark hair.

Matt McLane.

On impulse, she headed over to the woman as she walked back toward the kitchen to pick up an order.

"Hey, do you mind if I take table fifteen?"

Marny looked over her shoulder at her. "Matt?" She grinned. "Mr. Won't-sit-with-his-back-to-the-door?"

Riley blinked. "He won't?"

"Says it's a cop thing."

"Oh. Makes sense, I guess." And that it did, that cops had to think that way, would be unsettling, if she had time to dwell on it.

"I don't mind," Marny said, "but if you've got your eye on him, fair warning, he's well and truly taken."

"Oh, I know that," Riley assured her. "I've waited on him when he's been in with his fiancée, and she's amazing."

"All yours, then," Marny said. "But why?"

"It's sort of to do with why my car looks like it looks now." Marny had arrived at the same time she had, and commented in amazement at the change.

The other woman smiled now. "Oh. He recommended someone? He's good about that."

"Yes," Riley said, leaving it at that.

As she walked back to the booth in the back—where the occupant sat on the side with his back to the wall, indeed facing the entrance—she tried to formulate what to say. She didn't want to intrude on his lunch break, but she did want to thank him for the reassurance that Flynn was what Gracie had said he was. Or more importantly, that he wasn't what she said he wasn't, the worst kind of predator. She supposed with his background Flynn could be a predator if he had to be, but he'd clearly left that behind.

To create pure beauty. Amazing.

As it turned out, her ponderings were unnecessary, because Matt looked up at her and smiled widely. "I was hoping you'd be here. Can you sit for a moment?"

"Just for a moment, Officer McLane. I know you're on your lunch."

"Matt, please." He waved off her concern. "How'd it go with Flynn?"

"He's...a miracle worker."

His smiled widened. "In more ways than one. So the car's running?"

"Beautifully. And...I wanted to talk to you about that, since you know him. He clearly spent a lot of time on that beast, and he wouldn't let me even pay for the parts he bought."

"Don't worry about it. He says Shan pays him more than he could spend if that's all he did, look for ways to spend it."

"That's not the point," she said firmly.

Matt studied her for a long moment, then nodded slowly. "Good for you," he said quietly.

The simple approval warmed her. "I owe him more than thanks," she said. "Not just for the car, but he was so good with Gracie."

Matt drew back slightly, tilting his head quizzically. "He was good with her?"

She nodded. "So patient. And she made him laugh and vice versa. She laughed like I've never heard her when they got off into word play, which she loves."

Matt was staring at her now. "We're talking about Flynn, right? The guy who works at Dragon Hill?"

Her brow furrowed. "Yes. Why?"

The man opposite her toyed with the knife of the place setting, turning it over a couple of times. She waited. Then, seemingly decided, he looked back at her again. "There's a group of us, friends—"

"The Wild Oak Bunch?"

His eyes truly widened then. "Holy... He told you about that?"

She nodded. "It sounds like a wonderful group."

"It is. And we all worry about Flynn. Too often, it feels like he's on the outside, looking in. Like he doesn't think he fits, or belongs. But he'd do anything for any of us, and we all know it."

"And you for him?"

"Yes." The answer came instantly. "Problem is, I don't think he knows it. Or believes it."

"Why, do you suppose?"

"John—he told you about John?" At her nod, he continued. "John thinks it all ties back to what happened after he was hurt. But that's all he'll say. Says it's Flynn's story to tell."

"Or not tell?"

"Exactly." He studied her for another long moment. "You really want to pay him back?"

"I do."

"Then if what you said is true, and he opened up to your daughter, if she made him actually laugh...then the best thing you could do for him is see that continues." Riley hesitated. And Matt misinterpreted. "If you're worried about her, don't be. Flynn would die before he'd hurt a child, and there's not a twisted brain cell in his mind."

"Except maybe the ones that torture him?"

Very slowly, Matt nodded. And she got that feeling of approval again. "Yes," he said, sadly. "Those."

And as she went back to work, Riley felt, along with a powerful sense of sorrow for the price Flynn had paid, a gladness that he had people like this Wild Oak Bunch in his life.

CHAPTER THIRTEEN

That clematis was going to need trimming soon, or it was going to take over the arbor. Flynn mentally added it to the spring list, and thought for the first time since he'd come to Wild Oak, when John had needed him to keep Jen safe, that he might just welcome winter this year. He'd wanted to be busy, too busy to think, but Dragon Hill might just be a hair on the far side of that desire.

He walked past the stand of triteleia, picturing the explosion of purple flowers that would happen in just a few weeks. He wondered, once they were in bloom, if Gracie would be able to figure out why they were called triplet lilies. Or maybe she'd be more intrigued by the name of this particular variety, Ithuriel's spear. He'd bet she'd be tracking down the story of the literary angel the moment she heard it.

He stopped in his tracks, rattled as he realized where his mind had gone. Not simply that he was thinking about the livewire girl who had barreled into his life, but that he was thinking about her being around weeks from now.

You've got us...

The words of a child, a sweet, generous child, that's all. She didn't mean what it sounded like to an adult. And even if she had, in that childlike way, her mother would certainly have the final say. Even if Gracie was an amazingly smart kid, her mother was no pushover. The way she'd reacted at the mere idea of being, as she put it, a charity case proved that.

It was just that he wasn't used to kids, that's all that was causing these uncharacteristic thoughts. He especially wasn't used to little girls. He got on okay with Jimmy McLane, but he was a boy, and Matt's, so it was different.

With an effort, he shoved it all out of his mind and headed to check on the rock garden Shan had decided he wanted, kind of at the last minute. For that reason he'd gone with a reliable favorite for here, and the scattering of nemophila was already blooming. He liked the plant, despite the genus name that sounded vaguely like some kind of mental disorder, because it seemed to bloom forever, when other blossoms came and went quickly by comparison. He'd add in some other things eventually, but for now it looked quite acceptable, and Juliette had liked it.

"I like blue flowers," she'd said. And then, with a loving smile at Shan had added, "And blue eyes."

Blue eyes. Baby-blue eyes, the common name for the plant with the little blue flowers. The flowers weren't quite Shan's shade of blue; his eyes were darker. But they were someone else's.

Gracie. And her mother.

And just like that, he was back to where he'd been trying to escape. He hadn't seen her—either her—since they'd shown up Sunday. And he'd known her for less than a week anyway. Yet it was like that kid had burrowed into his mind so deep already he couldn't seem to shed her. The closest he'd ever come to that was Rashid, the kid they'd rescued on the mission that had gone sideways. The mission that had evolved into something entirely different when they'd encountered the terrorist band in mid-slaughter of an entire family.

The mission that had left him looking like this.

And the mission that had had John calling on every bit of medical training he had, first splinting Rashid's broken leg—after carrying him all the way back to the beach and the exfil boats—and then holding Flynn's face together after he'd dived for Hamdi when the dirty, cringing terrorist leader had gone over the side of the Zodiac in an escape attempt. Hamdi hadn't survived the encounter with the propeller, and Flynn nearly hadn't either. But John had held him together, long enough.

And little, scared Rashid was now a legal American citizen and going to medical school, inspired by those horrible minutes, and John's desperate wish to be able to do more for both of them.

It was strange, how the mind worked. He'd managed to put most of that out of his mind, most of the time, although it was an effort. But then Rashid had turned up, wanting to, as he'd put it, honor Mister Captain John and Mister Sergeant Flynn by showing them what he'd done with the chance they'd given him. Flynn knew it had moved John beyond almost anything except regaining the family he'd thought he'd lost forever.

And himself? That simple act by a grateful kid, had had a strange effect. It made him think about that mission, that life he'd left behind, and to his surprise he'd found it didn't hurt as much anymore. All because he could see then that it hadn't all been for nothing. Even though the rest of his family had died, Rashid had not. Something good had come out of that disaster, even if they had left too many of those killers alive to carry on. Now they—

He heard the faint brush of sound behind him. Instinctively, he dived right, for the cover of the brush. Hit the ground. Tucked up. Rolled. Was reaching for his sidearm before he snapped back to reality. Realized that thinking about that time had put his subconscious, that part of him that had kept him and others alive in combat zones, back on alert. And he'd reacted instantly, automatically at the sound of someone approaching from the rear.

Feeling more than a little sheepish, yet still wary—nobody should be here, on Shan's property, that he didn't know about —he slowly got up. And stood face to face with the nefarious trespasser.

Gracie.

RILEY PLAYED BACK what had just happened in her mind. Gracie had wanted to surprise Flynn, so had been tiptoeing very carefully. And had let out a startled yelp when he'd moved so quickly, without even looking. She herself had jumped, her heart giving a startled little skip, like at an unexpected sound at night. She wondered what on earth he'd been thinking about that had made him sense a threat in a child. Or maybe he hadn't realized, had only known someone was coming up behind him.

Or maybe some places he's been, a child could well be a threat. And she realized she'd just gotten a glimpse of the man, the soldier, he'd been. And despite the adrenaline spike it had caused, she'd still noticed the sheer grace and power with which he'd moved.

Gracie was looking at him steadily now. And once more, Riley decided to just let what would happen happen.

"Did I scare you?" her daughter asked.

Riley thought the idea that a child could scare a man with his background—*he was a hero, Riley*—absurd, but Gracie didn't know that. Then, to her shock, he admitted it.

"A little. But more startled. I didn't expect…anyone to be here."

"Mom didn't want to do this, she called it…what did you call it, Mom?"

"Trespassing," Riley said dryly.

"Yeah, that. But I wanted to surprise you."

"Mission accomplished," he said, and his tone was nearly a match to Riley's.

It took Gracie half a second, then she smiled. But then the smile faltered. "You're not mad at us, are you?"

He let out an audible breath. "No. But how did you get here?" He frowned. "You didn't try climbing that fence, did you?"

"No, Mom wouldn't let me but—" The girl cut herself off and gave him a doubtful look.

"Out with it," he said, and despite the gentle tone, there was no denying it was an order.

"I saw the code you put in, when we came in before."

His brow furrowed, then cleared. "When you followed me in."

Gracie nodded. Riley guessed he probably had a remote he used normally, but in that case had needed the gate to stay open long enough to let his truck and her car both through.

"Why did you do that? Go sideways like that?"

"It's what I was trained to do."

This time, Gracie's brow furrowed. "You mean to be a

soldier? To get away from somebody who wants to hurt you?" He nodded. Gracie's mouth curved downward. "I don't like that our soldiers have to do that."

Riley saw him draw back slightly. Saw him swallow. "Trust me, honey, neither do they."

And then Gracie ran to him, and threw her arms around him. "I'm glad you're not one anymore."

For a moment he stood frozen, staring down at her little girl. Then, rather awkwardly, he reached out one hand and laid it on her hair. Hair that was, Riley realized suddenly, almost exactly the same color as his, that sandy sort of brown, and she wondered if his went blond in the summer like Gracie's did.

Because she was looking at his hair she saw him swipe surreptitiously at his eyes with his other hand. And her breath jammed up in her throat at the expression of confused wonder on his face.

We all worry about Flynn. Too often it feels like he's on the outside, looking in. Like he doesn't think he fits, or belongs.

Was that it? Was it simply that Gracie was declaring her connection to him? Just as she had when she'd told him he didn't have to be lonely anymore, because "You've got us?"

She didn't know, of course. But she did know one thing. She was glad, in this moment, that Gracie had insisted on making this trip over here.

CHAPTER FOURTEEN

"**Y**ou didn't have to do this," Flynn said, staring at the array of food currently on his kitchen counter.

"It was the best way I could think of to show you what you've given me and saved me from,"

He blinked. That was a strange way to put some minor car repairs. "Saved you from?"

She took in a deep breath, and he wondered what on earth she was about to say. And when it came out, it sounded as if she'd rehearsed it.

"You've saved me from having to put extra time in every step of my schedule in case the car won't start. So you've given me extra time with Gracie. You've given me extra sleep. You've saved me from having to remember to leave the car running when I stop somewhere for just a moment, so I don't have to worry about it starting again, and then worrying about the gas I'm wasting. You've saved me from those moments of anxiety every morning as I wait to see if it will start. You've saved me from so much stress in general, I can't find the words for it."

He swallowed tightly. And his voice was a little rough when he said, "Those are pretty good words."

She smiled at him then, and for an instant he felt like he had in that first instant of jumping out of a plane, that moment of free fall that was punctuated by his common sense telling him how stupid that was, before the euphoria took over. It was as powerful, but very different than the feeling he'd had when Gracie had run over and hugged him.

"But still," he said when he thought he could speak without sounding like the fool he was feeling, "this can't have been cheap." He gestured at the various containers and boxes.

Her smile widened. "I get a discount," she said, pointing at the bags emblazoned with the Wild Oak Restaurant logo. "Especially on end-of-shift stuff. And today, the special was lasagna and they had a whole pan left over."

His stomach woke up at that. Audibly. And her smile became a grin.

"And she doesn't have to save to get the car fixed now," Gracie put in cheerfully. "I even got my favorite egg sandwich from the drive-through and we got to sit in the park and eat together on Monday before school. That's the first time in like, forever."

He hadn't thought of that, that Riley might have been scrimping even more than he'd already suspected.

"You should thank Shan for that," he said, rather gruffly.

"I'd like to, some day. And his lady, for the loan of her car. But it still holds, Mr. Flynn. None of it would have happened if not for you, and you did all the work."

"Just Flynn," he said, and for one of the few times in his life he added, "Please."

"All right. Flynn. Now," she said briskly, "you'll need to

warm up the lasagna— they put directions on the cover. And there's salad there, and garlic bread."

"So I smelled."

She lifted an arched brow. "Not a garlic fan?"

"I am," he said solemnly, "quite possibly the biggest garlic fan on the planet."

"Then you'll love that," she said, and the grin was back. "It's the only garlic bread I've ever had that actually has enough."

"Ew," Gracie said. "I don't like it. But Mom says I will when I get older."

"Assuming you got my palate," Riley said. "And your grandmother's."

"I got her name," Gracie said.

"Indeed, and you've done it proud, m'girl."

Gracie grinned up at her mother, who grinned back. She really did seem different. More lighthearted. Maybe the whole car thing really had been weighing her down that much.

"I…" What the hell was he supposed to say to her? He went for basic. "Thank you."

"Enjoy." She turned to pick up her purse.

He blinked. A crazy idea hit him. Crazy, but it only made sense, because he'd never finish this huge pan on his own, unless he had it breakfast, lunch and dinner for at least four days. And much as he liked it, that was a bit much.

He opened his mouth to speak, then shut it again when the words wouldn't come. Then Gracie moved, drawing his gaze. And he found he could say it to her.

"I'm going to need some help eating all this."

The child's face lit up. "I was hoping you'd ask!"

"Gracie, stop. Mr.— I mean Flynn, you don't have to do that."

Somehow breaking the ice with Gracie made him able to

answer her. "And you didn't have to do this." She hesitated, looking undecided. He dug a little deeper, found a couple more words. "Please, stay."

"Can we, Mom? Pleease?" He felt another crazed moment at the emphasis, the genuine plea in the child's voice.

Riley seemed to hesitate, then said. "All right." And then, while Gracie let out a cheer that seemed much larger than the moment deserved, Riley looked at him straight on. And the moment exploded when she said softly, "I was hoping, too."

SHE SHOULDN'T HAVE SAID it, but it was too late for that. She'd clearly made him uncomfortable, and the conversation over the meal—at least between them—was limited to the food itself. Gracie, on the other hand, had no problem asking him anything and everything that popped into her agile brain.

"When did you know you could grow things?"

"I don't remember not being able to. I just didn't see the use in it until now."

"But your garden is great! I just know the dragon loves it, 'cause I do." That got her the little smile Gracie always seemed able to coax out of him. Then it was, "Do you think the dragon likes lasagna?"

He blinked at that one before saying solemnly, "I've never asked him," which made Riley smile in turn. "I do know," he went on, "that the guy who made him does."

"Mr. Stone? The man who did the horses?"

He nodded. And then pointed at the food bags, which had the Oak Tree Restaurant logo on them. "He did that, too. Well, he did the sign out front, anyway, and that's where this came from."

Riley blinked. "Wait…the carved sign out in front, that's a Jake Stone?"

"It is. From long before he broke out as an artist."

"I had no idea."

"Is there other stuff he's done?" Gracie asked.

"The housing at the clinic. And the toys the patients play with and on there."

Gracie frowned. "You mean he builds stuff, too?"

"He used to."

Her daughter looked deep in thought for a moment before she said, "Mom says you don't always know what you're meant to do right away. Was it like that?"

"Your mother is very wise. It was like that."

"And like you growing things now?"

He looked surprised at that connection. "In a way, yes."

After another couple of bites it was, "Did you tell Mom why your name is funny?"

Riley blinked, looked at him. "Funny? Flynn is funny?"

He grimaced. "It is when your first name is Finnbar, which always ends up shortened."

"Shortened to—" It hit her then. "Oh, dear."

"Yeah."

"Whose idea was that?"

"My father. He was probably drunk at the time."

"I don't have a father," Gracie announced.

Flynn's gaze shot to Riley. She'd fielded this one so often it should be easy, but somehow in this moment it wasn't. Finally she said, "He's never been part of our lives."

She knew generally people assumed that meant they were divorced, separated, or had never been married, and most of the time she was happy to leave it at that. But right now, she had to stifle the urge to explain what she really meant, that the man who had fathered Gracie was never allowed into their lives, or thoughts. She didn't know how much longer she could get away with that with Gracie. Sooner or later, she was going to want to know, but she would hang onto the ignorance as long as she could.

"His loss," Flynn said quietly, and those two words, spoken with a wealth of sincerity, eased the pain of it all as nothing ever had.

And a bit later, Gracie was off to something else, clearly unbothered by the parentage discussion. "Do you ever go to my mom's restaurant?"

"Not very often. I don't eat out much."

"Why not?" Gracie asked. "Too expensive?" Riley winced at the child's repetition of her too often spoken reason.

"In a manner of speaking," Flynn said, his tone a little too even.

It wasn't much of a leap for her to realize he meant the stares he probably got. "It bothers you that much?" she asked quietly.

"What, Mom?" Then, looking at Flynn, Gracie demanded, "What bothers you?"

"It's not me it bothers," he said flatly, gesturing at the left side of his face.

"You mean the scars?" Gracie asked, sounding so surprised that Riley could have hugged her. Her girl had her head on straight. "They don't bother me. But if they bother you, can't they fix them? Like...like...what is it, Mom, where doctors do that?"

"Plastic surgery, you mean?" Riley said. She'd wondered herself, if only for his sake.

"Yes. That."

Flynn gave the girl a smile, but it was a little tighter this time. "Had three. You should have seen it before."

"Oh." Gracie gave a careless little shrug. "Well I don't care, and neither should you. Can I go see your TV? I've never watched one that big."

It wasn't, in fact, that huge, at least not compared to some she'd seen. But it was a lot bigger than the tiny old one they had. Not much point in thinking about anything else, since they couldn't afford any fancy viewing or streaming packages.

"Sure," Flynn said. "The remote's on the table."

"I'll second what she said," Riley said when Gracie had trotted across the room. "You shouldn't care. Although I'm sure that's easier said than done."

"Someone told me once a scar or two can be sexy, but that this is just a mess."

"If they walked away unharmed, you're a better human than I am."

"She did," he said bluntly.

She. Her stomach roiled, and she wasn't even sure why. "Because you'd never hurt a woman." He shrugged. "Who was she? Anyone who mattered?"

She heard the note of outrage in her own voice, saw him almost smile at it. With another shrug he said, "My fiancée. The first time she saw me with the bandages off."

Her eyes widened. "Whoa. You got lucky."

He blinked. "What?"

"What if you'd already married her and then found out she was a shallow, petty, small-minded...witch?"

She flicked a glance at Gracie on the last word, so he'd know that was the only thing stopping her from the word she would have otherwise used. When she looked back at him he was smiling, almost in wonder.

"I hope you never saw her again?" she said.

"Nope. When I finally got out of the hospital, she was long gone."

"I also hope you didn't waste time feeling bad about it. That was...beyond despicable. Unforgivable."

"You sound...angry."

"I am! And disgusted. It's enough to make you lose faith in humanity, that there are people like that walking around."

"You don't ever want to meet my mother, then."

Even in a negative context, the idea of meeting his mother rattled her. "I don't?"

"She walked out first. When she realized the scars were going to be permanent."

She studied him for a moment, telling herself not to ask. But she couldn't seem to stop herself. "How long did it take her to get over it?"

"She didn't. I haven't seen her since."

It was a moment before she could even think about speaking again. Finally, unable to help the sour tone of her voice, she said, "Well, if my mother had a long-lost sister, I think we just found her."

CHAPTER FIFTEEN

F lynn drew back slightly, at her tone and her words. This time it was she who shrugged. "She wanted me to—" she glanced at Gracie, who had found something with dogs to watch, which Riley had said would keep her rapt for the duration, she loved them so "—terminate. And when I wouldn't, she disowned me."

The thought that this bright spark of a girl might have been ended before she'd been born jabbed at him. He'd never had adamant feelings about it, and he could see situations where it seemed like the only recourse, but...this way? The thought of a mother demanding her own daughter not become a mother seemed off balance to him. But what did he know? His own mother certainly wasn't a stellar example; she'd almost done the same thing to him when he'd gone into the military— disowned him.

And in the end, she'd done it when he was at his lowest, in pain in a hospital bed and wondering what was going to be left of his life.

"I'm…glad you didn't. Even though it must have been really hard."

"It was. If it hadn't been for my grandmother...she took us in, was there for us. And when Gracie was born, she fell for her as hard as I did. When she passed, she left everything she had in a trust fund for Gracie, so she'll have something when she grows up. I loved that woman so much."

"Gracelyn?"

She nodded. "Gracie told you that, huh?"

"She said she usually only hears it when she's in trouble."

Riley laughed. "Good thing that doesn't happen very often."

"She seems like a good kid."

Riley's smile then was blatantly proud. He liked that. "She's amazing. She's the best kid I could ever have possibly had. She's smart and sweet and brave and caring and the best thing that ever happened to me."

"Then you're both lucky," he said.

She studied him for a moment before she said tentatively, "She really likes you, too. I've never seen her like this with anyone."

He lowered his gaze to his emptied plate. He didn't know what to say to that. That he'd never been like this with anyone, either? Especially a child? Most especially a little girl? She just looked at him with those eyes like her mother's, with that bright, crackling intelligence behind them, and he was lost.

And it struck him that his whole military career had been backward. Many of his brothers in arms had wanted to keep their loved ones safe and so they'd volunteered. He'd volunteered because John had, and it had seemed like a good idea at the time.

But now he understood. And suddenly his service, his

fighting, the horrible memories, even his wounds made sense to him. Because even though he hadn't known them, it was people like Gracie and her mother that he'd fought for, so they could be safe and Gracie could grow up to be the dynamo he was already certain she would be.

That realization gave him a feeling he couldn't put words to. Nor could he describe the feeling he got when, at Gracie's insistence, they all sat and watched an episode of her favorite dog-centric kid's show. He'd never experienced anything like this sensation of sharing this like...like a family. The kind he'd heard about, anyway; his own had been nothing like this.

But there was something about simply sitting there with Gracie and Riley, while the child laughed and pointed out her favorite parts, that was...soothing? Welcoming? Warming? Wonderful?

All of those, he finally decided as he watched the antics of the clever canine.

"How do they get him to do all that?" Riley said, sounding amazed.

"Dogs," he said, "can learn amazing things."

She looked at him, flicked a glance at Gracie as if to be sure she was focused on the show, then asked quietly, "Did you work with them? Overseas?"

"I was never a handler, but we had one attached a few times. They were incredible. Saved more lives than we could count."

"Don't they adopt them out when they retire? Maybe you should get one. Would your boss mind?"

"John's been trying to get Shan to get a guard dog for a long time. But I hadn't thought about getting a retired military dog. Shan might go for that. He's big on payback."

She smiled. "The good kind of payback, you mean?"

"Whichever is necessary," he said, remembering how Shan had pulled out the stops to help Matt when Jimmy's mother had, after years of pretending he didn't exist, had suddenly reappeared and threatened to take him away.

Her eyes widened. "I don't think I'd ever want him mad at me. He's got a lot of power."

"He's got the biggest power of all," Flynn said quietly. "Forgiveness. That's how he and Juliette wound up together." She was staring at him now, and he let out a long breath. "And I talk too much." *Around you, anyway.*

"Somehow I doubt that's something you'd ever be convicted of," she said with a smile. A smile that did more crazy things to him.

But the craziest thing of all happened after Riley had chivvied a reluctant Gracie along, saying she had to get home because it was a school night. He'd walked them down to her car, and stood feeling a bit awkward as they got in and Riley made sure Gracie's seatbelt was fastened before she fastened her own.

Riley started the car, and smiled. She looked up at him and said, "Thank you."

He thought of that impassioned speech she'd given him, and didn't try to brush it off this time. "You're welcome," he said simply.

Her smile widened. She looked down to put the car in gear, but before taking her foot off the brake, she spoke again. "Oh, and Flynn?"

"What?"

She looked up, right at him. "You could have twice as many scars, and you'd still be sexy."

And then they were gone, leaving him gaping at the receding taillights.

NEVER HAD Riley been more grateful for the relative darkness this time of year at nearly 9:00 PM. And that the moon was only a quarter and waning. Because she was sure her cheeks were so red Gracie would ask, if she could see.

She did not know what had possessed her to say it. Or rather, she knew what had made her want to—the fact that, to her, it was absolutely true—what she didn't know was where she'd gotten the nerve to do it.

"You like Flynn, don't you, Mom?"

Gracie asked it innocently enough, but her daughter was extremely smart and even more clever, and she wouldn't put it past her to be...whatever she was up to.

"Of course," she said, keeping her voice very level. "He's been very nice to us. Helpful. As has his boss."

"Mr. K?"

"Yes."

"And the lady who let us drive her car."

"Yes. Juliette, his girlfriend."

"They're nice, too, then."

"Yes."

"Jimmy said they were. He said when his mother showed up out of nowhere Mr. K helped them fight her off."

Riley blinked. "Fight her off?"

"Jimmy said she didn't want him, then she did, then she found out he'd been sick and didn't want him again."

The coldness of that boggled her. "That's...awful."

"Nah. Jimmy's glad she didn't want him. He loves Kelly."

And what had it taken, for Matt to trust that much? He obviously had more nerve than she did. She didn't trust. She simply didn't. It wasn't worth the price. She'd trusted too much once and—

She swerved off that old, beaten path. Yes, she trusted too much once and it had cost her everything she'd had. But it had also given her the most precious gift of her life, so she could not, would not, waste any more time in laments.

But neither would she trust that much again.

Absolutely you can trust him, with anything. He's the kind of guy you want on your side. He was a hero, Riley. He got those scars fighting for us.

Matt McLane's words echoed in her mind. She believed them, believed he meant them absolutely. And she trusted his judgment. Anyone who had gone through what he had with his son's illness knew what it was to face the end of life as you'd known it.

But with Flynn—Finnbar Flynn, really?—she was facing something very different. Something she had scrupulously avoided for nearly nine years now. Something she had long thought she would never face again.

Something she couldn't dare risk. Because the only thing worse than the kind of betrayal she'd known the last time she'd given her heart would be losing Gracie.

They were nearly home before she could breathe normally again.

CHAPTER SIXTEEN

Flynn heard the car approaching just as he finished the last of the trimming on the hedge out by the road. His pulse jumped, ridiculously. It had barely accelerated during this whole day's work. Hell, he'd been under fire with barely a jump, but at the sound of a car it kicked? He didn't even know what to do with that kind of feeling. He'd always been glad to see John, and he'd learned to welcome the presence of any of the Wild Oak Bunch, but this leap his gut took was something altogether new. And he didn't know how to deal with it.

Give me an unruly wisteria vine and I'm good. A band of insurgents or a terrorist I can handle.

But this, how could he handle it when he didn't even know what it was?

Finally, he couldn't resist a glance. And breathed again when he saw it was a marked police unit slowing to a stop. Matt or Lew, he presumed as he set down the trimmer and turned. Matt, he saw as the unit came to a stop a few feet away. The gray streak in his hair—a souvenir of his son's battle for life—was too distinctive to miss. He got out of the car, and as he walked over, he spoke into the radio microphone clipped to his shoulder.

"Unit two-fifteen, I'm 10-10 at Oak Tree and Dragon Hill."

The first number he knew meant Matt's shift and beat number. Ten codes he wasn't that familiar with. "What's 10-10?"

"Means I'm available, but don't bug me if you don't have to."

Flynn lifted a brow at him. The only brow he could lift. "Should I be flattered or worried?"

Matt grinned at him. He did a lot of that lately. "Just wanted to say thanks."

Flynn blinked. "For what?"

"Trusting me." Flynn drew back then, truly puzzled. "Don't think I don't know," Matt said quietly, "what it took for you to have her call me."

Riley. He meant Riley, and that he'd had her call him to vouch for him. "She's...protective," he said. "She wouldn't trust a stranger around her little girl."

"Sounds smart to me. I've seen too many parents who don't pay any attention, as long as the kid's out of their hair."

"Unlike you."

"Hey, I'm getting better. Jimmy's actually going on a school campout the weekend after this one." He grinned. "Of course, that consists of kids bringing sleeping bags to the gym, playing all day and watching a movie and eating popcorn at night, but hey, it gives Kelly and me a weekend to ourselves."

Flynn wondered if Gracie would be going to that, since she and Jimmy were in the same grade. Even as he thought it, Matt spoke again.

"He told me Gracie West is really, really smart. And nice. She's helped him with classwork a few times. Said she always gets it, and sometimes she knows it before the teacher even explains. And that she's reading stuff on her own, way ahead of the class."

"That doesn't surprise me in the least," Flynn said. "She's smart as a whip and twice as quick."

"You sound impressed."

"I was," he said honestly, but carefully keeping it in the past tense.

"You got their car running?"

"Yeah. It'll hold for a while anyway."

"Good. I get the feel things are pretty tight for them."

The memories came flooding back, of Riley's face as she stood up to him. *I may not be rich like your boss, but I'm not a charity case, Mr. Flynn.*

"Yeah," he said rather tightly. "So do I." But not so tight she'd completely surrendered her pride. And he admired that. Among other things.

You could have twice as many scars, and you'd still be sexy.

The words slammed back into him with the force of a blow. He'd swear he'd taken hits that put him on his ass that hadn't stolen his breath like that had. And no amount of telling himself she was just being kind seemed able to cool him down.

"Jimmy said Gracie practically lives at the library," Matt went on, giving him time to remember how to breathe again. "She's always checking out the maximum number of books, and is back in less than a week for more. He told her she needs an e-reader and said she just got sad. So I think we're right. And it's really good that you were able to help them."

He shrugged. They talked for a moment, mainly about Jen's imminent due date, and at seeing the ever-unflappable John Reese a nervous wreck, before Matt got a radio call and had to leave.

He watched the unit pull away. Thought. Wondered.

And then he loaded up the last of his gear into the truck and headed back to the garage. He'd worked up a sweat so took a quick shower, then settled in at his desk. He turned on the laptop, then opened the bottom drawer while it was booting up. Found what he'd wanted, pulled it out, then checked a couple of websites. Including the local library. Made a couple of notes. Then he leaned back in the chair and thought.

The approach was going to be the trickiest. He'd have to set it up carefully. Sort of like picking his way through a mine field. He knew what would be the easy way, but he couldn't count on that. To do so was a sure way to get blasted to bits. But he knew where the weakness was, the best infiltration point, and that's what really mattered.

He grimaced when he realized the terminology he'd been thinking in, but realized it truly felt that way, that he had a high, thick, solid wall to scale, and it was going to take some tactics. He spent some more time doing the "If this then that" game, before the true bottom line hit him. None of this would work, because he was dealing with an entirely unpredictable opposing force.

Sometimes you gotta just wing it.

John's phrase, usually heard when they'd exhausted all other options or were under such duress they had no time to think it through, rang in his head. It hadn't always worked out perfectly, but...they were still alive. In all the deployments, they'd only lost one man, when by rights half of them should be dead. That had to count for something. Giving a mental salute to Ryan Manetti, the one who had fallen, Flynn got to his feet. Putting this off wasn't going to make it easier.

He parked at the hardware store a couple of long blocks

away. He had to stop in anyway, since he'd used up the last of his trimmer string today. And if he left his truck there while he took a little walk, he spent enough money there they should cut him some slack.

He almost turned back twice. Once after he came out of the store and put the trimmer string in the truck. He stood there torn between just getting back in and going home, and completing the mission. Completing the mission won. It always had.

Second time was when he passed a group of kids, older than Gracie but still young. Heard the whispers, and a couple of opinions on his face. Some things never changed.

You could have twice as many scars, and you'd still be sexy.

A shiver went through him. He fought it down. That was *not* what he needed to be thinking now. And it almost made him reverse course.

But the mission came first.

He remembered the way, because it was instinctive him to always have a retreat path mapped out. Even—or especially—when you were carrying someone who was down.

He had to steady himself at the door before he knocked. Wondered if he should have set a time in his head, like if no one came to the door within a minute, he'd bail. Wondered if anyone was even home yet, although he knew Jimmy got out of school at two and it was almost five now. But when did Riley get off work? Did she always work the day shift? Did she always have weekends off or was this last one a fluke? Did she—

The door swung open.

"Flynn!"

There was no denying the happiness in Gracie's exclamation, or the delight in her face. It gave him that strange, swirling feeling again, and it was a moment before he managed to speak.

"Hi, Gracie."

"I was just thinking about you," she said excitedly, grabbing his hand and pulling until he stepped inside, never slowing down on her chatter. "Come in. I have more cookies and some milk, only I can't have those until after dinner so you'll have to stay and eat with us and then—"

"Whoa, Gracie. Really, I just stopped by to find out if you could…"

His voice trailed off as it belatedly occurred to him that this probably wasn't something he should do without clearing it with her mother first. Maybe she'd have some kind of objection over and above the ones he'd already thought of. So much for thinking of all the possibilities.

"Where's your mom?" he asked instead of finishing his original sentence.

Gracie gave a careless wave. "Oh, she's in the shower. Some clumsy guy spilled stuff on her at work."

Riley. In the shower. Naked, water sluicing over her slender body, finding every curve and hollow. He'd never envied water before.

If there was a muscle in his body that didn't lock up tight at the images that brought on, he didn't know where they were. And knew distinctly a couple of places where they definitely weren't. Places he hadn't heard from in a very long time. Places he'd thought long numbed into oblivion, maybe permanently.

"—been worse."

Abruptly he tuned back in to Gracie's chatter. "Worse?"

"At least it was her Wild Oak shirt, so they'll give her another one. And she didn't get burned."

He blinked. "Wait. What did the guy spill on her?"

"Coffee."

He went still. "Hot coffee?"

"I guess. But she said it wasn't bad. Not enough to go to the hospital or anything."

And run up a bill for the ER? He didn't doubt she didn't think it bad enough for that. He'd bet anything short of third degree burns wouldn't be bad enough for that. She'd been falling-down sick just days ago, and had fought him at every step until she'd finally passed out. Just as she'd fought him over the car.

"How long has she been in there?"

Gracie frowned at that. "Kind of a long time. We're usually out of hot water by now." Then she brightened. "But she's probably not taking a hot shower, right? Probably a cool one, 'cause of the hot coffee."

Gracie smiled, clearly glad to have figured out that puzzle. But Flynn stood frozen. There wasn't a shower in the world cold enough to shove the images that were parading through his mind to rest. He fought the urge to go hammer on the bathroom door and demand to hear her say she was all right. It wasn't his place. Besides, if she didn't answer, what was he going to do? Break the door down? Storm in to find that she just couldn't hear him over the water? And end up standing there gaping at her, with her thinking the worst while his suddenly unruly body betrayed his every thought?

"Gracie," he said, and his voice was tight and rough, "go check on her, will you please? Just make sure she's all right."

Gracie frowned again. "Why wouldn't she be?"

"Sometimes…" He tried to think of a way to say it that wouldn't scare the child, but couldn't. Finally he just said it. "Sometimes burns get worse than they seem at first."

Gracie's blue eyes widened. She spun around and ran

down the hall. She stopped in front of a closed door and knocked, loudly.

"Mom! Mom, are you all right?"

He couldn't hear her answer, but judging by Gracie's body language, the way she relaxed, she'd apparently gotten a satisfactory answer and he breathed again. Gracie said something else, too quietly for him to hear. And again, and then she was running—did she ever not?—back.

"She's okay. She was just running cold water on it. She'll be out in a minute."

Suddenly, he wanted more than anything to get out of here. He should do what he'd come to do, and if Riley didn't like it, she could handle it. Except that was kind of scapegoating her, making her the bad guy, and that wasn't really fair. She probably had to do that too often already.

"You'll stay and have dinner with us, won't you?" Gracie asked. "I don't know what Mom has planned, but it'll be good. Sometimes it's boring to have the same stuff all the time, but it's never bad."

"Thank you, but I really don't think you should ask people to stay without checking with her first."

"Why? She likes you. I know she does."

He blinked. "You do?"

"Sure," Gracie said with a shrug. "And not just 'cause you helped with the car."

Interesting, that she thought that disclaimer was necessary. He wouldn't have expected a child her age to even get that. She truly was unlike any other kid he'd come across. Of course, given how low that number was…

"She talks to you," Gracie explained. "She doesn't talk to men, but she talks to you."

Flynn's jaw tightened. He supposed she'd gotten tired of

guys hitting on her. It had to happen, a woman like her. Hell, she'd probably think that's what he was doing, when she came out.

He needed to get out of here. "You…told her I was here?"

"Of course. That's why she's hurrying."

"She doesn't have to hurry. Some other time would be better, so just let me see she's okay and then I'll head home and—"

"No! Don't go. Please?"

She reached out and grabbed his hand, holding on as if in desperation. Flynn looked down at that little hand that couldn't even reach all the way around his, and knew that he could no more walk away from Gracie West than he could fly.

CHAPTER SEVENTEEN

F *lynn was here?*

Riley suppressed a shiver that had nothing to do with the cool water running over the patch of skin on her side that looked like she'd fallen asleep in the sun in a shirt with a big hole it in. She dried that area gently with the old, worn towel that was at least soft. She hastened through the rest, grateful she hadn't washed her hair.

Then the gratefulness vanished when she remembered what clothes she'd brought in here to put on when she was done; she was in for the night, so she'd gone straight for pajamas. Or, at least, what passed for pajamas for her—a faded T-shirt and a pair of knit shorts that had once been full-length pants until a renegade washing machine in the laundry room at her last apartment building had chewed them up from just past the hip down. They were soft and comfortable, so she'd just cut them off.

They were also too damned short to be wearing in front of Flynn. Not to mention she hadn't planned on a bra, either.

Maybe she could sneak into her bedroom and grab her

jeans. Or maybe she could call Gracie to get them for her. That would be better. She pulled on the T-shirt and shorts, figuring she could just put on her jeans over them for now, and went to edge the door open a little.

Just in time to hear Gracie plead, "No! Don't go. Please?"

Riley closed the door again, feeling a sudden weakness in her knees at the tone of her little girl's voice. Gracie did without so much, and she never complained. The only way Riley knew she was aware at all of what was missing was by the way she reacted when an unexpected treat came her way. Like riding in a new car. That simple fast-food breakfast and the time in the park the other day. The now-working A/C in their car.

All courtesy of Flynn.

That's all it was, she told herself. She was grateful to him, for all his help, his generosity. That was why she overreacted to the idea that he was here.

She sucked in a deep breath to steady herself, then cracked open the door again. "Gracie? Can you come here please? I need you for a moment."

She heard a brief scramble, then Gracie's light, quick steps as she called out, "Are you okay? Did it get worse?"

"No, I just need—"

Her words broke off abruptly as she heard a second, much heavier set of steps coming down the hall, almost drowning out Gracie's.

"Are you all right?"

She nearly groaned aloud at the sound of Flynn's voice from so close, while at the same time the concern in that deep, rumbling voice made her feel something. Something she didn't have words for.

Or something she didn't dare name.

"I'm fine," she said, and it sounded rather weak even to her own ears.

"Let me take a look."

"No, I—"

"I've dealt with burns before, Riley. Let me see how bad this one is."

"It's no worse than a sunburn," she protested.

"Anyone ever tell you you're stubborn?"

Gracie giggled. "Grandma did. But she said it nasty, not funny like you did. Huh, Mom?"

"Yes," Riley said, her voice going very quiet as she remembered the first time her mother had thrown that at her. When she'd told her her decision about her baby was final. And her mother had called her a stubborn bitch.

"Well don't be now. Gracie can't afford it."

She blinked. "What?"

"If it's worse than you think, and it goes septic—"

"All right, all right," she said, all her resistance draining away as if she'd pulled the plug in the tub. "But it's not that bad."

She backed away from the door, then wished she'd stepped out instead; the bathroom wasn't large anyway, but he made it seem...too small to contain him. And if he noticed what she was wearing—or almost wearing—he didn't react, unless she was so unattractive that was the cause of him clenching his jaw. But he said nothing except, "Show me."

She lifted the worn T-shirt, careful to keep her breasts covered. But he was focused on the reddened patch over her ribs.

"Ouch," he muttered as he tilted his head to see where it wrapped slightly around her side.

"It hurt," she admitted.

"Still does, I'm guessing," he said. Then he straightened up. "You have anything? Preferably something with lidocaine or something?"

"I...no."

"That's what you need."

"I need to fix Gracie's dinner and then she has homework to finish and—"

"No cooking for you. Being around heat's the last thing you need. I'll go get something and bring it back."

"Take out? Cool!" Gracie yelped.

"That's not necessary—"

"Stubborn," he muttered, "isn't the word for it."

"What is?" Gracie asked, her attention caught.

Flynn looked at her. "Obstinate? Maybe intractable?"

"Do those mean the same thing?"

"Pretty much. And," he added in a tone too pointed to miss, "they're more polite than mulish and pigheaded."

Gracie giggled again. And it hit Riley that she'd heard more of that delighted giggle in the last week than...ever. And that, too, was thanks to this man.

Her daughter looked at her pleadingly. "Come on, Mom. Take-out! Can we get it from the diner?"

"Honey, that's clear across town, too far to—"

"That's fine," Flynn interrupted. "Their roast beef sandwich is great, so I'll grab one for me, too."

"Chicken for me," Gracie piped up. "And Mom, too, right? She loves the chicken sandwich there, but we don't get it very often. Then you can eat here with us, and I can show you my room and then—"

"Gracie, slow it down. I'm sure Flynn didn't come over here intending to spend the evening."

"Of course not," Gracie said. "'Cause we hadn't invited him yet."

Flynn looked away abruptly, but she thought she saw the corner of his mouth twitching. He cleared his throat and said briskly, "Let me go get it first."

"I'll give you money for—"

"You will not," he said firmly. "I offered. That's how it works. And I was going to pick something up for myself anyway."

"Clear across town?" she asked, as pointedly as he'd made the pigheaded comment.

"Well, no, but now that my stomach's set on it, nothing else will do."

"See, Mom! Can I go with you?"

He gave Gracie a look Riley couldn't interpret. She opened her mouth to save him from having Gracie chattering at him—because apparently around him the child couldn't shut up—all the way over and back. But he spoke first, gently.

"I'd like the company, but maybe you should stay and help your mom. Make sure she doesn't do anything that will hurt that burn."

"Oh!" Gracie gave her a startled look. "I'm sorry. I'll stay here, Mom. I can get stuff for you, and I'll finish my homework out here, so you don't have to call me if you need something."

Riley felt her eyes sting as once more, as she'd done count-less times, her little girl floored her with her generous spirit. *Some things are worth any price. My baby girl is one of them.*

"Now that's some good planning," Flynn said, and Gracie beamed. "I'll be back—" he glanced at his watch, a big, black thing that looked like a holdover from his time in the Army "—by six, six-fifteen latest."

He was gone before Riley could say another word. And her daughter, darn her, was grinning from ear to ear.

IT ONLY TOOK Flynn a couple of minutes to find what he wanted at the drugstore. The checkout line took a little longer, so he texted ahead with his order for the diner, a convenience the owner's son Sebastian had instituted, over his traditionalist mother, Lucinda's, protests. But now even she admitted it had been a good idea. After all, every tradition was new in the beginning, she'd said. Which he'd thought very wise.

Not to mention it saved him time doing what he was doing now, enduring the stares. The clerk, at least, when he finally got there, smiled at him, but then she knew him from when he'd occasionally stop in here.

He was on his way back, the smell of the food waking up his stomach, when he drove past the nursery, which was open for another ten minutes or so. He glanced at the clock; thanks to texting the order he was right on time to be back at six. But he had given himself that window...

Wondering all the while when—and why--he'd stopped listening to that little alarm in his head, he made the turn.

CHAPTER EIGHTEEN

Riley watched Gracie look at the clock on the oven. Again. 6:14. The child was supposedly doing her homework there at the kitchen counter, but Riley doubted she was focusing much, not the way she was glancing up at the time every minute or two.

"There could be traffic or something, honey."

Gracie shook her head. "He said 6:15 latest. He wouldn't be late. He just wouldn't."

"I know what he said, but—"

The knock on the door cut her off, and her daughter gave her a triumphant smile. "Told ya'!"

She was off the stool and running for the door before Riley had time to get out of the kitchen.

"I knew you wouldn't be late!" Gracie yelped as she yanked the door open. Without, Gracie thought with a smothered sigh, even thinking about checking the peephole.

But it was Flynn, a couple of large white bags bearing the diner logo in his hand. "I wouldn't," he agreed. "I'm sort of a better half an hour early than five minutes late guy."

That caught Gracie's attention—as just about everything he said did—and she looked up at him. "Why?"

"Because if you're late, unless it's completely out of your control, it's like you don't think the other person's time is important."

"Oh," Gracie said thoughtfully. This man was, whether he intended it or not, teaching her little girl a lot of important things.

"Besides," he added with that delightfully crooked grin at the child, "there's nothing worse than having some guy in a much fancier uniform chew you out for being late."

Gracie laughed. "You should meet Principal Morton. He's the worst about being late."

"Take one of these, will you?" he asked, and Gracie grabbed the closest bag and trotted toward the kitchen. Then he reached for a smaller bag he'd been holding with a couple of fingers and held it out to Riley.

"Here. Go put this on that burn. It'll feel better right away."

She stared at the tube that slid out of the bag. He'd done this, too? Then he bent and picked something up that he'd apparently set on the mat outside her door. Surely not three bags of food, that would be—

Her thought ended abruptly. She stared at what he was holding out to her. Then her gaze shifted to his face. He was looking just slightly to his left, which hid most of the scars from her. And it struck her yet again how breathtaking he was. She wondered if that turn away was intentional, perhaps even automatic. That jabbed at her, and made her look down again at the beautiful bouquet of cheerful daffodils in a pretty yellow vase. Belatedly, she reached out and took them, because she didn't know what else to do.

"I thought they'd go well in here," he was saying when she tuned back in.

She looked around rather numbly, only now realizing he'd picked these to go with the few decorative touches she'd been able to manage in here, in an effort to add some cheer; the throw across the back of the worn sofa—the one with more knitting mistakes than she cared to admit, but the yarn had been free from a giveaway bin at the thrift store—and a couple of pillows. All yellow, nearly the same shade as the flowers she now held.

That he'd done this, all of it, noticed the color and actually bought her flowers, stunned her. "Flynn, I...thank you." *This is the nicest thing anyone's done for me in years.*

She managed to stop the pitiful words before they escaped. And then his next words came, and they were like ice water.

"I had them put it in a vase because I wasn't sure you had anything."

"Of course I don't," she said stiffly. She had nothing. Nothing at all.

He tilted his head slightly, frowning. "Not something everybody keeps on hand."

Riley smothered a sigh. He was only being kind. Generous. Which she already knew he was.

She just wished he wouldn't pity her.

She was being touchy and prideful, as her grandmother used to say. He hadn't meant anything by it, he'd just been being thoughtful. Again.

And right, since she didn't have anything to put flowers in, nor anyone to give them to her. Not in this life. And there was no room in that life for this man, either. No matter how much she might wish otherwise.

"Come on, Mom, I'm starving!" Gracie called out from the kitchen.

"Come in, you must be hungry too."

He gave her an odd look then, but he stepped inside. When they got to the counter, she saw her little girl had laid everything out neatly, with silverware and plates that seemed unnecessary for sandwiches. But then she saw the big tub of the diner's delicious coleslaw, and another of their famous mac and cheese, which was probably Gracie's favorite food in the world.

Even as she saw it Gracie crowed, "He got mac and cheese, Mom! A ton of it." She shifted her gaze to Flynn. Looked at him almost adoringly. "How'd you know it's my favorite food ever?"

"Just a guess," he said solemnly. Then, in a whisper, he added, "Because it was mine too, when I was eight."

Gracie grinned at him. "Were you little when you were eight?"

"And skinny," Flynn said.

Gracie laughed. Even Riley smiled as she tried to imagine a little, skinny Flynn. Then Gracie pointed at the middle of the three places she'd set. "Here, you sit in the middle. That way we both get to sit next to you."

He looked beyond bemused at the idea, as if it was as foreign to him that people would want to be near him as it was to her that someone would bring flowers.

We're a pair....

And she immediately cut off that line of thought.

"Go put that cream on," Flynn said. "Do it for three days or so, and it should be much better."

Since her side was protesting even in her looser jeans, she

didn't argue with him. But she retreated to the bathroom to do it. And he'd been right; the moment she smoothed the stuff on, the burning pain eased. She glanced at the directions, which said up to three times a day if needed.

She left the tube on the bathroom counter and went back out in time to see Gracie scramble up onto the barstool where she'd been doing her homework, but had shoved her things aside.

Flynn looked at her. He'd shed his jacket, which now lay over the back of the couch. Under it, he had on a long-sleeved knit shirt that did a little too much to remind her of his broad, strong chest and flat stomach. She swallowed hard.

"Better?" he asked.

"Yes. Much. Thank you."

He smiled, and she thought she definitely liked the way it was made kind of quirky by the pull of the scar. "Are you working tomorrow?"

"No. They told me to take the day off, after the spill." She sighed, wondering how many more times they would be that kind to her. A day off for being sick, now another for this.

"They're good people. It'll be fine."

It was as if he'd read her mind and her concern. "I hope so." It had to be, because she couldn't lose her job.

"What's that?" Gracie asked. She was pointing at a small jar she'd put by Flynn's plate, so Riley assumed it had been in the bag with his roast beef sandwich.

"That," he said with great import, "is horseradish."

Gracie laughed. "That's a funny name."

"It's a root that you grate up and use on things to enhance the flavor."

"Can I try it?"

Riley smiled inwardly at the idea as she took her apparently assigned seat on his right.

"You could," Flynn said neutrally. "But fair warning, it's powerful stuff."

Gracie stared at the little jar. "More powerful than garlic?"

Flynn laughed. What a wonderful sound that was, if only because he seemed so surprised that he was doing it at all. "It can be. And this is my boss's special blend. I talked them out of it since he's not here right now."

"Mr. K? Wow." She gave him a curious look. "What's he do? I mean I know he's really rich, everybody knows, but what does he do?"

"Now? He runs a company that has offices all around the world. A long way from inventing one little phone app. He's definitely the moneymaker of the Wild Oak Bunch."

Gracie laughed. "Jimmy talks about them. He said everybody does something different, so everything's taken care of. So you grow things and fix things, Mr. K makes money?"

He nodded. "And Jimmy's dad protects, Jake creates, John organizes. And now Shan's Juliette preserves things in pictures, Matt's Kelly teaches people things, John's Jen builds buildings, and Jake's Rachel, in a way, heals people."

"Sounds like you have the perfect little community there," Riley said with a warm smile.

"Why are you the only one alone?" Gracie asked innocently.

"Gracie!" Riley yelped, appalled.

But Flynn just shrugged. "Reasonable question. But besides the obvious, I guess it was just meant to be."

The obvious? Did he mean the scars? She couldn't deny, being seated on this side where she couldn't see them, what he must have looked like before. But he was still the same person, if a little damaged. Surely the women he encountered weren't all that shallow. Somebody had to see the amazing man he was.

"Here." Flynn twisted off the lid and held out the jar to Gracie. "Take a sniff. It'll make your eyes water."

Gracie hesitated, but then leaned in. And her mother had the sudden feeling that she would try just about anything this man asked of her. And Riley didn't quite know how that made her feel.

"Eww!" Gracie yelped. "You *eat* that?"

"Told you it was powerful."

"I don't think I want to grow up, if you have to eat stuff like that."

Flynn set the jar down and watched the child for a moment before he said quietly, "Just don't be in any hurry, kiddo. Being an adult isn't easy."

Gracie's gaze shifted to her, and what Riley saw in her daughter's eyes made her own tear up. "I know," the little girl said.

Flynn turned to look at her, just as Riley took a swipe at her eyes. "I must have gotten a whiff of the horseradish," she said.

"Or something," Flynn said neutrally, and she knew he knew perfectly well how Gracie had gotten to her with that too-adult understanding.

Riley could tell it was with barely contained excitement that Gracie waited until they'd finished eating before she grabbed Flynn's hand and pulled him to his feet. Or rather he let her do it; she knew he could have easily resisted.

"Come on and see my room!"

"At your own risk," Riley said dryly. "She is eight."

"It's not that big a mess," Gracie said, grinning uncon-cernedly.

Riley followed, curious for reasons she didn't want to

admit about his reaction to Gracie's little world. She saw him smile at the posters, as if they weren't what he'd expected. "Beautiful," he said at the aurora, and he laughed at the dragon. "No wonder you got along so well with Shan's guardian of the gate."

She saw him take note of the bookshelves, at the additional stack of books on the small, desk. The desk that was nearly buried in clutter. The small corkboard that was as cluttered as the desk. Then he went still.

"You saved the bandage?"

Gracie nodded. "It's all healed," she said, showing him her arm. "But I wanted to save it. To remind me of the day I met you and the dragon."

Riley couldn't put a name to the expression that came over his face then, but it wrenched at her. She spoke rather hastily, with a grimace at the piles. "Sad part is, when she says that's not that big a mess, she's telling the truth."

"It's holding a lot," Flynn said. "But then, so does her brain. So fitting, maybe."

"See, Mom?" She smiled widely at him. "I knew you'd get it."

Almost against her will her gaze went to the shelf over Gracie's bed. But the spot her eyes went to was empty. She frowned. Then spotted what she'd been looking for, moved back to the old place of honor on her pillow.

Snowball. Gracie's old, much loved, worn—and scarred— teddy bear.

Her gaze darted to him then, as she wondered if he'd seen it, if he even remembered what Gracie had said. But he was staring at the little bear, and suddenly she was certain. He did remember. Because he didn't seem to forget anything.

Especially that some people looked at him as they would

that stuffed bear. His fiancée, for instance. Or even worse, his mother. They'd looked and seen a man ruined. Not worth a second glance.

Discardable.

Whoever you both are, wherever you are, you're both fools.

CHAPTER NINETEEN

He should leave.
 He didn't want to leave.
Which was why he should.

Flynn smothered an inward sigh. He wasn't making sense even to himself. But he was just liking this too much. And when Gracie had asked him to wait while she showed him something, he'd been unable to resist and had sat down on the couch near where the bright yellow throw was folded. The throw that had made him pick daffodils at the nursery.

Riley had refused to let him help her clean up, so he sat there listening to the sound of dishes and silverware clanking. The apartment did not have a dishwasher, so she was doing them by hand. He didn't like that, but he did like that she was moving more easily, and not favoring her side as much, so he knew the salve had worked.

And he clamped down hard on the wish that he'd applied the stuff himself. Stroking his hands over that satin skin of hers would have been a recipe for something far hotter than that horseradish. And utterly, completely stupid. Because it would put Riley in the awkward position of rejecting him, and that would change everything. And crazily, he was afraid of them slipping back out of his life. He knew it was only temporary, but he still wanted this...whatever it was, for as long as he could have it.

Then Gracie was back, a large book in her hands.

"See what I got at the library? It's about plants, and look, I found the dragon plants and the fireworks!"

She had plopped down right beside him, leaned over, and opened the book to a full-page color photo of a firecracker plant. He saw a piece of paper marking another page that she turned to and there was a similar shot of the dragon wing begonias. And she was so sweetly, innocently excited he couldn't even describe how it made him feel.

"I see that," he managed to say, but his voice was tight.

"What's the name of the blue ones, growing by the rocks?" she asked.

"Nemophila," he said. "Better known as baby blue eyes."

She smiled at that. "I have blue eyes."

"I noticed. Almost exactly the same color. And just like your mom's."

The smile widened. "What are the big bushes out by the road and the dragon? Will they have flowers?"

"You mean the ones you scratched yourself hiding in?" he asked, his brow raised exaggeratedly.

Gracie laughed. "Yeah, those."

"Those are bougainvillea."

"That's a hard name."

"The variety is New River. That's easier. And in the summer there should be so many purple flowers you can hardly see the green."

"Wow!"

He couldn't believe she was this interested. Wouldn't most kids find this the most boring thing ever? But she paged through the book and asked him questions, and he found himself explaining about climate zones and growing seasons, and she listened with every evidence of rapt attention.

He glanced up as Riley came back from the kitchen and sat in the armchair that was at right angles to the couch. Those and a battered coffee table and the corner table that held the ancient television were the only things in the room. And he couldn't help wondering what else they were doing without, beyond what he already knew. Clearly, they were barely getting by, if that. And yet she was raising the most amazing child he'd ever seen.

It occurred to him to wonder if Riley was piling up debt. She was a loving mother who clearly hated seeing her child do without. But he discarded the idea quickly; the car, the budget cell phone, the worn clothes...

The image of Riley in the bathroom, wearing that old T-shirt and those short, cutoff pants, slammed into him and he had to look away. He stared down at a photo of an exotic orchid Gracie had turned to, trying not to think about those incredibly long, shapely bare legs and the sway of her breasts beneath the thin cloth. It took him a moment to rein in both his thoughts and his suddenly uncooperative body. He found silently chanting every name in the Orchidaceae family he could remember helped.

"Do they grow here?" Gracie asked.

"They can," he answered. "In fact, there are some that like growing around rocks."

The girl's smile was immediate. "You could plant some of them near the blue eyes!"

"Been thinking about just that."

Then they were on to philodendrons, with Gracie seeming quite content to go through the thick book page by page. But when they hit the big section on rhododendrons Riley spoke.

"Gracie, don't you have homework to finish?"

The girl looked up at her mother. "I can do it in the morning, Mom, honest."

"What's the rule?"

Gracie let out a pained sigh. "Do it now, because I don't know what might happen in the morning."

"Finish it in your room, if you can find space on your desk."

Gracie made a face at her, but she got to her feet, picking up the book as she did so. Then she looked at Flynn. "Don't just leave, okay?"

"I'll say goodbye," he promised, feeling odd, almost off balance now that she wasn't right next to him.

"I'm sorry we ate up your Friday night."

He shrugged. "Just another night." And it had been a very long time since it had been anything else.

"Gracie is...she's never...she's not used to having an adult male to talk to. Not like she talks to you."

Should we call someone? Your dad?

Don't have one.

Gracie's easy answer echoed in his mind. And he wondered if perhaps she hadn't been better off, if her father had been the kind of man who would let her slip out of his life.

"I...she's easy to be with."

She started to speak, stopped, and when she went on, he was certain it wasn't what she'd been going to say. "Thank you for being so patient with her. She's a bit...voracious."

"She likes to learn. That's good to see." He suddenly realized he'd never gotten around to why he'd come here in the first place. "Sort of in line with that...and given her fondness for every kind of book there is, judging by the pile on that desk of hers, how would you feel about her having an e-reader?"

Her mouth—that luscious mouth—thinned slightly. "Not in the cards, I'm afraid."

"But you wouldn't have an objection otherwise? I mean, you can put parental controls on it."

She drew back slightly. Studied him for a moment, then said flatly, "I think you'd better just say it, Flynn. But if you're going to say you want to buy her one, then don't bother."

At least she hadn't slipped back into calling him Mr. Flynn. That would have sent a message he didn't want to hear, given the way he was feeling around her tonight.

"No. I know you wouldn't...let me do that. But Shan gave me a new one a while ago. After," he added with a wry smile, "he laughed himself silly over my old one, which worked perfectly fine but not to his technological standards."

He'd managed to make her smile with that. "I can only imagine," she said.

"Anyway," he went on, reaching into the pocket of the jacket that was behind him and pulling out the thin device, "this one's just been sitting in a desk drawer ever since. It's a little scratched, because I carried it around a lot, but it still works great."

He held it out to her. She looked at it, probably saw it was indeed a little worn. Then she looked up at him. "Carried it...where?"

"Let's just say it's well traveled."

"Over there?" she asked quietly. He nodded. Didn't speak because he didn't know why that made her look so...intense. "And you want to give it away?"

"I've got enough souvenirs." She drew back as if he'd snapped at her. It took him a moment to get to what she'd thought he'd meant. "I didn't mean that," he said hastily. Then, as he realized the truth of his own words, he added, "I wasn't even thinking about the scars. I swear."

"Then I believe you," she said simply.

"Just like that?"

"Yes. Because I trust you." She stopped, as if she were hearing her own words. And then, in a tone of wonder, she repeated, "I trust you."

And all Flynn could think was that if he ever met the man who'd done this to her, he'd be lucky to walk away alive.

CHAPTER TWENTY

"The big thing is," Flynn said, "you can download a ton of books from the library." He gave Riley that crooked grin she was coming to like altogether too much. "Might save you a couple of trips a week. You just go to the library website, check the e-book selection, tell it what you want, and it'll send it to the vendor and you download it like any other book. I tried it to make sure."

He'd done all this. For them. Did he never stop?

"I didn't deregister it," he went on, "but you can if you have an account and want to re-register it on yours."

"I don't. I don't dare," Riley said, still not quite believing this was happening. But how could she turn this down? This was for Gracie, who so rarely asked for anything. And this, this would be the biggest gift she'd had in her young life.

"Then it can stay on mine. I'll make sure you've got access so you can have control over what she sees."

Riley couldn't help but wonder at the look he gave her then, even as the idea of a joint account of any kind with him made her a little breathless. Was that why he looked hesitant?

It wasn't like sharing an online account for book downloads was some kind of declaration. Should she reassure him that she understood that? Or would that just betray her silly thoughts? Thankfully, before she blurted out something stupid, he went on.

"I cleared out my stuff. Not that I had anything really...inappropriate on it," he said, a little hastily. "For her, I mean. But there's not any kids' books on it. Not yet, anyway. She'll change that, I imagine. Although I'm guessing she reads way above what most people would think is her level."

His words sounded like her thoughts had, short, choppy. He was nervous, she realized suddenly. And she wondered why, wondered what it would take to make a man who had been through everything he'd been through nervous.

And she thought it was the sweetest thing in the world, that he was worried about his content and Gracie. "Yes, she does. Is there any plant stuff? She seems to have developed a...strong interest."

Heaven help her, she'd almost said passion. And that was a word that hadn't been in her mind in conjunction with a man in a very, very long time. But it had been about a subject, not the man she was discussing it with. Hadn't it?

But he smiled at her question, and suddenly she wasn't so sure. She was far too fond of that crooked smile, in far too short a time. *Your judgment about men sucks, remember?*

True, but she didn't think Jimmy's dad's judgment did.

"Yes," he answered. "She can re-download those, if you want." He hesitated, then asked, "Does this mean...you'll take it? For Gracie?"

She drew in a deep breath, and gave him a wry smile. "You know she's my weak spot. My vulnerability."

"I thought of it more as the best infiltration point," he said neutrally.

That nearly made her laugh. "I appreciate you clearing it with me first."

"I didn't want you to have to be the one to say no if you didn't want her to have it."

The simple admission nearly did her in. She had to say no to her precious, sunny child so often...that he realized that should embarrass her, but instead, she was impossibly moved by his understanding. How did a man who'd had a mother who walked out on him when she saw his scars end up like this?

"All right," she said, giving in. Although she doubted she could have said no to this opportunity for Gracie. "Thank you. Thank you...a lot. This will mean the world to her."

He smiled, that endearing little smile she was coming to treasure. He got out the charging cable and gave it to her, then powered the device on and put a couple of his garden references and plant guides back in place. As he did he said, "You might want to disable the purchase capability. It's kind of easy to buy something by accident."

She smiled back at him. "Voice of experience?"

He finished and looked up at her. "Let's just say I'm more at home with a pruning saw."

She laughed. "Why don't you go give it to her?"

He shook his head. "You can. I've taken up enough of your—"

"Stop." He blinked. But stopped. "It's your gift to her, you give it to her."

"If I meant it as a gift, I'd have bought her a new one. This is just...recycling."

That did make her laugh. "Are all you heroes so reluctant to accept credit?"

He went very still. "I'm no hero, Riley. You want a hero, go talk to John Reese, or Matt McLane."

She studied him for a moment before saying with quiet determination, "They are, no doubt about that. But you see, I get to decide who I think is a hero." She stood up. "Come on. I want to see her face."

He still hesitated, but then gave in. "I need to say good-night to her anyway."

"Because you promised."

"Yes."

She again studied him. "Do you have any idea how much that means, always keeping promises to a child?"

Again he shrugged. It seemed to be his go-to when he didn't know what to say. She wondered if he'd always been so reticent, or if that was a side-effect of his injuries and the resultant scars. Crazy, she thought, that if it had happened differently, and if the scars had been somewhere where they could be hidden, he might be an entirely different person.

And how crazy was it that her next thought was that she was glad they weren't, because she quite liked the man he was now?

GRACIE LOOKED up as they stepped into her room. The door hadn't been closed, and Riley had whispered to him that she'd probably left it open so she could make sure he didn't leave without that goodbye.

The child smiled at him so instantly, and so widely it made

his throat tight again. "Hey," he said, the short greeting all he could get out.

Gracie's suddenly changed, saddened. "You're leaving?"

He was, wasn't he? Once this was done, his mission here was done. So of course he'd be leaving. "I just wanted to give you this first. Your mom says it's okay."

He held the device out to her. She took it before she really looked at it, but when she did her eyes widened. "An e-reader? For me?"

"It's my old one, but it works fine." She was staring at him now, shock showing in her bright blue eyes. "You can get books from the library on it, so you don't always have to lug home so many."

"I know, I've seen my friends do it. But...really? It's for me? For keeps?"

She looked so astonished, he thought his heart might break. "Yes, Gracie. It's yours. Your mom will have the say on what you get on it, still, but it's yours."

The girl erupted into motion, unexpectedly climbing up to stand on the seat of her chair. And then she threw herself at him, and he had to move quickly to catch her. Her little arms went around his neck and she hugged him so tightly it was a little hard to breathe. But he didn't care, not one bit. He held her securely, thinking he'd never felt anything like this, the revelation of having the complete trust of a child. And he didn't know how to deal with it.

He needed to think. And he couldn't do that here. Gracie was disconcerting enough, but Riley was...again those images of her in the shower hit him, and he knew he had to get out of here before he said or did something unforgiveable.

He wasn't even sure what he said to Gracie, and then he and Riley were at the front door.

"You're all right? The burn—"

"Can't even feel it right now. Thank you. I'll put some more of that cream on it before I go to bed."

And that opened another door he didn't dare even glance at. Or think about. How easy it would be to slide that old shirt off of her, those short things off those long, long legs...

"Flynn," she said quietly, "everything you've done—"

"Don't. You've thanked me enough. More than enough."

"No, I haven't. Because I can't."

He stood there, willing himself to move, hell, willing himself to run. But he couldn't seem to get the message to his feet. And then Riley moved, with that lovely grace. She leaned in and stretched up at the same time. And kissed his cheek. The scarred cheek. Heat rippled through him instantaneously. But shock rippled through him at almost the same moment. No woman had ever done that. Mostly, they avoided even looking at it, to the point of always standing on his right, so they would only see the undamaged side.

Except Riley never did. His mind raced to confirm the realization that had just hit him. She never did. She was almost always in a place to see the left side, the ugly side, the side that made people's eyes dart away.

Most people.

Obviously Riley West was made of sterner stuff.

For a long, silent moment he just stood there, staring at her, into those bottomless blue eyes, barely aware his lips were parted and his breathing had quickened.

Her cheeks looked pink. She was probably embarrassed. Wishing she hadn't done it?

He didn't know what to say.

So he left without saying a word.

CHAPTER TWENTY-ONE

E ven hours later, Riley still couldn't believe she'd done it.
But even more, she couldn't believe the effect it had
had. On her, anyway. It was if she could still feel it. Her lips
still tingled, and she felt echoes of the warmth that had
flooded her even now.

The scars hadn't been rough or stiff, but merely a slightly
raised line she could feel. But Flynn himself had gone utterly
rigid, then had turned and left without a word. As if she'd
done something horrific.

And maybe she had.

She'd only been trying to say the heartfelt thank you he
wouldn't let her speak, or merely shrugged off.

She smothered a sigh and turned over. Another mistake,
since that put her in line with the clock beside her bed, which
declared uncompromisingly that it was 3:00 AM.

She couldn't even say she was out of practice, since she
hadn't had much practice in the first place. She simply didn't
know how to deal with a man she'd somehow failed to keep at
arm's length.

Because she hadn't really wanted one any closer since that night nine years ago. Which was likely why her one try had been such a disaster.

The memories, held at bay for so long, slammed into her. She was tired, her guard was down, and it was the dark middle of the night, and after all this time she knew better than to fight it. So she curled up, grabbed a pillow to muffle any sound, and hung on.

Flynn looked at the rather crooked cut he'd just made in the board he'd meant to replace one in the hedge support near the gate, and stood there debating whether he should be handling anything with a slicing edge today. He wasn't doing any better than he had yesterday, when all he could think about was the night before. How it had ended, anyway.

No, sharp edges were not his friend on this Saturday morning.

Cutting yourself shaving should have been the first clue.

But he hadn't expected the already somewhat tricky job of shaving his scarred cheek to go completely awry when the memory of a pair of soft, sweet lips kissing that twisted flesh had risen up to swamp him. He had thought he'd hammered that down in the restless hours of last night—after the entirely sleepless night he'd spent immediately after she'd shocked the hell out of him—but he'd been wrong. In this case, bloody wrong.

At least it wasn't your throat. Although maybe it should have been.

He heard a car approaching and his gut knotted. He steeled

himself to look, and breathed again when he saw it was Jake's truck. He liked that the man, who could now afford probably any car he wanted, still drove his old carpenter's truck. The same way Shan still drove his pickup from years ago, when he wasn't careening around on that motorcycle that Flynn imagined gave his people at Kelleher nightmares.

Jake parked, got out, and walked toward him. There was a bit of a breeze this morning, and it tangled his dark hair.

"Come to check on your guardian?" he asked with a gesture at the dragon when Jake came to a halt.

"He's Shan's now. And your guardian as well, Rach says."

"She would," he answered quietly; Rachel Stone was one of the most generous, loving human beings he'd ever met. She'd had to be to break through Jake's walls.

Jake only smiled, the smile of a very contented man. Flynn had time to ponder the oddity that his eyes were almost the same color gray as his blue-eyed sister's husband, Flynn's best friend. The guy who had been as close as Jake had had to a big brother—maybe even a father—in his life.

For some reason, the memory of the first time he'd come to the Bunch's monthly gathering at Jake's place at the end of the road came back to him. He'd been edgy, not certain he should have come, and only there because John had flat-out made it an order. And just because they no longer wore the uniform didn't mean the man still didn't have that right now and then.

Flynn had stayed on the periphery that day, watching, seeing them all laugh and talk, until Jake had walked over to him.

"Don't like my place?"

"What? No, it's great." He'd meant it—he liked the spacious grounds, the comfortable, homey cabin, and the huge workshop, all of it shaded by a stand of the glorious oak trees the town had been named for.

"Then why the isolationist act?"

"I...people get weird around me. Not their fault, it's just...they don't know what to say."

"The scars, you mean?" People weren't usually that blunt with him, and he'd appreciated that Jake was. "John ever tell you about me?"

"He told me your father was an ass who once burned all your work. Didn't need to hear anymore."

"True story. Want to know why I believed him for so long, that my work was worthless?"

"Why?"

"Because it wasn't perfect. I'd see the perfect image in my head, but I could never translate it with my hands. I figured that meant I wasn't any good."

Flynn had stared at him then, thinking of the brilliant work he'd seen at a couple of Jake's shows. "That's...crazy. Your work is amazing."

"It took Rachel to show me that yes, they weren't the perfect replica of the image I had in my head." He'd grinned then. "They were better."

"She's right."

"Come tell her that, then."

He'd done so, at Jake's urging, and once Rachel had latched onto him, there'd been no more hiding on the edges. She'd made sure he was involved, and he'd been amazed at how they'd accepted him. And Jake's personal lesson about perfection—and the lack of it—had stayed with him.

It hadn't, however, helped him much with Riley West.

Now Jake nodded toward the dragon. "I hear he made a new friend."

That snapped him back to the present. *Damn, word gets around fast.*

If there was a downside to the Wild Oak Bunch, it was that nothing, but nothing, stayed secret for long. But he trusted them all, so he hadn't worried about it much. At least, not until now.

"Local kid," he said casually.

"Smart kid, Matt says."

"Very." He knew this wasn't why Jake was here. In fact, he had a pretty good idea why he was here. And a moment later he was proved right.

"How long are you going to keep John hanging, Flynn?"

His jaw tightened. "He can do a lot better than me."

"Last I checked, there wasn't a list of qualifications."

"I don't know the first or last thing about dealing with kids."

Even as he gave the by now-practiced response, he realized that maybe, just maybe, that wasn't strictly true anymore. But there was a huge—and terrifying—difference between a smart eight-year-old and a baby. More terrifying than wading into a terrorist stronghold.

"He doesn't care about that. And the chances are really good you'll never have to do much. So just say yes, damn it. Tell him you'll be his kid's godfather." Jake shoved a hand through his tangled hair. "Be my nephew's godfather, Flynn."

Flynn's breath caught in his throat. He hadn't really thought about that, that by resisting this he was not just saying no to John, but to Jake, too. And Jen. And the baby's Aunt Rachel. Damn, why did it all have to be so intertwined?

It was crazy how this rattled him. He'd been in firefights that hadn't gotten to him like this did. Of course, those were over and done with pretty fast, one way or another. This, this would never be over. Until he died, he would be responsible for another human being, should the worst ever happen. He couldn't. He just—

Another car pulled in behind Jake's pickup. He'd been so distracted, he hadn't even heard it. He looked, and this time his breath slammed to a halt. A bare instant later, the door to the all too familiar old vehicle opened, and Gracie was headed for him, balancing a plate carefully in her hands.

His gaze flicked to Jake, who lifted a brow at him. "His new friend?" he asked, indicating the dragon.

Flynn only nodded, because he couldn't speak if he'd wanted to. And then Gracie was there, and Flynn was fighting not to look toward her mother, who had stayed in the car.

Gracie held out the plate, which held more cookies, and as he took it, he could tell they were even still warm.

"You didn't have to—"

"Yes, I did!" she yelped, cutting him off. "I love it, Flynn, I've been having so much fun looking for books and I already have so many downloaded I won't run out for days, and Mom won't have to drive me to the library so she's happy too to save the gas and time and—"

The girl stopped suddenly, and gave Jake a shy, sideways look. "I'm sorry. I know I interrupted. Mom told me since you have company I have to be quick."

Mom, who still wasn't getting out of the car. Probably too embarrassed, and wishing she'd never done...what she'd done the other night.

His gaze flicked to Jake, who was half smiling as he watched Gracie. Flynn wondered if he was seeing his own future; his little Cammie was already showing signs of being a very bright girl.

He didn't quite know where the urge came from, but he did it anyway. "Gracie, meet the creator of your favorite guardian of the gate. Jake Stone, this is Gracie West."

The child's gaze shot to Jake, and she stared up at him with eyes nearly as big as the cookies she'd brought. "You're him? You made him—" she pointed almost wildly at the dragon "—and the horses at the Atrium?"

Her voice was full of awed excitement, and Flynn smiled to himself at the look on Jake's face. He probably should have asked before he introduced him, but Jake deserved to be gushed over. He might be one of the hottest artists in the country now, but Jake had never, ever forgotten his battle to get there, and it still amazed him sometimes how people reacted to his work. Even—or knowing Jake these days, probably especially—children. He'd spent a lot of time doing work for Shan's children's cancer clinic, and it had left a mark.

"That'd be me," Jake said with a crooked smile, and Flynn knew he'd done the right thing.

Gracie turned and yelled at the top of her young and very healthy lungs. "Mom! Mom, come here, you have to come here! Right now! It's him, it's the man who made the dragon! And the horses! Hurry!"

When her mother didn't move instantly, she ran toward the car, and if she bodily dragged Riley out Flynn wouldn't be surprised.

"Should I be glad Cammie is still fairly nonverbal?" Jake said, his tone rather wry.

"Not for long, I hear," Flynn said.

Jake sighed. "Yeah. She's working on Mama and Dada, and I swear she said 'Hi' the other day."

Flynn laughed, but it died away the moment he looked

back toward Gracie and saw her indeed pulling her mother this way.

"Whoa," Jake said. Then he shifted his gaze to Flynn. "You neglected to mention Mom's a looker."

"Didn't notice," he lied gruffly.

Jake's gaze sharpened. "I know you're a bit sour on women, and I don't blame you, but if I thought that was true, then I'd be more worried about you than I already am."

He'd be the first to admit that his history with women—be they fiancées or mothers—had curdled his outlook. But Gracie was just a kid, a little girl, so it had seemed harmless at the time to let her in a little.

Gracie's mother, on the other hand...

And then Gracie was back, and he had no choice but to repeat the introduction. But he kept it as short as possible. "Riley West, Jake Stone."

The two shook hands. Knowing exactly what touching Riley felt like, the sight made his stomach knot. It took Flynn a moment to recognize the sensation.

Jealous? He was jealous of a friendly handshake? Between Riley and Jake, who was so crazy in love with his wife no woman could tempt him? Not even one who looked like Riley....

When he snapped out of it—damn, if he'd been prone to these fanciful moments back in the day, he'd never have survived, and probably would have taken the whole team with him—Gracie had commandeered Jake and made him go with her to the dragon, no doubt to pelt him with questions.

"I'll go rein her in," Riley said, clearly uneasy.

"He'll deal. He has a baby girl of his own now."

"But he's a famous artist, and she's taking up his time."

"Jake doesn't see himself that way. He spent too long thinking he was a failure to ever go pretentious on us."

She stared at him. "A failure?"

He nodded. "Thank his father for that one."

"Parents can be...well, some just shouldn't be."

Riley looked around the garden, toward the house, and along the sheltered, flower-festooned path they'd walked to show her the dragon. Then she looked back at him.

"Is that why you don't see yourself as the artist you are? Your parents?"

He nearly gaped at her. "What? I'm not an—"

"You are," she cut him off firmly. "This entire place is a work of art."

"That's—"

"In fact, you should be designing places like this. The way you took this place and made it suitable for the guardian there...people would pay a ton of money to have that kind of thing done."

"This was...different. It was for a friend."

"I still bet you could have a thriving career at it. Just throw up a website with some photos of this place, and within a year you'd be not only in demand, but famous in landscape design circles."

He couldn't help it, he laughed. The very idea was downright silly. She was just joking. She had to be. And judging from the way she dropped it, he was right. She glanced over at Jake, who was showing Gracie something on the dragon's tail.

"So...he just dropped in to visit?"

Flynn grimaced. "More to harangue."

She blinked. "You? About what?"

"Being a godfather." It was out before he thought. Damn, why couldn't he keep his mouth shut around her?

"To his little girl?"

"No, John's her godfather. Well, and her uncle, but he's up to it."

"If he delivered her, I should say so. Who, then?"

He let out a compressed breath. "John's son. Who's due any minute now."

She studied him for a long moment, and somehow that made him more nervous than if she'd started right in on some chatter about it being an honor. Which he already knew.

"And you don't want to do it?" she finally asked.

"I'm not up to doing it."

"You, Mr. Flynn, are full of bull." He drew back sharply at the blunt words and tone. She didn't waver, just crossed her arms and stared at him. "Don't forget I've watched you with Gracie."

He was a little taken aback at her fierceness. At the same time, he admired it; despite everything life had tossed at her, Riley West was no coward. It took him a moment to formulate an answer.

"That's different. She's not a baby."

"No, she's not, but—"

"Mom!" Gracie came back at a run, Jake following more slowly and wearing a thoroughly bemused expression. "He showed me how he did the tail. That's what I couldn't figure out."

"Your daughter," Jake said to Riley, "is quite something."

"I know," Riley said, but she looked pleased.

"Figure you got a glimpse of your future?" Flynn asked.

Jake rolled his eyes. "If so, I'm in trouble."

"A lot of people don't think they're up to it," Riley said quietly. "But then it happens and most of them manage to measure up."

Flynn shot another glance at her, but she was innocently looking at Jake, not even hinting that that had been aimed at him. But he knew that choice of phrase hadn't been an accident. In her way, Riley was just as smart as her gifted daughter.

Especially when she was making a point.

CHAPTER TWENTY-TWO

R iley stared at Melanie, the restaurant manager. She'd been terrified when she'd called her in to the office, afraid she was about to be let go. She hadn't noticed any change in the business level, but maybe it was worse than she thought. She hadn't done anything to warrant being fired, that was certain. She was so careful it sometimes grated on her, but she didn't dare lose this job. She had a tiny bit of breathing room now, thanks to Flynn, but the money she'd been saving for those repairs were already earmarked for other necessities. Flynn. The man she'd spent far too much time thinking about all day Sunday, after the joy he had brought to Gracie with that simple, thoughtful passing on of his old e-reader, something that was so far down on the list she might never have gotten there.

She gave herself an inward shake and made herself focus. "I...don't understand," she said hesitantly.

"It's simple. I'm recommending you for the day shift lead position, now that Marny is leaving."

Marny had told her just a couple of days ago that her

boyfriend had gotten transferred at his work, and they'd decided to move together. But Riley had assumed...

"But...Brittany. She's been here much longer than I have."

"Yes. But she's also made it clear she has no interest in the job. I presume you do?" Melanie smiled. "It's not a huge raise in pay, but it is a raise."

A raise. Even a small one would help. But this also meant more work; she knew Marny spent time checking time cards and helping with the supply inventory, and probably more. And Riley had other things to consider. Gracie, and her school schedule. She was so good about staying in various after-school programs until Riley was off work, and that covered all but two days a week.

"And of course this is subject to an interview with Mr. Carlson. He has the final say."

She'd only met the owner of the Oak Tree restaurant once, when she'd been hired. She'd been too afraid, too desperate for the job to do much more than give yes or no answers. But she'd seen an approving glint in his eyes when she'd told him she'd decided to stay in Wild Oak in large part because of the wide selection of schools for her documentedly brilliant daughter.

And because he'll never find me here.

A chill rippled through her at just the memory of the thought, and again she fought for focus. "Of course," she echoed.

"So shall I schedule it with him?" Melanie asked.

"I..."

"Riley," the older woman said gently, "I know this would mean a change in your schedule, including working an occasional weekend day, and that you have other things to consider, your daughter especially. We're not rushing you, but we will need an answer fairly quickly."

"I'm sorry. Please don't think I'm an idiot. I just never expected this."

Melanie gave her a smile. "You're a hard worker, and clients love you. We're very aware that you have regulars, who ask to be seated in your area. That says a lot to me, and it means a lot to Mr. Carlson. So, even if you decide not to take the promotion, your job is safe, if that's a concern."

Riley let out a breath. "Thank you. It was." She sucked in more air so she could go on. "I would have to figure out scheduling, with my daughter."

"Perhaps with the extra money you could pay someone to watch her?"

"Perhaps," Riley said, although her stomach roiled at the very idea of entrusting her girl to a stranger. There had to be another way. Another school program, something at the library, anything. As for those weekend days, she had no idea. But surely there would be something. But it had to be okay with Gracie, too.

"The only other issue is that Mr. Carlson is heading out of town in the morning, so he would need to meet with you at seven this evening. Can you manage that?"

Riley couldn't help wondering of those last words were a test, because if she couldn't manage a last minute thing like this, she probably couldn't handle the job, either. Seven o'clock only gave her two hours from her end of shift to arrange something for Gracie, who she normally picked up from the YMCA today at 5:15. She'd think of something. Somehow.

"I'll manage it."

Melanie's smile was wide and welcoming. She'd always liked the woman, found her more than reasonable, especially about Gracie, perhaps because she had two girls of her own. "I know you will."

When she picked her up, Gracie was so excited at the news, it almost surprised Riley. "Mom, that's great! A promotion is a good thing, right?"

"Yes. Yes, it is. But it would mean more time at work for me. Not a lot, maybe half an hour or so, more on Fridays, but—"

"I can stay longer at the Y, and I can read in the library after the kids' group ends. It'll be fine."

Her sweet, clever girl, instantly realizing and solving the problem. Riley almost teared up and had to turn her head away.

"There's one more problem, though," she said after a minute. "The owner of the restaurant wants to talk to me personally. And he can only do it tonight. In an hour and a half." She went on with the only thing she'd been able to think of, and only because the man had offered his help before. "I thought I'd call Jimmy's dad and see if—"

"He's working tonight, Jimmy said so. But it's okay, Mom," Gracie said quickly. "I can go stay with Flynn."

She couldn't deny the thought had occurred to her, but she didn't really want to impose on him any further. Not to mention, it was a step she wasn't sure she was ready to take. Was fairly sure she wasn't ready to take.

"Honey, I think he's done enough for us already, don't you?"

"He's done a lot, but not because we asked him."

Because he felt he had to, because of his boss and his innate instinct to help.

She threaded her way through a busy four-way stop intersection as she thought, and before she realized, Gracie had grabbed her phone and started to tap.

"Gracie—"

"There, I've got it. It's okay, I'm calling, Mom. You drive."

"Honey, don't—"

"Hi, Flynn, it's me!" her daughter said happily into the phone. With full confidence her voice would be recognized. Then, with a too aware glance at her mother, she added, "Mom didn't want me to bother you, but I grabbed her phone and called because I knew you wouldn't mind, because this is important, like a promotion at work important, but she has to talk to the boss right away to get it, and you know how she is, she won't leave me alone even though I'd be perfectly fine, but she still won't, and she was going to call Jimmy's dad but he's working tonight, and so I told her I could come stay with you."

The girl at last paused for a breath. And after a moment, the first trace of worry creasing her young brow, she said, "Flynn?"

"He's probably still trying to sort all that out," Riley said rather dryly as she tried to think of a way to get poor Flynn out of this benignly, without hurting Gracie's feelings. "And he's also probably busy, honey, so—"

Gracie waved her off as apparently Flynn finally spoke. And after a minute, Gracie lit up. "Thanks, Flynn! We'll be right there."

Gracie tapped to end the call and gave Riley a triumphant look. "I told you it would be okay. Let's go."

She stared at the whirlwind that was her daughter. "Now?"

"Yeah! He said he has to make a trip to the nursery to pick up some stuff, and I can come with him. That's cool, isn't it, Mom? I want to see all the plants they have there. Oh, he said come in the back way, he's at his place. I'll have to see the dragon later."

Sometimes she wondered how she kept up at all with this child. And ten minutes later, as she was pulling in the gate—after Gracie keyed in the code Flynn had apparently left the same, or maybe told her on the phone—she still felt a tiny bit breathless. And even more so when she saw him walking in that way of his, clad today in a pair of black jeans and T-shirt that made him look slightly dangerous. Then she remembered who and what he'd been and mentally removed the "slightly."

Gracie had jumped out and run, then jumped at him from three feet away. As the child had clearly known he would he caught her, held her safely. And Riley was struck by how much smaller her little girl seemed in the arms of this man. But then she saw the smiles they exchanged, and nothing beyond that mattered. Because she hadn't seen Gracie ever smile like that before, and she somehow knew it had been a very long time since Flynn had smiled like that, too.

After a moment he set Gracie down, told her to put her things in his truck, and continued over to Riley.

"Congratulations."

Flynn's deep voice made her yet more breathless. "Haven't got it yet, but...thank you. I wasn't even sure you got all that, as fast as she went on."

That crooked smile again. Yes, she definitely adored that smile. "It took some sorting, but I got there."

"I'm so sorry, I didn't know she was going to call—"

She stopped when he held up a hand. "It's all right. This is a special circumstance, after all. Job promotions don't come along every day."

"I don't even know if I should take it, I have to think about Gracie after school. That's if Mr. Carlson even really offers it."

"That's your interview?" She nodded. He studied her for a moment. "He and Shan are pretty tight." She stared at him. Why would the billionaire of Dragon Hill be close with the owner of the Oak Tree? Then he added, "Want me to have him call and put in a word?"

Her eyes widened. "No! No, I don't want you to. If I get this promotion, it'll be because I got it, not because of somebody pulling strings."

The gold flecks in Flynn's hazel eyes seemed to gleam, and he slowly smiled. "Nice to know you're exactly who I thought you were."

She drew back. "What was that, a test?"

He shrugged. "Just a question."

"You mean if I'd said yes—"

"I would have called Shan."

She studied him for a moment before saying slowly, "And thought less of me, but never have said a word."

Another shrug, an answer in itself.

"Judge people often?" she asked, an edge creeping into her voice.

His brow furrowed. "More assess. Out of habit, and training. Feeling judged?"

She sighed. Of course he did; how often had his life, and others, depended on the accuracy of those assessments? "Too often," she admitted.

"By anyone harder on you than yourself?"

That was a question she had no answer for, and she was happy when Gracie ran back to them, and pointed out she'd better go or she'd be late.

"Not the way to start a promotional interview," he said gravely.

"No. I'm nervous enough already."

"Think about something else, Mom. That's what you always tell me."

But the only thing she could come up with to think about was the man standing right here.

"Need a distraction?" he asked, and something had come into that voice of his, already so deep and male, that sent a quiver through her.

And then he leaned forward, held her shoulders, and kissed her.

CHAPTER TWENTY-THREE

"Y̶ou kissed my mom."

Flynn couldn't look at the little girl who had turned on him the moment her mother's car was clear and the gate had closed behind it. He didn't dare look at her. In fact, he wished, at this moment, he was anywhere but here, somewhere alone, to process what had just happened. Because he'd only meant to do just what he'd said, distract her.

He hadn't expected to light up like a flamethrower himself.

But he had. His entire body had, in a way he'd never felt before. From a simple kiss, delivered in a purely non-romantic way.

Purely non-romantic. Nonsexual. Non...wanting.

Right.

"Why?" Gracie demanded.

He searched for some remnant of the cool under fire guy he'd once been. "You said it," he told her. "She needed something else to think about. I figured that would be enough of a shock."

"Oh." There was a long, silent pause. He was on the verge of looking at her when she spoke again. "I was hoping it was 'cause you liked her."

He froze. Her voice was sad. As if she had genuinely been hoping...that.

"Gracie..." It was all he could get out.

"It's okay," the child said, with a far too adult sigh. "Mom says we're enough, the two of us. But we can't always be together. I know she gets lonely sometimes." She gave him a sideways look. "Like you said you do, sometimes."

It took every bit of battlefield nerve he'd ever had to pull himself together enough to say evenly, "But like you said, I've got you now, right?"

He would have crossed that battlefield for the smile she gave him then. And suddenly, that simply, she was herself again. As if he'd somehow righted her world with those words.

"Are we going to the plant place?" she asked excitedly.

"We are," he said. "Get in the truck. I have to stop by the house and lock up, since I was up there earlier."

"Does that mean we'll go out by the dragon?"

He couldn't help but smile, despite the roiling in his mind. "Yes, so you'll be able to say hello."

He waited until she was in and had her seatbelt fastened. Then he started the truck and headed toward the house. His thoughts were an impossible tangle the entire way, between what Gracie had said, how that had made him feel, how the fact that Riley had trusted him with the most precious thing in her life made him feel...and that kiss.

He should have known. Should have known after that friendly kiss she'd given him the night he'd taken the e-reader over. He'd overreacted to that a hundredfold. Had been feeling pretty pitiful that such a casual thing could have impacted him like that. In fact, he wouldn't have thought he could have a stronger reaction than that,

Until now.

He'd been busy telling himself he wasn't remembering right, that it hadn't been that hot, really, that she couldn't possibly have tasted that good, when they reached Shan's house. He pulled to a stop on the driveway that curved in front of the front door.

"Could I peek in?" Gracie asked, almost shyly, for her. "I've never seen a dragon owner's house."

How very...Gracie. Most people would probably have said they wanted to see the inside of a billionaire's house. And given that was what she'd asked, he knew what Shan's answer would have been, had he been here.

"I don't think he'd mind a peek," he told her, and she scrambled out of the truck.

He smiled when the child only took a single step inside and then stopped. She had her own boundaries as to what consti-tuted a peek in mind, clearly. She looked around the entry and into the living room that, Shan admitted, didn't get all that much use.

"Mr. K is really rich, isn't he?" she asked, looking puzzled.

"He is."

"This looks like a regular person's house," she said.

"That's because he's a regular person first. He just got rich sort of by accident. It's not why he does anything he does."

"Mom says he gives away a lot of it. Like to the clinic that saved Jimmy."

"He does."

"Does he—oh!" He wasn't sure what she'd spotted, but it made her take two more steps before she stopped herself.

"What?" he asked.

"He has a piano!"

The corner of the instrument Shan had said was called a baby grand for being smaller than a full-sized grand piano was visible in the room to the right.

"Yes. It was here when he bought the place."

"He doesn't play it? Mom says pianos should be played."

He gave her a curious look. "She does?"

Gracie nodded. "Can I go look?"

"Sure." She ran over to the instrument while Flynn closed the front door for now. Then he walked over to where Gracie was reaching out to touch the polished wood with a single finger.

"Does she...play?" he asked.

"She used to, at Gran's, before Gran died. I was little, but I remember all the beautiful songs. She's really, really good. Gran used to say she'd be famous some day. She used to teach at a music school by where Gran's house was."

Flynn frowned. She was a music teacher but working as a restaurant server? "Why doesn't she still do it?"

"She said she can't. I'm not sure why. She just says it's one of the things we had to leave behind." That was an odd way of putting it. Gracie sighed. "I think she really misses it. She won't even listen to piano music. She just gets all sad."

He was still pondering the revelation when they arrived at the nursery, but after that, he didn't have time. Gracie was voracious, wanting to know the name and growing habits of any plant she saw that she liked. And he noticed she liked them for reasons ranging from the size and color of the blooms to the shape of the leaves, with a special fondness for the out of the ordinary ones, the unusual shapes, the variegated colors.

Finally, she hit one he knew nothing about, and he told her they'd have to call someone from the nursery over to ask, because he didn't have a clue.

Gracie looked up at him consideringly. "I suppose even you can't know everything."

Even you? He couldn't stop his smile at that. Didn't even try. Damn, she was smart. And sometimes so adult she threw him.

He watched her as she wandered through the display of petunias, carefully reading the signs amid each variety. She was about at the maximum distance away he was comfortable with when it happened.

"Hey, dude, nice scars!"

He went still. Looked to his left where the words had come from, saw two boys who looked like they were barely into their teens. They were alone, and he wondered what they were doing here, since the place had technically closed a few minutes ago.

"Yeah, you could make a horror flick, man," the second one said.

"They wouldn't even need makeup." Back to the first.

They both laughed. He said nothing. Failing to get whatever they wanted, they wandered away, toward the back exit. He looked back at Gracie, glad she'd been too far away to hear them. It pretty much flowed off his back by now, but he had the feeling it would have upset the child. And he didn't want her upset. Ever. Over anything.

On impulse, he picked up one of the indoor plants she liked, a bright blue African violet, and a pot with an owl painted on it that she'd giggled at, and added them to the flatbed cart which already held several flats of plants and bags of mulch. And on a more reckless impulse, he grabbed a bouquet of cut lilies—thankfully minus the bright orange pollen—and added it, hoping congratulations would be in order.

"Hey, Mr. Flynn! Here's the fertilizer."

He turned to see Kevin lugging two big—and heavy bags —of the stuff which he dropped on top of the mulch. "Thanks, Kev."

"Thank you, man. My mom had the best time at dinner when we used that gift card you gave me."

He smiled. "I'm glad."

It wasn't until he'd walked away that Flynn realized he'd sent them to the place Riley worked. Depending on when they'd gone, maybe she'd even waited on them.

As if the thought had made it happen, his phone chimed a text. He pulled it out, tapped the icon that had popped up.

Riley.

But all it said was *Done. On my way for Gracie.*

He frowned. Gracie was watching him, clearly wondering, so he held it out so she could see.

"She didn't say!" the girl exclaimed.

"My thought exactly," he agreed. He hoped it wasn't because it was bad news. It would be easier for her to talk to Gracie, if it was. He brought up the dialer and handed the phone to the child. "Why don't you call her?"

"Thanks," Gracie said. "Sometimes she's just so...Mom."

He laughed at that, and went back to loading up the truck while Gracie made the call.

"Mom, why didn't you tell us?" A pause. "Well, what happened?" That was a demand. Flynn grinned to himself. And then he heard a shriek of delight. "You got it!" He let out a relieved breath. He dropped the last bag into the truck, then stopped in the act of reaching for the houseplant when Gracie held the phone out to him, the call still live.

"Congratulations," he said into it.

"Thank you." Riley sounded a little shaken. "And thank you for watching Gracie for me. I'll come get her right now."

"No hurry. We're just finishing up at the nursery."

"Then I'll come there, get her out of your hair."

"She wasn't in it. But we're parked out back, near the greenhouse."

"I'll be right there."

And she would, barring traffic, since the restaurant was barely five minutes away. "Don't rush," he said. "We'll wait."

"Do you think she won't worry so much now?" Gracie asked him when he ended the call and turned to put the last flat of plants in the truck bed.

"I hope so," he said. "Although she worries about you more than money."

"I know. I wish she wouldn't. I'm fine." Gracie frowned. "At least she's not so scared anymore."

Scared? If there was anything he'd learned about Gracie it was that she didn't use words idly. "She used to be scared?"

"When I was little," she said again. "After Gran died and she said we had to move."

"Had to move?"

Gracie nodded. "I thought we were going to stay in Gran's house, but after a while, Mom said we couldn't anymore."

They'd lost their home? That would explain a lot. He remembered what Riley had said about Gracie having a trust from her grandmother, and it said a lot about her that as executor, she hadn't broken it to help their financial situation.

She'd rather do without now so that her daughter wouldn't have to later.

"Here," he said, setting the house plant and pot on the open tailgate of the truck. "While we're waiting, let's get this potted up."

The child dove in eagerly, scooping potting soil out of the smaller bag he'd gotten for the purpose, then he slid the little plant out of the plastic pot and into the ceramic one with the snowy owl on the side.

"There," he said when it was tamped down. "You put that in the window of your room, it should do well there. Remember to water it, but not too much. Try not to get the leaves wet. Let me know if it doesn't seem happy."

Gracie stared at him. "My room? You mean it's mine?"

Flynn grinned at her. "It's a little girly for me."

"You bought this...for me?"

She looked almost as stunned as she had when he'd given her the reader. And it squeezed at him that such a simple gift —maybe any gift—could be such a shock to her.

When Riley arrived, she had to park out near the street, which gave Flynn the chance to watch her walk across the back parking area toward them And watch her he did, with a pleasure a little too reminiscent of that kiss.

"Mom, Mom! Come look at what I got!" Gracie yelped.

Riley smiled at the excitement, and as she reached them, she looked at her daughter's hands.

"I gather it involved digging in the dirt?"

"Look! It's got blue flowers and there's an owl! Flynn says it will grow in my window."

Riley looked at the little pot and its new occupant, then up at Flynn. He gave a half shrug because he didn't know what to say.

She looked at Gracie. "Do you have your things?"

The girl nodded. "In the truck. Mom, I had so much fun! I learned about a ton of plants, and got to—"

"Slow down, sweetheart. Why don't you take your school bag—and your new owl—over to our car. But don't touch anything else, until we get your hands cleaned."

"There's a sink with soap over there, on the side of the greenhouse, for just that reason," Flynn said, nodding toward the glass structure. "She should be able to reach it."

"Excellent," Riley said briskly. "Gracie? After you put the things in the car."

"Yeah, yeah," the girl muttered, and darted over to the cab of the truck to grab her school bag, slinging it over her shoulder so she had both hands free for the violet. Then she was off to the other vehicle.

"Does she ever," Flynn asked, "do anything at less than a run?"

"Rarely," Riley said. Then she added, "You keep finding things I can't say no to."

He lowered his gaze, but smiled as he reached into the back of the truck. "Hopefully here's another one." He brought out the bouquet of lilies and held it out to her. "Congratulations on the promotion."

Riley stared at the flowers. "I still have the daffodils."

"Can't have too many flowers around." Her gaze shot to his face. And again, he shrugged. "Believe me, there's nothing you can say about a guy like me liking and growing flowers that I haven't already heard."

"I think it's a gift. Darn near a miracle," she said softly. "But then, a guy who's like you, after all you've been through, is a miracle to me."

For the umpteenth time since he'd met Riley West, he

wondered how on earth any man who'd had a shot with her had let her go. Wondered if the fool who had fathered Gracie and then vanished had any idea what he lost. Wondered—

"Flynn!"

Gracie's horrible scream tore through the air. He was running before he thought.

CHAPTER TWENTY-FOUR

Riley's heart slammed up to her throat and she stood, frozen. Gracie had sounded both angry and scared. And then her brain kicked in and she realized Flynn was well ahead of her, running faster than she'd seen anyone move in a long time. She started after him, toward the car where Gracie had been after dutifully—she'd watched—washing her hands. But she wasn't there now. She was out in the driveway, standing near two young boys, older than Gracie, maybe twelve or thirteen.

Riley was close enough to hear when one of them said to Gracie, "Oh, nice, little bitch, scream for your daddy."

"Just stop hurting him!"

"Hey, look, it's scarface," one of the boys said, glancing at Flynn as he cleared the parking area and headed toward them.

"Ah, he won't do nothin'. He didn't inside." She had no idea what they were talking about, but clearly Flynn did.

"He got the scars protecting you, even though you're mean and nasty!" Gracie shouted back at them, and Riley's heart quailed at the fearlessness of her little girl and ran faster.

Flynn halted beside Gracie, and things happened fast. "All right?" he asked.

"I am," she said as Riley skidded to a halt next to her daughter, for the first time seeing the tears streaking her little girl's cheeks. "But they were hurting him!" She pointed toward the street.

From her angle, Riley couldn't see anything but Flynn was closer and taller and clearly did. He spun around on the two boys, who had seemed to finally realize they were in trouble and started to back away. But too late; moving so swiftly she nearly jumped, he had them both by the scruff of the neck. They weren't small, but he lifted them both at once as if they weighed nothing. They were pale now, staring up at the man they'd insulted. And Riley found herself staring at the powerful flex of his arms, the muscles holding steady, as if this were no effort at all.

"How does it feel to be helpless?" he said.

He was barely whispering to them, but Riley thought she'd never heard anything more ferocious. Even if she hadn't known who he'd once been, she'd have been intimidated. She put her arm around a trembling Gracie as the boys started to squirm.

Flynn never wavered.

"Don't like it?" He nodded toward the curb of the street. "Neither did he." He lifted them higher, and they started to gulp back frightened tears. "And you can call me all the names you want, because I'm bigger and stronger than you and you don't matter. But you don't ever—" higher yet "—*ever* call someone littler and weaker than you names. And if I see you within a hundred feet of this girl again, you will not be walking around looking for people or animals to torment for a very long time. You won't be walking, period. Are we clear?"

Riley could barely hear the muttered, tearful agreements from the two bullies who weren't thinking about bullying anyone at the moment.

"That's yes, *sir*," demanded the man who never raised his voice, yet commanded attention. He got two meek "Yes, sir's" in return.

He set them down. "Now let's see if you're grown up enough to not go scream to your parents about something you know you had coming. Or go ahead, so we can tell them and everyone exactly what you were doing. Get."

They turned and ran. He turned back to Gracie, who threw her arms around him. "I knew you'd come, I knew it."

"Always," he said, hugging her back.

"But we have to help him now."

Only then did Riley take a step forward to look over the edge of the curb. When she saw the dirty, whimpering little puppy who looked as if he shouldn't even be away from his mother yet, with singed patches of fur as he lay in a muddy stream of runoff water, she felt a wave of nausea.

"They were trying to set him on fire, Flynn! They had matches and—"

"Shh, honey," Riley said as Gracie's voice rose. "We don't want to scare him any more than he is."

Gracie bit back the rest of her outburst as Flynn knelt beside the little animal. "Easy, there, buddy. It's over now, you're safe. You don't know that yet, but you are. Nobody's going to hurt you now."

He was barely whispering to the frightened animal, and yet it was a world away from the hissing, warning whisper he'd used on the two boys. He held out one hand, the backs of his fingers to the puppy. And kept speaking, softly, almost crooning.

"I need to check you out, little one. Don't be scared. We just need to know how bad it is, okay? I'll try not to hurt you, but if you feel scared and have to nip, that's okay, I'll understand."

When he finally reached to touch the pup, the animal twisted slightly, made a token effort at defense, but the moment Flynn's fingers gently stroked his head, he gave in.

I know the feeling, little one. And Riley felt tears well up in her own eyes.

She watched as he ran his hands gently, so gently over the little creature, then more firmly, poking here, prodding there. The puppy shivered, but didn't pull away. And to soothe the terrified dog Flynn, he who was so often without words, kept talking, and always in that soft, soothing whisper so different from that ominous, menacing tone of before.

"Singed on one side, muddy on the other, that must be confusing. But we'll fix it up, buddy."

The puppy lifted its head and looked at him, but as if that had been all the strength it had left it went back down in the mud and no doubt cold water. And shivered again.

Then, without looking at her or changing his quiet tone Flynn said, "Gracie? Did they do anything else that you saw? Kick him or hit him?"

"N-no. Not that I saw."

Flynn nodded. Then, still kneeling beside the puppy, he straightened and, to Riley's surprise, pulled off his T-shirt. She had an instant flashback to when he'd answered the door just out of the shower. Barely had time to recognize that the unveiling of taut abs and a broad, strong chest was having a dizzying effect on her all over again—and that this was hardly the appropriate occasion or location for her reaction—before he leaned back down and gently, still so gently, wrapped the shirt around the little animal. Then, slowly, he slid his hands under the puppy and lifted him out of the gutter.

"Is he going to be all right?" Gracie asked anxiously.

"I think so. He's cold and wet and scared, mostly. They didn't burn much more than fur. He might feel a bit like you do if you get sunburned, that's all."

"Does he need to go to the doctor?"

"It's Sunday, honey," Riley said, tearing her gaze away from the way Flynn's jeans rode on his narrow hips, giving her too clear a view of that slight arrow of hair leading downward. "I don't think they're open."

And according to Marny, who had a big, loveable but goofy golden retriever who had a tendency to ingest socks, the closest emergency vet was twenty miles away.

"I don't think so," Flynn said. "We'll watch him for a while to make sure."

Riley watched as he brought the little bundle up to cuddle against his chest, and something seemed to break and run warm inside her.

"We can't have pets at our apartment," Gracie fretted.

"I'll take him back to Dragon Hill," Flynn said. "He'll be safe there, until we can find where he belongs."

"What if we can't?" the girl asked. Riley winced inwardly; she could see where this would go. Gracie had always wanted a dog, but it just wasn't feasible, location or money wise.

"Don't go meet that boat until it docks."

Gracie blinked. "What?"

"We'll worry about that if it happens."

Gracie thought about that for a moment before she nodded, clearly having figured out the analogy to her satisfaction. Flynn was so good at that, playing with words with her.

Then Gracie looked at her mother. "We have to go with him. He might need help."

Riley wasn't sure if she meant the puppy or Flynn, but it seemed pretty obvious to her that Flynn knew what he was doing. And she supposed field first aid, or whatever they were trained for in the Rangers, made this seem routine. But the way he'd handled that frightened pup was anything but routine, to her. And one look at her daughter's face made it clear; they were headed to Dragon Hill. No way she would add to the upset her little girl had already suffered.

"All right. If it's all right with Flynn, we'll go until we're sure he's okay."

Gracie's smile was well worth the small sacrifice of time. "It's okay, right, Flynn?"

He gave Gracie a smile that gave her another tug inside. "Always," he said.

I knew you'd come, I knew it.

Always.

The earlier exchange slammed through Riley's mind. And she realized, belatedly, that Flynn had meant that quite literally. This was not a man who would toss this around lightly. That simple exchange meant exactly what it sounded like; if Gracie ever needed help, he would come.

CHAPTER TWENTY-FIVE

F lynn walked over to where Riley was standing looking out the west windows and handed her the half—at her request, since she'd be driving later—glass of wine he'd poured. "Should be champagne, I guess, to celebrate, but..."

She gave him that smile that did crazy things to him every time he saw it. "This is more than I expected or would have done on my own."

"Congratulations on the promotion, again." He clinked his own glass with hers. He rarely—almost never—drank, but this was worth it.

"Thank you."

He stood for a moment, trying to decide what to do that would be a safe distance away from Riley, then laughed at himself. She was in the same room; there was no such thing as a safe distance. Especially with the image of the way she'd looked at him when he'd pulled off his shirt to wrap up the puppy. For the first time, he truly understood the people who thought he was amused when he was far from it, because of the way his mouth was torqued.

So, do people always think you're joking, or not serious? You use it, don't you? Heck, you'd be crazy not to.

She'd seen that so fast, that first time she'd shown up here after she'd passed out. Few people realized that sometimes he just didn't say anything and let his involuntary expression speak for him. And that was just the first of the many times she'd seen, noticed, or understood things few did.

She smiled at him. He smiled back. It still felt strange. He'd smiled more since the day he'd found Gracie hiding in the bushes than he had in the entire time since he'd left the service. He hadn't had much to smile about back then, and half the time people thought he was about to laugh at inappropriate things or times anyway, because of that tweak.

He looked down at his glass, swirled the wine in it for something—anything—to look at besides Riley. Then he looked back to where Gracie was sitting at his desk, purportedly doing homework, but stealing glances every few seconds at the nest of blankets on the floor near her, where the now-clean puppy was curled up.

When they'd gotten here, he'd headed for the sink to bathe the pup, and he'd handed Gracie his phone and given her the task of finding out what they could feed him temporarily. During the bath, he'd found he was right—he was more singed than anything. So, clean and dry and with a tummy full of left-over rotisserie chicken and rice, the dog was a much happier little guy than he had been. And Gracie had found it delightful that they were eating the same thing as the puppy, when he suggested they finish it off.

"What shall we name him?" the girl had asked excitedly as they'd dug into the makeshift meal.

Flynn had seen Riley's worry flash across her face; the child was become attached already. "Maybe he already has a name," she said warningly.

Gracie's chin came up. "If they named him, they should have kept him safe." Then she turned those bright eyes on him. "What would you name him, Flynn?"

"I…don't know."

"It needs to be something that fits," Gracie said thoughtfully. "Like we could name him after the place we found him, but he's a boy and begonia is a silly name for a boy."

"That I wouldn't argue," Flynn answered neutrally.

Riley seemed to give in, on this aspect at least. "But you wouldn't want to name him gutter, either, even though we found him in one."

"We could name him rainy because he was wet. Or muddy," Gracie said with a laugh.

"Muddy," Flynn murmured.

"Cute," Riley said, "but I'd hate for it to plant ideas in his head."

"No," he said, not sure what made him say it, "I was just thinking. There's an Irish name that means you're from a muddy place."

"What is it?" Gracie asked.

"Brody."

Gracie looked thoughtful. Riley smiled. "I like it."

"Me, too," Gracie said. She turned to look at the pup. "Do you like it? Would you like to be Brody?" The puppy had lifted his head, tilting it as if listening. "Look, he likes it!" Gracie had exclaimed.

"So it seems," Riley had said.

And so the puppy had a name, and Gracie was one step closer to heartbreak if his owners—underserving though they might be—showed up to claim him.

"Shall we sit outside?" Riley suggested, stirring him out of the memories.

"You trust her to do her homework and not end up on the floor with the dog?"

"I trust her to do it, yes. She's very good that way." Riley smiled. "I don't count on her not ending up on the floor with him to finish it, however."

And again he smiled back. He wasn't quite getting used to it, but it didn't feel quite as strange as it once had. He opened the sliding door onto the balcony and they stepped outside. In another month, it would likely be too hot to be out here in the afternoon, but today it was merely warm.

He only had two chairs out here, since he rarely had more than one person visiting, unless the Bunch descended on him, which didn't happen often unless he missed a monthly gathering. Fortunately for his equilibrium, there was a small table between them, giving him a couple of feet of distance from her.

They sat in silence for a while, until he finally risked a look at her and saw her deeply furrowed brow.

"What's the biggest problem?" he asked, since she obviously was trying to figure something out.

She gave him a fleeting smile before the worry settled in again. "My new work hours."

"As in more of them?"

"Yes." She sighed. Took a sip of wine. "Not your problem."

He wondered how many times in her life she'd said that to people. Riley West was a very determined woman. So he chose his words carefully. "Sometimes thinking out loud helps. Feel free."

The smile was better that time. And she did lay out the issue. "I've always worked the earlier shift so I could be done in time to pick Gracie up. But with this new job, in order to keep up with scheduling and paperwork I'll need to stay after my shift."

"How long?"

"Hopefully only a half an hour during the week, and Gracie can stay at the library and the after-school programs that much longer. But Fridays, I'll have to do weekly reports and inventory type things, and that's going to take longer. At least an hour, likely two. And finding something for her on a Friday evening is going to be hard." Another sip of wine. "I even thought of hiring someone to watch her, but she'd hate that, and it would be tough to find somebody who'd think it's worth it for an hour or two, not to mention that it would likely eat up the raise that comes with the job."

"Kind of defeats the purpose," he said neutrally.

"Exactly!" She sighed. "Maybe I shouldn't take the job. I can't do this at Gracie's expense. She's the whole reason for...for everything."

"I know," he said quietly. She lifted her gaze from the wine glass. "You're doing an incredible job with her, Riley. She's an amazing kid."

The smile he got then seemed brighter to him than the sun that was gradually sliding down toward the horizon. "She is, isn't she? It's like the universe sent me the best kid in the world, to make up for...everything else."

He frowned slightly at the sudden change at the end of her sentence, but focused on the problem at hand. It was what he did, after all. After a moment, he asked, "Do you trust me, Riley?" When she gave him a wary look, he added, "As much as you trust anyone, I mean?"

"I...yes. How could I not, after everything you've done for us?"

He drew in a deep breath. Wondered if he had any idea what he was letting himself in for, yet knowing he was going to do it anyway.

"She could come here, on Fridays."

She stared at him. And then color rose in her cheeks. "No, no, Flynn. I wasn't asking for help or even hinting—"

"I know that. You never would." He gave her a wry grimace. "Even when you probably should."

She shook her head slowly. "I couldn't let you do that. I'm sure you have better things to do, on Friday nights, than babysit an eight-year-old."

"Eight going on thirty," he replied dryly, and got the fleeting smile again as the color faded slightly. Then he lowered his gaze. Decided it would be far too pitiful to admit he hadn't had anything better to do on a Friday night for years, and said simply, "No. I don't." But then he looked up and met those blue, blue eyes and said quietly, "Besides, I'm not sure there is anything much better than hanging out with this particular eight-year-old."

Except kissing her mother.

"Flynn," she whispered, then stopped as if her throat was too tight for any more words.

"I'll put her to work," he said, in a warning tone and a purposefully lowered brow.

"She would love that. Absolutely love it. And it won't be forever, Flynn, I promise. With the raise I'll be able to catch up, and when I get even I'll be able to pay for someone, or get her into a program, or—"

She stopped and visibly swallowed. Hard. Crap, she sounded like she was going to cry. He couldn't handle that. Gracie's tears over the puppy had about done him in. He tried to think of something, anything to say. Couldn't find a single damned word.

And then the slider opened and Gracie came out onto the balcony. *Saved.*

But then he saw what was in her hands, and the idea he'd been saved vanished. She held out the box that had been shoved to the back of a desk drawer.

"What're these, Flynn?"

"Nothing. Old souvenirs."

"I like the purple one. Is that George Washington?" He sensed rather than saw Riley go very still. "And there's a star on this one. And this one has—"

"I know, Gracie," he said, trying hard to keep his voice level, and not to grab the box away from her. Then, when Riley took it from her daughter, he wished he had grabbed it.

She looked into the box, reached in with an index finger and moved the contents around as carefully as if they were spun glass.

"They're medals, honey."

"What do they mean?" Gracie asked.

"They mean," Riley said, "that Flynn is a true hero."

Gracie frowned. Then shrugged. "But we already knew that."

Riley lifted her head then and looked Flynn straight in the eye. "Yes. Yes, we did know that already." He swallowed tightly, and knew words were beyond him. "But these mean he's not just a hero to us. He's a hero to all of America."

"Oh." Gracie looked from the box back to him, studied him for a moment in that intense, head-tilted way he'd come to know. "That's okay, I guess. I wish he was just ours, though."

And for the first time in a very long time, Finnbar Flynn indulged in something he'd written off years ago.

He wished for the very same thing.

CHAPTER TWENTY-SIX

Picking her up at school that Friday brought on a bewildering rush of emotions. First, he'd had to identify himself and confirm he was indeed the guy Riley had said would be picking Gracie up with her permission. He wasn't quite sure what he felt, standing there while they studied his ID. He was glad they were being careful, but the way the woman kept sneaking glances at his scars was wearing.

"You don't mind if I wait for her with you, do you?"

The words had been a question, but her tone had made clear there had only been one acceptable answer. And so he had an escort to the building that held Gracie's classroom.

They'd just rounded the corner of the building when a woman called out, "Flynn?"

He looked up, surprised, but then realized he shouldn't have been when he spotted Kelly Burke, Matt's fiancée, and Jimmy's soon to be stepmom. In his nerves over this, he'd actually forgotten Jimmy was in this class too.

"You know Mr. Flynn, Ms. Burke?" the school official asked.

"I do," Kelly said, her dark ponytail bouncing as she trotted over to them. Her golden brown eyes were warm with welcome, and Flynn found himself breathing easier. "Jimmy said Gracie West said you'd be picking her up."

"I...yes. I am."

Kelly smiled at him, in a way that made him wonder what else that exchange had included. "I know her mother from the Oak Tree. She's a sweetheart. I get the feel she's had a rough time, but she'd do anything for her little girl."

"I know." *So would I.*

And then three classroom doors slammed open at once, and kids began to spill out. And in that moment he felt stranger than he ever had in his life. What was he doing here, taking responsibility for that most precious of things, a child? He looked at the oncoming horde, thinking he'd been less nervous when it had been an armed force.

But then, in the same instant he spotted her, Gracie spotted him. Her face lit up, there was no other way to describe it, and she yelled "Flynn!" as if she'd just seen home after a long time away. His stomach knotted as she ran toward him, and he was so focused on that look of elation on her face he didn't realize Jimmy was beside her until they skidded to a halt. Or rather Jimmy did; Gracie kept coming and threw her arms around him as if she hadn't seen him in a month instead of just four days ago.

He hugged her back, and it was a moment before he could clear his throat enough to say, "Hey, Jimmy."

"Gracie says she's stayin' with you on Fridays now, out at Mr. K's house." Flynn nodded. "Cool."

"Obviously my work here is done," the school official said with a smile. "You have a good afternoon."

Kelly smiled at the woman who then turned and walked back toward the offices. Then she winked at Flynn, and leaned down slightly to greet Gracie. "Hi, Gracie. I'm Kelly. I've heard a lot about you from Jimmy."

"You're going to marry his dad, aren't you?"

"I am. Soon."

"Then I get to call her Mom," Jimmy said with obvious pleasure. "Maybe one Friday you could come out to the stables with us." The boy looked up at Kelly. "That'd be okay, wouldn't it?"

"Of course it would, if it's all right with her mom." Kelly straightened, and gave Flynn a sideways look. "And you, of course." He blinked. What did he have to do with it? He was the babysitter, not...a parent. "Because you would have to bring her," she explained.

Oh. Flynn couldn't meet her gaze because obviously she'd known exactly what he'd thought. And the look she was giving him was a bit too...something. Speculative? No, she'd gone beyond speculation in a big hurry—that was a knowing look.

"I'll ask Mom," Gracie said excitedly. And she was practically bouncing as she walked beside him to his truck. "Did you bring Brody?"

"I did," he told Gracie. "I think he missed you."

"I missed him, too. I thought about him all day."

He wasn't surprised. She clearly was already very attached to the animal. He'd done some searching, on line and around the nursery, but hadn't been able to find anyone who laid claim to a missing puppy. And he was still trying to deny he was glad about that. The big-footed, clumsy little critter was more company than he'd ever imagined. And if he grew into those feet, he was going to be a big boy.

"Did he like the ride in your truck?" Gracie asked.

"Seemed to." And he'd been remarkably well behaved,

seemingly content to just stretch up his full length, paws on the armrest, to look out the window. "More than the last one, anyway."

"That's because he's happy now," she pronounced confidently. "And he knows he's safe. Mom says feeling safe is the most important thing."

Her words unsettled him. He'd thought in the beginning Riley was simply a worry-prone parent, but the more he was around her, the more he thought there was something else going on. She wasn't just worried, she was nervous. Edgy. As if she was constantly expecting...something.

Brody was indeed happy, more like delighted, when Gracie climbed into the truck. The pup scrambled into her lap and began to diligently wash her face, making the child laugh in just as much delight.

Once back at Dragon Hill, Gracie alternated between playing with the puppy and helping with the afternoon's work. And between planting ranunculus around the outer edge of the new rock garden and keeping an eye on the two youngsters, Flynn's afternoon had raced by. Gracie had immediately fallen in love with the flowers because she said they looked so perfect, like they were made from tissue paper instead of real. And she couldn't wait to show them to her mother when she picked her up after work.

Flynn was about to suggest they head back to his place for just that when Gracie called out, "Mom! You found us!"

He looked up to see Riley walking under the arbor, reaching out with one slender hand to brush her fingers over a flowing firecracker plant. She must have parked by the garage and realized when they weren't there they'd likely be here. And suddenly he was glad they hadn't gone back, just because this gave him the chance to watch her walk.

Then she focused on her daughter, the smiling expression on her face reminding him of...something. Gracie ran to her, jabbering excitedly as Brody gamboled around her feet. Riley bent to kiss her daughter and pet the dog as the words flooded out. "We saw Jimmy's new mom at school, and she knows Flynn, and she said I could go out to the stables with them one Friday if it's okay with you. And Flynn an' I are planting 'nunculous, those are the ones that look like paper, and you have to say hello to the dragon or he'll get mad and oh! The piano! Can she see the piano, Flynn?" He got a split-second glance before she barreled on. "And we have to stay for dinner 'cause Flynn wants to know about your new job and I have to finish my homework and my stuff is here —"

She finally stopped when Riley held up a hand. "A breath, honey. For me, if not for you. I gather you had fun?"

"This was the best day ever!" Gracie crowed.

Riley looked at Flynn then. "Thank you," she said. "So much."

He shrugged. "We had a good time."

And he meant it. Crazy as it sounded, for a man who'd been who he was and done what he'd done, this afternoon spent with a little sprite of a girl had been the most rewarding he'd had in a long while.

"How about your week in the new job?"

"It's a learning curve. I never gave Marny enough credit for all the paperwork she had to do. But I'm enjoying the challenge."

"Look, Mom!" Gracie crouched down to show her mother the flowers, while Flynn planted the last two. "I helped. We got them all done super fast, huh, Flynn?"

"We did."

Gracie straightened. "Can she see the piano now, before we go back?"

"Sure," Flynn said. He'd mentioned it to Shan, who had immediately said yes, although he'd said it in a strange tone of voice Flynn couldn't put a name to.

"Piano?" Riley asked.

"It's Mr. K's," Gracie explained. "But only because it came with the house. He doesn't play, and you always said they should be played." Riley drew back slightly, staring at her daughter. "Well, you did."

"Yes. Yes, I did."

Gracie scampered toward the steps that led up to the expansive patio outside the big house, where the sets of glass French doors looked out onto the garden he'd created here. But Flynn was looking at Riley as she watched the girl.

"What's wrong? You looked...shocked."

"I was. I said that, but...Flynn she was two years old. How could she possibly remember that?"

"Gracie? Are you really asking that?"

She shifted her gaze to his face. And then, suddenly, she was laughing. And it was one of the two the best sounds he'd heard all day, the other being Gracie's delighted yelp of his name at school.

"I stand reminded," she said.

And suddenly it hit him, what Riley's expression had reminded him of. Gracie's expression when she'd spotted him there.

An expression that had a name, one he was dodging like crazy.

Love.

He swallowed, called up more discipline than he'd had to use in a long time but had been digging out ever since Gracie had tumbled into his life and brought her mother with her. "She said you were really, really good. On the piano."

"Bless her. I had big dreams, but then...reality bit."

"She said you used to teach."

"Back in the dark ages."

He didn't push; it clearly wasn't something she wanted to talk about. Gracie called out to them to hurry up.

"Never less than top speed," he said as they started that way.

"That's my girl." Riley hesitated at the top of the steps. Glanced up at him. "Are you sure this is okay? I don't want to trespass."

"I'm not Matt McLane, but I'm pretty sure if you're invited, it's not trespass. And Shan invited you to look at it."

"He did?"

"He did." He shrugged. "I asked him after Gracie talked about it."

Something came into her expression then, a sort of longing that tightened his throat.

"Mom, hurry up! You've gotta see!"

"If it was me," he said neutrally, "I wouldn't keep her waiting."

Again she laughed, which made him smile as they reached the doors. He pulled one open and they stepped into the house. Gracie ran, but oddly—or perhaps not—Riley stopped dead just like Gracie had when she'd seen the piano. But from here there was a clearer view of the whole instrument.

"Oh!"

"Your daughter said the same thing."

"I thought maybe she meant a keyboard. I didn't expect a baby grand." They walked over to the alcove the instrument sat in. And again, much as Gracie had, she reached out to touch the gleaming wood.

"It's beautiful," Riley whispered.

"Shan might not play, but he's not the sort to let something like this deteriorate."

"Play something, Mom," Gracie said eagerly.

"Oh, I couldn't."

"Forget how?" Flynn asked.

"I could never forget." He'd known that would be her answer, just from the look on her face as she stared at the piano. "But I haven't played in so long, it would be awful."

"Shan was wondering if it's out of tune. If it can get out of tune just sitting. Maybe you could tell him." Okay, that wasn't too bad, for having made it up on the fly. He just had to hope Shan would forgive him for tossing his name around like this.

"They can." Her expression changed. Her brow furrowed and she looked up and around the room. "It mostly depends on the room environment. Heat and cold, and especially humidity. The strings are one thing, and always the first suspect, but the soundboard is just that, a board, and wood absorbs moisture in humid conditions, and dries out in dry conditions. That changes the crown, the curve in it, which changes the pressure on the bridge and hence the strings."

Flynn stared at her. He wasn't even sure what a soundboard was. But no matter how long it had been, she had indeed never forgotten. And the longing in her expression was almost painful to see.

She walked around the instrument, still talking. "It's not near a window, so that's good. But a humidifier to keep it constant is also a good option. And even if it's not played much, a yearly tuning is good in a home." She smiled, rather sadly. "Not like a concert piano—that can need tuning more than once a day."

He blinked. "A day?"

She nodded, back to looking at the keyboard now. And he didn't think he was mistaking the curling of her fingers as resisting the urge to touch.

"Stage lights, equipment, and overhead doors, moving it from under the lights to off stage, or even a different spot on the stage, can all affect the humidity and thus the sound."

"I never realized," he said. "Piano tuning must be quite a business."

She reached to, at last, touch a key. Not press it, but just brush a finger over it. And there was no mistaking the yearning in her eyes. "They have digital tuners now. A lot more accurate than the old methods, although nothing replaces a good ear. But these days, the digital helps when playing in a band or group with, for instance, electric guitars. Because they're tuned electronically most of the time, if the piano isn't sometimes they don't blend well."

"So play something, Mom. So you can tell Mr. K if it's okay," Gracie prodded.

Still, she hesitated. And Flynn didn't know what to do. Finally he just said, as neutrally as he could, "It would be a favor to him." And pulled out the bench.

As he'd hoped, that did it. He felt a little guilty, like he'd played her somehow, but he couldn't take that ache in her expression any longer.

And finally, very slowly, Riley sat down.

CHAPTER TWENTY-SEVEN

She hadn't been at a keyboard in over five years.

She hadn't expected to ever be again.

Especially not at the keyboard of a beautiful instrument like this one.

She held her breath as she touched the keys. Settled her hands into position. And let the breath out as she lightly ran a scale, up, then down. It sounded surprisingly good. It had been a very long time, but she thought she might try testing the intervals. She started on middle C and headed up a third.

"Can't you just play each note?" Flynn asked.

She smiled, but was fixated on the keyboard. "I'm not that good. I'm just listening for a wobble. And you can't compare the middle with the treble or bass keys, you need to do each within its range."

"I think," Flynn said, "I'll stick to tuning engines."

She did look up at him then, and he was grinning at her. And that made her grin back at him.

"Can't you play a real song?" Gracie complained.

And before she even thought, she'd started. The old,

familiar tune rolled out, as if she'd been practicing every day. It was simple, yet with a beautiful swell and rise and lift, and she had always loved it. It built to a crescendo that made her heart swell, forcing her to admit how much she had missed this, this that had once been such a part of her. And then it slid down into a slow, aching last few notes, ending with an upward flourish, and totally unexpectedly ,she was fighting tears.

"I know that song!" Gracie exclaimed.

"Yes," she said, her voice almost painfully tight. "I used to play it to get you to sleep."

"If you were aiming for the heart, you hit it dead center." Flynn's voice was low and rather gruff, but in a way that gave truth to his words. He truly meant it. And she had to look at him, even knowing he'd see the tears. He did. And slowly reached out to brush away one that had spilled over. Even that small touch added a nearly unbearable pressure to what she was already feeling.

She hastily looked away, because she had to. She was feeling too much for this man already, and now, now he'd given her this. This gift she shouldn't have taken. The only thing she was sure of was that she'd been right to stay completely away from anything resembling a piano. Because even this small taste was going to take her forever to get over.

She tried to clear her throat. Failed. Tried again and managed to speak. "It's really in pretty good shape, considering. The upper and lowers are a bit off, but the middle sounds good. I think it would only need a professional tuning."

"I'll tell Shan." She only nodded. And stood up. "You don't have to stop," he said gently.

"Yes. Yes, I do." How could she explain that the more she played, the more it would hurt to walk away?

"Why did you leave it behind, Riley?"

"No choice." And that was not a discussion she wanted to have. With anyone, but especially this man who constantly had her so off balance. Who seemed to see so much, in his quiet way. This man her daughter already clearly loved.

This man she could so easily fall in love with herself. And that was an impossibility she didn't dare think about.

And yet she was still thinking about it as she sat at the bar-height counter in his sleek kitchen, watching him proficiently chop up an onion for a salad. She'd never seen anyone do it that way, cutting the onion in half, then cross-hatching each half, then cutting it as you would slices. The chopped pieces fell to the cutting board as neatly as if he'd done it all laboriously slice by slice, or with some fancy device.

She glanced over at Gracie, who was doing her homework at his desk again, seemingly as comfortable here as at home. Odd, since at home she liked the privacy of her room. But here, she seemed to like being with them.

Be honest. She likes being with Flynn.

And she couldn't blame her girl for that.

After a steak dinner that tasted like ambrosia to her after months of whatever was cheapest at the market or left over at the restaurant, and a healthy shot of Flynn's wonderful crooked smile when she said as rare as his would be fine for her—Gracie required a bit more cooking time, which he managed deftly so they all came off the grill at once—Riley insisted on cleaning up, and he let her while he went to show Gracie the intricacies of the home theater system.

"Mom, he's got everything!" Gracie yelped excitedly when she came out of the kitchen.

"Only because Shan does, and I'm on the same system. He's got every possible channel and streaming app, some from places I've never even heard of," Flynn said.

"I imagine he has to keep on top of things like that," she said.

Flynn nodded. "He says it sparks ideas for him. For new apps or services. Or he'll see something he likes that he wants to invest in. A startup he'd like to help."

Gracie paused on the latest in a series of kid's movies for a moment, but went on.

"Don't like them?" Flynn asked her.

"I only saw the first one," she said. "And I liked the book better."

He didn't look in the least surprised. "You could read instead."

She shook her head quickly. "We don't have all this, so this is cool."

She finally stopped on a film about a dog who finds his way home, and within minutes she was snuggled up on the end of the couch with Brody happily on her lap.

"I'm worried about how attached she already is to that dog," Riley whispered as she came over and sat beside him.

Telling himself she'd only sat so close because she didn't want Gracie to hear, he managed a fairly level reply at the same low volume. "I've checked a bit, neighborhood online groups, asked at the nursery, and in the area. Nobody'll cop to missing a puppy."

"You think he was just abandoned?" She sounded upset, and he knew her caring didn't stop with her daughter.

"Probably. Or they don't care enough to look for him."

"I don't get people sometimes," she said. And yet again he had the feeling there was a much deeper level to the words. Then she looked up at him. "I know Gracie pulled you into this. And we can't have him at our apartment, even if..."

She trailed off and shook her head, and he knew the next words would have been "we could afford him."

"Don't worry about it. We're doing okay, for now. He even seems partially housebroken. He goes to the door, anyway. He's kind of puppy clumsy, and all those stairs are a bit much for him, so I usually end up carrying him."

"You're very kind, Flynn."

Kind? He'd never thought of himself that way. He tried not to be mean or cruel, but that was about as far as it went, in his mind. "I just try not to hurt anyone." He'd had enough of that. And sometimes knowing it was necessary didn't help much.

"As I said, kind." She sighed. "And look where it's gotten you."

He sat there silently for a moment, unable to think of any words to describe how he felt about where this supposed kindness of his had gotten him. To describe how it felt to have a clumsy, now-happy puppy and a little girl too clever for words right here, and a beautiful woman by his side. It wasn't permanent, and it wasn't what he foolishly wished it could be, but it was still more than he'd ever had, more than he could put into words.

Because there were no words big enough. Not that he knew.

Gracie fell asleep before the movie was over. Riley watched her for a long, quiet moment before saying, without looking at him, "I can't thank you enough for this. She so obviously had a wonderful time today."

"Check back when she gets bored with digging in the dirt," he said, wishing she'd quit thanking him.

She got up, and he immediately felt colder. Gave a sharp shake of his head, to clear out the image he'd let form in his mind, of this going on indefinitely. She walked over and bent down to wake her daughter.

"Gracie? Time to go."

"Wha?"

"Now, honey. We need to give Flynn a break."

"Didn't ask for one," he said, standing up. "Want me to carry her down?" He didn't want to, but he tried not to dwell on it, because that led only to the fact that he didn't want them to leave at all.

Gracie snuggled deeper into the pillow she and Brody had been curled up half on. "Gracie," Riley repeated patiently.

"Don' wanna."

"I know. But it's time to go home."

The child grumbled, but sat up. She rubbed at her eyes, yawned widely, and said, clearly still half-asleep, "Who's Regina?"

Riley froze. Visibly stopped breathing. And as Flynn watched, she turned not pale, but an almost sickly gray color that scared him. A long, silent, and somehow tense moment spun out before Riley sucked in an audible breath and spoke.

"Nobody, honey."

"But I heard someone call her. In my dream."

"It's just someone we used to know. A long time ago."

But Flynn had no doubt there was much, much more to it than simply someone they used to know.

CHAPTER TWENTY-EIGHT

"How are things there?" Shan asked.

Flynn put down the bag of mulch and shifted the phone. "Quiet, at the moment."

"Which, knowing you, means you're working even though it's Saturday."

Flynn ignored that to ask, "How goes the project?"

Shan laughed and let him get away with it. "This is good for me. I somehow avoided all the handyman and building type skills until now, so I'm trying to learn."

"And you're happiest when you're learning."

"That's what Juliette says."

"Where do you think I got it from?"

Again, he laughed, and Flynn wondered if the day would come when the haunted, tortured Shan from the photograph Juliette had taken at his son's funeral would one day vanish forever.

"Juliette wants to know if you got that car fixed?"

"I did." His mouth quirked, even though his boss couldn't

see him. "And she'd better brace herself when she gets back. Those two are big on thanking, thanking, and thanking again."

"And you're as bad as ever at accepting, I presume?"

This was what he hated about talking on the phone; a shrug didn't suffice. He went for a quick change of subject instead. "I...sort of acquired a puppy. Temporarily," he hastened to add.

"That has to be a story."

"I'll try to clear him out before you get back—"

"Hey, I have no objection to having a dog around. John's been nagging me forever to get one to patrol the place."

"It'd be a long time before this little guy's up to that."

"That's fine. It'll keep your old boss off my back longer. How'd you...acquire the pup?"

He told Shan the story, finishing with, "I didn't hurt them, but they were pretty scared, I think. It hasn't boomeranged on me yet, but that may just be because they don't really know who I am. If they told their parents, they could be coming after me."

Shan laughed. "Let them try. If there's one thing Kelleher's got, it's good attorneys."

"I...but they don't do this kind of thing, do they?"

"They do what's needed," Shan said. "And I made it clear when I hired them that theirs was not to question."

"I don't work for your company, technically."

"You work for me," Shan said. "And you're my friend, Flynn. I've got your back. The whole Wild Oak Bunch would have your back." He didn't know what to say to that. His mouth was suddenly a little dry, and he swallowed. "Get used to it, buddy. No more lone-wolfing it."

"It's...a change."

"I know. Speaking of changes in your life, how is...Riley? That's her name, right?"

"She's..." Amazing? Wonderful? Beautiful? All of those.

"That good, huh? About time, buddy."

"No, it's not...like that." *Not that I don't want it to be.*

"Yet," Shan said, but to Flynn's relief he didn't dwell on it. "She like the piano?"

"More in awe, I think. And it's not badly out of tune."

"What'd she play?"

"I don't know what it was, but it was amazing." She was amazing. "Something she used to play to get Gracie to sleep, when she was little."

"Sounds like quite the pair you have there."

He didn't know what to say to that, either. Especially when he remembered the look on Riley's face when she made herself stop playing when it was obvious she could have happily gone on for a very long time.

And then it hit him that he hadn't told Shan the biggest news. Well, at least as big as the dog. So he explained about Riley's promotion, and that he was watching Gracie on Friday afternoons until she got everything figured out.

Shan made a strange, choking kind of sound. *Uh-oh.*

"If you'd rather I didn't, I—"

"No, no...I was trying to picture you babysitting an eight-year-old girl."

"You haven't met this one. She's way smarter than your average eight-year-old."

"Jimmy's pretty smart."

"Yeah, he is. Gracie's more...wise, I guess." He let out a breath. "And I think she's learned it the hard way."

"We'll go to work on that when we get back. Hey, time for a second coat of paint here. Wish me luck!"

Flynn put away his phone, marveling not for the first time how his life had changed since he'd come to Wild Oak. He'd done it because he would lay down his life for John Reese, as John would do for him, but he'd never expected it to turn into...so much.

And when he found himself counting the days until Friday —again—he shook his head at himself.

THE TEXT CAME in the middle of the night.

Flynn jolted awake, out of a dream he'd been having variations of almost every night. The kind of dreams he hadn't had since he'd been a teenager with hormones running amok. And all of them featured Riley West, in ways that had him groaning with the ache of it when he awoke hard and needy.

On the other hand, at least he'd been sleeping, something that had always been a fairly rare commodity for him.

There were only two things he could think of that would bring on a middle-of-the-night text, John's baby—finally— or...Gracie. He grabbed the phone from the nightstand and tapped in the code to open it, then the messaging app. And was almost relieved to see John's terse, WE'RE ROLLING.

As they'd agreed—and the others had demanded—he sent out a group text to the Wild Oak Bunch. Then, as he scrambled to get dressed, he thought about how changed his life was, that he actually had people to worry about besides those he'd served with. He had the Bunch, that amazing group that ran the gamut.

And he had Riley and Gracie now. Just as the child had said. And they had taught him so much; Riley that maybe the scars didn't matter as much as he thought, at least to her, and

Gracie that perhaps he wasn't quite as bad with kids as he'd assumed.

He was smiling as he put on his shoes, remembering the Friday babysitting experiences. He'd assumed it would be a hassle, having to always keep an eye on her, but instead, it had turned into an adventure. Challenging, yes, because of Gracie's insatiable need to know, but the way she took what he said with such solemn acceptance, the way she grinned at him when he made some play on words, and most of all, the way she so seriously told him he was being silly when a mood crept up on him, kept an unaccustomed smile on his face all afternoon.

And he had the niggling feeling that somewhere down deep something was changing in him. They were changing him. In ways he'd never expected, because he thought he'd lost the capacity for it long ago.

He picked up the puzzled puppy from the bed on the floor —he'd finally broken down and bought a real one—and deposited him in the makeshift pen he and Gracie had made in a corner of the kitchen. He would borrow, as Shan had insisted, one of the cars out of the house garage rather than try and drive his big truck and find a place to park at the hospital. And he was willing to bet that Shan, and Juliette—who had become close to everyone in the Bunch but was a bit in awe of the dynamic Jennifer Reese—would be on Shan's jet on their way back by sunrise.

He had farther to go from Dragon Hill, so John and Jen were already there when he arrived. He had no fondness for hospitals, but even he had to admit this ward was different. It was more about joy and the future than pain and farewells. As he followed the directions the nurse at the desk had given him, he found himself wondering if Gracie's father had even been around for her birth. Surely he must have been, even if it had fallen apart after. Apparently before Gracie had been even old enough to know.

When he found them in the small room down the hall, John, not at all to Flynn's surprise, was pacing. He smothered an inward smile; the man had been cool as could be when he'd personally delivered Jake and Rachel's baby in their home after Rachel had fallen and the irrepressible Cammie had decided if her mother was going to do silly things like that it was time. But now he was showing signs of stress he never had even on the toughest battlefield.

"Flynn, thank God," Jen said when she spotted him.

He blinked at the overly-effusive—and clearly thankful—greeting. He loved Jen like a sister, but—

"Will you please slug him or something? He's driving me mad."

This time the smile broke free as he walked into the room. "Getting on your nerves, is he?"

"Hey," John protested, "this is my kid's arrival we're talking about here."

"And your wife's biggest project," Jen said sternly to her husband. Which was saying something given the building projects scattered around Wild Oak that had her name on them. "The doctor says it will be at least another hour if not longer. So if you don't calm down, I'll kick you out and Flynn can stay."

John shot him a look. Flynn looked back at him without a flicker.

"That didn't panic you," John observed with interest.

At least he'd managed to distract him, and out of the corner of his eye he saw Jen mouth a silent "thank you."

"Nope," he said. "It's the least I can do."

"Still think you owe me, huh?"

"Yes," Flynn agreed, because he forever would owe this man who had saved his life three times. "But that's not what I meant."

John frowned. "What did you mean?"

"I meant it was the least I could do—" he held the gaze of the man he'd more than once followed into a hell that had turned out more than figurative "—for my godson."

It was a moment before John said, "Nothing like leaving it to the last possible moment, buddy." But he was grinning when he said it, and pulled Flynn into what Jen called the tough-guy hug, which involved a couple of heavy thuds on the back. "Thanks, my friend."

"I knew you'd do it," Jen said airily, in the instant before she paled and a gasp escaped her. John spun around and was back at her side in a single stride. She let him take her hand, but after a few moments, assured him it had passed. Then she looked at Flynn and picked up as if nothing had happened. The woman was beyond cool. "And it will make it a lot easier to explain to our son someday why his middle name is Flynn."

Flynn gaped at her. They'd already told him some time ago they were going to name the boy Ryan, for the one who didn't come home from that last mission. He'd been all for it, and had accepted a rare glass of wine to toast the choice.

But they'd neglected to mention this.

"I..." His voice trailed away because he couldn't think of a single thing to say.

"Good, no argument," Jen said with a grin. "Now, you sent out the group text?"

"I did," he said with a shake of his head at the quick change of subject; sometimes he forgot just how much force of will this woman had. She was the strongest woman he knew.

At least she had been, until he'd met Riley.

"So how's the new job going?" Jen asked cheerfully.

He blinked. "New jo—" He stopped as he realized what she meant. "How did you—"

She waved him off. "I talked to Kelly who talked to Matt who got it from Jimmy."

"More importantly," John said, almost as cheerfully as Jen, which was noteworthy, "when do we get to meet this pair of miracle workers?"

He had absolutely no idea what to say to that. And before he could think of anything, Jen gasped again, and her grip on John's hand went white-knuckled. And stayed that way for a solid minute. And John was suddenly the same edgy man he'd walked in on.

"Another hour, my ass," he snapped. "That was less than five minutes."

"I think you may be right," Jen said, panting a little now. "That one lasted a while, too."

By the time it was over, Flynn was convinced of the old saying that if it were up to men to give birth, the human race would have died out long ago. He'd had his share of painful time in a hospital and then some, but the logistics of childbirth were something he'd managed to avoid thinking about much.

And he thought of Riley, of her long, slender body in relation to the actual size of a baby in real terms, and it made him shudder. And truly hope she hadn't been alone. Surely at least the grandmother she'd spoken of so lovingly had been there.

And when John came out, his expression awestruck as he carried the tiny being in his arms, and introduced Flynn to Ryan Flynn Reese, the two brothers-in-arms looked at each other.

Neither one tried to hide the moisture pooling in their eyes.

CHAPTER TWENTY-NINE

It was another joyous, slightly delirious Wild Oak Bunch barbecue that next Saturday at Jake and Rachel's. When John, Jen, and little Ryan arrived, their first outing since bringing the baby home, Flynn couldn't begin to describe the feeling that came over the entire gathering. But even that was nothing compared to the moment when Jen walked over to him and deposited Ryan in his arms, "So I can eat, I'm starved."

He had no idea how long he stood there frozen, aware only of the slightness of the bundle he held, the tiny size, the barely perceptible weight.

"Breathe," Rachel suggested as she walked by, also headed for the table where Matt and Jimmy were already laying out platters full of Matt's Uncle Lew's famous grilled hot dogs and hamburgers and chicken.

"You get used to it," Jake said with a grin as he passed by next, holding his own little one, Cammie. At a year old, she seemed huge in comparison to the small being in his arms.

He stared down at the baby, who slept so peacefully it almost scared him. How the hell did you tell if something was wrong?

"You look like a natural," Shan said as he and Juliette headed for the tables under the big oaks.

"Hardly," he muttered.

"Come, sit with us," Juliette insisted.

He didn't want to admit he was afraid to move, afraid he might drop the kid, or maybe worse, wake him up. He didn't know how much lung power a one-week-old had, but he guessed it was enough to get attention when necessary.

He sat down gingerly, his back to the table because he didn't want to tackle sitting normally with the baby. But he didn't really breathe right again until John came over to retrieve his new son.

"You passed, bro," he said with a grin as Flynn handed over the blanket-wrapped bundle with obvious relief.

"Fair trade," Jen added, setting a plate full of food down on the table for him.

He was still feeling a little odd when he swung his legs around to face the table to eat. He had maybe two bites of chicken, with Lew's terrific barbecue sauce, swallowed when Shan nearly brought them back up again.

"Sort of expected you to bring your ladies today."

His head snapped up to stare at the man who was both boss and friend. He didn't know what to say. Because he had thought about Riley and Gracie, about bringing them here. Gracie would love it, and she already knew Jimmy, Matt, and Kelly, and it was likely inevitable, given how much time she was at Dragon Hill, that she would meet Shan and Juliette soon.

"Aren't you supposed to head back to finish that project?" he said in an effort at diversion even he admitted was lame.

"Dad said to take our time," Juliette said blithely. "Why didn't you bring them?"

He lowered his gaze to his plate. *Because I know what it means. Because you only bring people here that...are going to be part of the Bunch.*

"Busy," he said shortly, leaving it to them to decide if he meant Riley and Gracie, or himself.

"Hmm," Shan said. Something in the tone of the noncommittal response made him look up. And what he saw in the eyes of the man across the table was understanding. Then, unexpectedly, Shan said, "When do we get to hear her play?"

Flynn blinked. "What?"

"The piano," Shan said patiently. "I want to hear if it's worth keeping."

"Oh, it's worth it." The words broke from him almost without volition.

"Then arrange it," Shan said with a shrug.

"Spoken like the true despot he is," Juliette said with a teasing smile. Flynn couldn't help it, he smiled back. Because there couldn't be a less despotic billionaire in the world than Shan Kelleher.

"I'll see what I can do," he said.

"And that," Shan said with satisfaction, "is as good as cash in hand."

THE SCENT WAFTED OUT, catching her attention first. That sweet smell of that yellow rose, the one that had mysteriously tripled in number practically overnight, after she'd said they were the most beautifully scented things she'd ever smelled. When she stepped into the room, her eyes widened; the roses were everywhere, vases full of them, on tables, the floor, even the piano itself, including two small bouquets in the holders at each end of the keyboard.

She looked up at Flynn, astonished.

"I wanted you to be able to smell the roses while you played." He gave her that crooked smile she so loved.

"I..."

"You will play for me, won't you?"

She would do anything for this man, but he asked for nothing. Until this. She owed him more than she could ever repay. She sat down, stretched her fingers, chose the keys, and began to play. She started with the same soaring, building melody she'd played the first time she'd sat down at this instrument. She segued into her favorite classical piece, that moonlit sonata she had loved since she'd first heard it. Then, feeling more confident, she went into a quick, rapid-fire piece she'd learned as an exercise but liked the sound of as well.

And as she went, it flooded back into her, the love of this, of playing, of the music itself. Even the wrong notes she hit out of sheer rustiness didn't bother her. The last remaining hollow place in her was filled, leaving no room for unhappiness or haunting memories. That man—she refused to name him even in her mind—didn't matter anymore, and never would again. She had too much precious in her life now to let him sully it.

When at last she stopped, more because she knew her out-of-practice fingers would be paying a price than anything, one look at Flynn's face gave her all the compensation she could ever want.

For a long moment, she simply looked at him. And then a movement from the back of the room caught her attention, startling her; she hadn't realized anyone else was here. When a man stepped forward, her breath caught. Because she knew him at first sight, not as those who made a habit or a hobby of knowing people whose wealth was in the stratosphere did, but as many in Wild Oak did. Because this was the man whose work, whose response to his personal tragedy had put this quiet little town on the map.

Shan Kelleher.

"He told me how good you were," the man said with a glance at Flynn. "I wondered if he was letting his feelings color his judgment. He wasn't."

She curled her fingers tightly, nerves pinging. "I...thank you, Mr. Kelleher."

"Shan, please." He came over and leaned an elbow on the top of the piano as he looked at her. "I won't ask why you quit. Flynn told me you had good reason, and that's your story to tell or not. I will ask...what now?"

"Sir?"

The billionaire rolled his eyes. "No 'sir,' not in the Wild Oak Bunch."

"But I'm not—"

"Oh, but you are, Ms. West. You see, we've been wishing you would come along for a long time."

She blinked. "What?"

"Oh, we didn't know it was you, but clearly it is. You're the one to save the last of us, the one we all worried about the most."

Flynn made a sound, shifted slightly, and she knew he wasn't comfortable with what his boss—and clearly his friend —was saying. Shan ignored him.

"But we'll get to that. Right now, the question before the

house is...what do you want to do with this amazing talent you obviously have?"

"Do with it?"

"A fully funded concert tour? A place with a prestigious orchestra? A deal with an agency? Recording contract?" The man grinned at her. "Or maybe your own video channel and outlet? With an app all your own?"

She knew she was probably gaping at him, but couldn't help it. "What?"

"I could do that last one myself," he went on as if she hadn't spoken. "Might be fun. Haven't done any musical things before."

"Yourself?" God, she sounded like a very slow student.

Flynn spoke for the first time since this had started. "As opposed to calling in one of the hundreds of favors people owe him that would get all those other things."

She really was gaping now. "For...me?"

"For the most talented musician I've heard in a long while." He smiled at her, and an image shot through her mind, of a man in a photograph, a broken, devastated man who'd looked as if he'd rather be the one being lowered into the grave he stood beside. It seemed impossible this was the same man.

"I don't know what to say," she answered honestly.

"Why don't we start local," Shan said briskly. "The annual fundraiser for the clinic is in June. Does that give you enough time to work up a program?"

"I..."

He turned on Flynn before she could formulate an answer. "And you will need a tux, my friend."

The look on Flynn's face wiped away all her nerves. "To see that," she said solemnly, "I would solo at the Met with no rehearsal."

Shan burst out laughing. "Oh, you're the perfect, final addition to the Wild Oak Bunch, Riley West. Welcome."

She smiled back, only wishing it were true, because there was nothing she'd like more than to be a part of this group that had formed such bonds, and included such a diverse group...and had taken in Flynn, she suspected whether he liked it or not.

CHAPTER THIRTY

G racie shrieked with delight as they made the turn around the corner of the house. This third Friday of babysitting was going even better than the first two.

He leaned the handles as far as he safely could on the turn, because she seemed to love it even more. He never would have thought a ride in a silly wheelbarrow would make a kid so happy in this day of video games and smartphones. But then, Gracie likely hadn't had much experience with either. And while it made him ache inside to think of them doing without, he wasn't sure she might not be better off.

He hit the driveway at a run, and Gracie squealed her delight again. They were headed for the dragon, which probably half of her excitement; he had solemnly asked her if she thought she was up to helping take care of his home domain. The grass he was stationed on needed some trimming, and there was no way any mechanical trimmer was getting anywhere near the beast.

With an exaggerated, brakes screeching noise—when the hell did he drift into making sound effects for a kid?—he brought them to a halt. Gracie jumped out and ran over to her beloved creature. He watched her go, clumping in the little rubber boots he'd gotten for her. Riley didn't know about those, yet. He'd had to guess at the size by age, but fortunately they fit. And Gracie had been thrilled. And yet again, his gut had knotted at her amazement at such a simple thing.

Yes, she was teaching him a lot about the job he'd taken on, as little Ryan's godfather.

Riley had called him the Sunday morning after the baby had been born, to thank him yet again for watching Gracie, and been startled when he'd told her he'd just gotten home. But when he told her why, she'd been delighted.

"Do you need help shopping, or did you already give them a gift?"

"Sort of," he'd muttered, stifling a yawn.

Being Riley, as smart as her daughter, it had only taken her a split second to get it. "You said yes! You're his godfather!"

He let out a breath and half smiled even though she couldn't see him. "I did."

"What a lucky, lucky little boy," she'd said, and it was so clearly heartfelt, it knotted him up inside.

"It was only thanks to you and Gracie."

"You would have done it anyway, for John."

"I'm not so sure."

"I am," she had said firmly, with full confidence.

He snapped back to the present as Gracie came back from patting the dragon.

"What do we have to do?"

"Trim the grass around him. It has to be done by hand. Wouldn't want any scrapes or marks on his feet."

"He wouldn't like that," she agreed gravely. "But that's harder, huh?"

"It takes longer," he agreed. "But I don't mind. Gives me more time to hang out with him."

Gracie grinned at that. And went to work with the small pair of manual clippers he gave her with such care that it made him glad Shan hadn't given in to his suggestion of making the sculpture's cement foundation, there only to protect the wood base, bigger.

As they worked, he mused that he'd never gotten around to asking Jake what he used to protect his pieces that would be displayed outside. Obviously something, because this beast was holding up well, as was the big lion out at the winery. For that matter, one of his earliest pieces, the sign at Riley's restaurant, had been there for years and was still in great shape. There must be a secret—

His text notification went off, and he stopped to pull out his phone.

Riley.

He spent a moment, not for the first time, thinking he needed to assign her a special tone. He hadn't yet, because he couldn't decide what it should be. It occurred to him now, though, that the piece she'd played on the piano would be perfect. But he didn't know if it was out anywhere. He'd want her playing it anyway. Maybe she'd play it again so he could record it.

He snapped out of the reverie that always seemed so easy to slide into when he was thinking about her. Opened the message app.

RUNNING LATE. HOUR'S WORTH OF WORK LEFT. I'M SORRY.

She'd told him that today would be the first day she was totally responsible for everything that needed to get done; Marny had left mid-week. And he was fairly sure, knowing her, that she would be double-checking everything to be sure.

No problem, we're good, he sent back.

Thank you so much.

Stop it. We're having fun grooming the dragon.

It was a moment before an answer came, and when it did he laughed. It was an emoji. A dragon.

She really was feeling better. Hopeful. And it was damned good to see.

"What's funny?" Gracie asked, darting over to him.

"Your mom," he said, and showed her the screen.

Gracie grinned at the image. "She's pretty cool, my mom."

"Yes."

And then some.

The afternoon grew hotter as they finished up the dragon. May in California, even this far north, could be like midsummer in other places. He kept an eye on Gracie, and when she started to pause more often, and finally wiped at her face, he quickly finished it up and called a halt. And he was glad of it, because by the time they walked back to his place— her conveyance of choice, the wheelbarrow was full of clippings now—she was getting a bit red in the face. There was never a word of complaint, however, not a single "I'm hot," whine. Not from his Gracie.

His Gracie?

Whoa.

The possessive feeling still sat uneasily on his mind, and his heart. He'd been so used to being alone, it had taken the entire Wild Oak Bunch to prod him into coming to the monthly barbecues at Jake's. And they'd become as close to family as he had, and he'd do anything for any of them.

But what he felt for Gracie was different.

What he felt for Riley was very, very different. Than anything, ever.

I want to be able to bring them to the next barbecue. To have it mean what it's meant for the rest of the Wild Oak Bunch. That we're...together. The three of us.

"I should clean my boots," Gracie said, looking down at the bright blue footwear with the owls on them; her second favorite animal, after dragons, she'd said seriously.

"The hose is over there," he said. "But use the smaller one, the big one's what I use for cleaning equipment and your owls might drown."

She laughed, and ran over to the double hose bib while he went into the garage to wash his hands. The cold water felt good, and he realized he'd gotten a little warm himself. A couple of cold sodas sounded good about now.

He stepped back outside to suggest it and—

A blast of cold water hit him dead center in the stomach. And Gracie, holding the hose with the nozzle aimed straight at him, giggled.

"Oh, you've done it now," he said, his voice full of mock threat.

She giggled again, just as she triggered the nozzle again. This time, the stream hit him in the chest, and water splashed all over his face and hair. And, he admitted, felt darn good.

On impulse, he grabbed up the bigger hose, switched the selector on the nozzle to a harmless spray, and spun around on her. Gracie yelped and backed up, but she was grinning so widely he kept going. And when he let loose the shower, she laughed again, and instead of running, just stood there and let the water drench her.

"That feels good!" she exclaimed.

"Yeah," Flynn admitted, "It does."

When they were back inside, both sopping wet, he kicked off his shoes just inside the door, and Gracie set her boots neatly beside them. And yet again he felt that tug inside, this time at the sight of those little boots next to his much bigger shoes.

Gracie looked down at her dripping clothes. "Oops," she said as little puddles began to form on the floor.

"It's tile, won't hurt it. Hang on for a minute." He went down the hall to the bathroom and bedroom, came out with a towel and a clean T-shirt. "Here, dry off, head to the bathroom and put that on, and we'll get your clothes in the dryer so you can put them back on."

She scampered off. He went back and changed into dry clothes himself, toweled off his hair and ran a comb through it, and by the time he was done Gracie was coming out. His shirt hit her at the knees, and she twirled gracefully.

"Do you like my dress?" she teased.

He grinned at her. "It does look like a dress. I'll never be able to wear that thing again."

"Where's the dryer? I'll put these in. I know how, honest."

"I'm sure you do. It's in that closet back there."

He heard the footsteps on the stairs just as Gracie trotted off. He went over to the door and pulled it open just as Riley arrived. She looked a little tired, but satisfied, as if she were certain she'd done a good job. He hoped so. Because he was certain.

"Hi," she said, and he realized he'd just been staring at her. He'd been into the restaurant a few times, but he'd never noticed how the knit shirts kind of...clung.

"Hi," he finally got out, stepping back to let her in.

"I'm sorry I'm late—"

She stopped when he held up a hand. "Please don't do that anymore. It's been...fun. A new experience, but fun."

"I don't know how I'll ever—"

This time he grabbed her hands to stop her. "If the next words are 'pay you back,' please don't say them."

She lowered her gaze, and her chin went down with it. He tucked a gentle finger underneath it and lifted her head. And in the next instant he wanted to kiss her again more than he wanted his next breath. Only this time not as a distraction, this time with full intent. The urge exploded inside him, and he leaned in, unable to stop himself. And she tilted her head back, as if she'd read his intent, in fact as if she were welcoming it. He—

Gracie plowed into her mother. It took Riley a moment, but then she scooped her up and hugged her. He guessed Gracie weighed about fifty pounds, but she handled it easily. *Never underestimate the strength of a real mother.*

"Mom, it was so fun! I got to ride in the wheelbarrow and—"

Riley ran a hand down Gracie's back. "What are you wearing?"

Gracie grinned. "My new dress. Flynn gave it to me to put on."

"He...what?"

Riley's expression changed. Her gaze shot to Flynn, her expression going from shocked to horrified to afraid so fast he didn't know what to think.

"Riley?"

"What have you done?" she said hoarsely, backing away with Gracie in her arms.

His brow furrowed. He stared at her, trying to figure out what was wrong.

"Mom, don't hug so hard, that hurts!" Gracie yelped.

"What else hurts, baby?" Riley asked, still backing up.

"Nothing," Gracie said, puzzled.

"Where are—" She gulped in a breath. "Where are your clothes? Why did you...take them off?"

It hit him then, with more force than an IED. Nausea exploded in him with the same kind of power. For a moment he thought he was going to vomit right there. He stumbled backward. Came up against the counter. Grabbed it. Held on like he was trying to break off a chunk of the granite.

Gracie was staring at her mother. Then she looked at Flynn, as if for explanation.

"Go," he said from behind clenched teeth. "Get out."

"What's wrong?" Gracie asked, starting to sound anxious.

"Get your things. You're leaving. Your mother doesn't trust me anymore."

Gracie squirmed loose from her mother. She spun around to face Flynn. "What's wrong?" she said again, but it was nearly a wail this time.

"Honey—" Riley began. Flynn didn't look at her. Couldn't.

"Get your clothes." His teeth were starting to complain and his throat was starting to burn, but he was certain if he relaxed, he was going to puke all over the floor.

"But they aren't dry yet!"

"Get them. And go." He heard the puppy whine. Knew what he must sound like.

"Stop it, you're scaring Brody!" Gracie was staring at him, tears welling up in her eyes. He was already so nauseous it didn't make him feel any worse.

"Just go."

Gracie spun around and darted down the hall.

"Flynn," Riley began.

"Just get out," he said flatly. And finally he looked at her. "I would rather you had run screaming at the sight of my scars than think what you just thought."

And then, because he couldn't take another second standing there with a woman who thought him capable of the most heinous of crimes, and because she was between him and the door, he spun around and headed for the balcony.

And when it turned out that wasn't far enough, he grabbed the railing and went over the side.

CHAPTER THIRTY-ONE

Gracie was crying harder than Riley had ever seen her. It took her a minute or two to calm her down even a little. Even Brody, who crept over and licked at her cheek didn't soothe her.

"Why are you mad at Flynn?" the child choked out. "I started it."

That caught her off guard. "You started...what?"

Gracie sniffed hard as she nodded. "We were hot, from working, and...I thought it would be funny. He wasn't mad, why are you?"

"You thought...what would be funny?"

"I sprayed water on him." Riley drew back slightly. Gracie gulped and went on. "He pretended he was mad, but he was teasing. And he grabbed the other hose and sprayed me right back."

She stared at her child. "Water?"

"It was a water fight, Mom, like we used to do at Gran's house when it got hot. Why are you mad?"

"You had...a water fight? That's why you...took off your clothes?"

"They were dripping all over the floor. So Flynn gave me this shirt and told me to go in the bathroom and change, then put my clothes in the dryer."

Gracie shoved the wadded up bundle of jeans, T-shirt, socks and underwear at her. They were still warm, proving the truth of what she'd said.

"And that's...all that happened?"

Gracie stared at her mother as if she'd lost her mind. "What's wrong?" she demanded for a third time.

Dear God. What was wrong was that she'd made a horrible, insulting, disgusting, and borderline abusive accusation. To a man who had done nothing but help them. Take care of them. Given them so much, in so many ways. Especially Gracie.

An image shot through her mind, of the moment when Flynn had realized what she in essence was accusing him of. He hadn't just looked stunned, he'd looked physically ill. He'd actually turned almost gray before her eyes.

Flynn would die before he'd hurt a child, and there's not a twisted brain cell in his mind.

Matt McLane's words shot through her mind. She should have thought of them before she'd jumped to conclusions. But she hadn't been thinking at all. Her protective instincts had ricocheted off her past history and gone from zero to condemning in a split second, and she'd hurt a wonderful, generous man, badly.

I would rather you had run screaming at the sight of my scars than think what you just thought.

Shaking now, she looked down at her precious little girl. "Honey, I made a big, awful mistake. I hurt Flynn, because I misunderstood. And I have to try and make it right."

"Are you gonna say sorry to him?"

"If he'll listen." *And if I can find him.* Because something this bad couldn't be dealt with on the phone or worse, by text. This needed to be done in person, face to face. She owed him that much, and so, so much more. "But I need you to do something for me while I try. Will you stay here, not go outside or wander? I can't be worried about you, too."

"I'll stay with Brody. You have to find Flynn. That's more important." Gracie crossed her arms and glared at her. "That's *most* important."

"You're right, honey. It is. I just have to figure out where he would go."

"His truck is still here."

She hadn't realized it until her clever girl said so, but the big truck indeed hadn't fired up; they would have heard it.

"So he must still be here, on the grounds." Riley wasn't sure that helped much, given all the acreage that was Dragon Hill.

Even as she thought the name, Gracie spoke again. "Go to the dragon."

She blinked. "What?"

"The dragon," the child said impatiently. "He talks to him sometimes."

"He...talks to the dragon?"

"Sure. So do I. He doesn't answer, but Flynn says sometimes it helps to sort things out if you say them out loud."

Yet another gift given to her precious child. And suddenly finding him and making this right—*please, let me be able to make this right*—was the most crucial thing in her world.

She ran down the outside steps and kept going. Followed the firecracker trail, the shortcut he had cleverly delineated.

She searched all around her with every step, in case he was somewhere else, but there was no sign.

She reached the secluded arbor. Empty. Passed the new rock garden, with the amazing flowers Gracie had helped him plant. No sign. She kept going, her heart hammering not with exertion but in time with her silent pleading, a heartfelt *please* with every step.

She cleared the hedge. Spotted the curled tail of Jake Stone's magnificent creation. And then she spotted a pair of long, strong, jeans-clad legs stretched out between the fearsome creature's front feet, with their formidable talons. And if the thing came to life and ripped her to pieces with those talons, she didn't think it could hurt any more than it already did.

She walked until she could see that he was sitting with his back leaning against the carved belly of the beast, his head tilted back and his eyes closed. He still looked pale, although not that terrifying gray any longer.

She stopped, drawing in the deepest breath she could to steady herself. She'd had to do some difficult things in her life, but this was going to rank right up near the top. What on earth could she say, what could possibly make up for what she done, what she'd accused him of?

There was only one thing she could think of, and it was the last thing she wanted to talk about. Ever. But it was also the only thing big enough to outweigh her unwarranted and cruel leap to judgment. He deserved that much from her. And more.

He deserved everything she could give. And if that meant she had to splay out her sordid past for him to see, then so be it.

"You're supposed to be gone."

She should have known he would sense that she was there.

A man whose life had once depended on being aware of his surroundings wouldn't forget those lessons.

"Flynn, I—"

"Don't want to hear it."

"I don't blame you, but—"

"Just go, Ms. West."

Somehow that last jabbed her more than anything he could have said. She gathered her nerve and sat on the ground facing them both. And right now, even had the creature behind him been real, she would be more afraid of Flynn. Because right now, he had more power than she had ever willingly given anyone.

And besides, she wouldn't put it past this man to have that beast at his command.

"You can turn your dragon loose on me, but I have something I have to say first."

"Don't want to hear it," he repeated. And he had yet to open his eyes. As if he couldn't even bear to look at her.

"But you're going to," she said determinedly. "Even if it rips me to pieces."

"That'll be the dragon," he said sourly.

"No, it won't. I'd rather fight that dragon than tell anyone this. Other than a counselor, I've only told one person the whole story. And she's dead now, so you'll be a party of one."

That at least got him to open his eyes. His brow furrowed. "Why?"

That he'd even bothered to ask gave her a tiny shred of hope. She drew in a deep, almost rattling breath. "Because, it's the only way to make you understand. Why I...reacted that way. It's the only thing big enough to make up for...what I thought."

He stiffened. And now he looked at her, his gaze colder

than she had ever seen it. "You really think some words can make up for that?"

"That's up to you. All I know is this is all I have, and if it doesn't make you see, then nothing can. And if you still can't...forgive me, then you'll never have to see me again."

"Sounds pretty good right now."

He didn't sound angry, but almost bitter. And that clawed at her as if that dragon sheltering him truly had struck out with those talons. He leaned back again, tilting his head back against the sculpture and closing his eyes once more. As if she had never come here, never disturbed him. She wondered what the dragon had heard, when he'd first come here. Had he spoken to it, told it of the idiot woman he'd left behind?

"Then you'll listen?"

He shrugged in that way of his that she'd most often seen when he was declining any thanks. But he said, "Hit me with this mass of words that's going to explain all and make it all right."

"It's not a mass. It's only six."

That made him open his eyes again. And with one of the greatest efforts of her life, she met his gaze. And spoke the words.

"Gracie is a child of rape."

CHAPTER THIRTY-TWO

I t was a warm spring evening, but Flynn suddenly felt as cold as he had on that joint training exercise above the arctic circle. He'd heard the words she'd said, but couldn't quite process them. He was feeling nauseous all over again. The only coherent thing that formed in his mind was a name.

Gracie?

No. How could such an abhorrent act result in a child like her?

Through the fog that had descended on him he heard Riley's voice. Tried to hone in on her words.

"—when, how and who doesn't matter anymore. We're safely away from him now. What matters is that since she was born, I've lived in fear of something like what happened to me happening to her. And for an instant, back there—only an instant, Flynn, I swear—all those fears rose up and swamped me. What do they call it, the lizard brain? That's all that was working in that moment. I wasn't thinking straight. I wasn't thinking at all. If I had been, I would have known how utterly, completely, totally wrong even the thought was."

"But you still thought it."

He'd never heard himself sound like that. Broken. Beaten. In the worst days after he'd been hurt, he'd hated the sound of the groans of pain he couldn't hold back.

This was worse.

"I'd grovel if I thought it would do any good, Flynn. But I've earned your anger, your disgust tonight. I only wanted to...explain why. And right now, Gracie is angrier at me than she's ever been in her life. For your sake. And I deserve it." She let out an audible breath. She started to speak but stopped at a catch in her voice. It was a moment before she tried again. "Even if you can't forgive me, I beg you, please don't turn your back on Gracie because her mother is a fool. Please. She...loves you, Flynn."

I love her, too.

The words formed immediately in his mind. And he didn't even argue the truth of them. But he couldn't say them.

He couldn't say anything.

And for a long, wire-drawn moment, silence spun out. Then, so quietly he had to concentrate to hear her, Riley spoke again. "When you were overseas, in those combat zones...did you ever misinterpret something that ended up costing someone else?"

His breath stopped, as if the autonomic process had been somehow short- circuited. The memory exploded into his brain, of the time when he'd done exactly that, when in the middle of a fire fight he'd misinterpreted a man's movement and it had almost cost a young father only trying to get food for his child his life. As it was, the man would probably limp the rest of his years, and that was on Flynn. He would carry that for the rest of his life, just as he would carry his scars.

"We'll leave," she said quietly when he didn't speak. He

couldn't, he hadn't remembered how to breathe yet. "It's up to you now."

And then she was gone, leaving him to sit in the shadow of the towering beast who, for all his listening abilities, was absolutely no help at all. Nothing could help with the maelstrom of thoughts careening through his mind. He liked none of them, and for the first time in a very long time, wished he had enough booze on hand to get stinking drunk.

But he didn't. He'd written that off as a viable path long ago. Not for anything would he take his father's way out, even if he did now look upon it with a lot more understanding than he'd had as a kid.

She loves you, Flynn.

"Gracie."

He said it out loud, not even sure why, since the dragon was the only one here. He'd only been half-kidding when he'd told the girl he talked to him sometimes.

This apparently was one of the times.

Gracie. That sweet, loving child who was sometimes too smart to believe. That child who had broken down every wall he had, simply because she refused to let him hide behind them. The child who had made him feel things he'd never thought to feel, not just again but ever.

He spoke out loud again, although he was barely aware of it. "She made me laugh again. I thought I'd forgotten how."

And again the dragon merely listened. Kind of like John had, when he'd given him all the reasons why he should pick another for his child's godfather.

"She did that, too," he whispered into the dark to the dragon. Because it truly had been Gracie who had unknowingly allowed him to make a vow to the one man who had the inalienable right to ask it of him. A vow to always be there for his son.

You don't want to do it?

I'm not up to doing it.

You, Mr. Flynn, are full of bull. Don't forget I've watched you with Gracie.

"Faith," he muttered. Riley had had more faith in him than he'd had in himself. The dragon stayed silent, as if that were obvious.

But Riley had also jumped to the most heinous conclusion he could have ever imagined.

Because she was raped.

Riley saying Gracie was a child of rape had somehow put the emphasis on her daughter. Knowing Riley it was probably intentional, because Gracie was ever and always her main focus. Gracie, who fell in love instantly with his fierce, silent friend here.

An image shot through his mind, from that day Riley's car had broken down. When he'd told Gracie her mother was right to be wary, because people weren't always what they seemed. Riley had gone rigid, and something dark and painful had flashed in her eyes. And he'd known in that moment that Riley had learned that wariness the hard way.

And now he knew exactly how she'd learned it.

She had been raped.

And yet out of that rape had come the most amazing child. It was a dichotomy he couldn't balance in his mind.

"How does she do it?" More dragon-silence.

Riley's words came back to him, as they so often did. As if everything she'd ever said was etched permanently into his mind. But this time they came in a flood.

We're safely away from him now.

She's the best kid I could ever have possibly had. She's smart and sweet and brave and caring and the best thing that ever happened to me.

It's like the universe sent me the best kid in the world, to make up for everything else.

And now he knew what that "everything else" was.

When you were overseas, in those combat zones...did you ever misinterpret something that ended up costing someone else?

But that had been in active combat.

And rape isn't?

Some man had forced himself on her, in that most intimately horrible way, and the thought made him as nauseous as her accusation had. In that moment, he wanted more than anything to know who had done it, so he could hunt him down and end him. That fierce, primal urge brought his reeling mind finally to the bottom line.

Was he willing to throw away everything good that had come into his life since the day he'd found Gracie, because of one mistake? No matter the size of it?

The dragon loomed over him, guarding the gate to Dragon Hill. Shan's hill. And as he sat there in the darkness, his own words about Juliette and Shan came back to him.

She worked incredibly hard to make up for an understandable mistake she made once. She's a good person.

He's got the biggest power of all. Forgiveness.

Wasn't Riley's mistake just as understandable? Even more so?

The dragon had no observation to make, no words of wisdom. Clearly the unhelpful beast was going to make him do this on his own.

And then a final memory struck. From the day he had taken Gracie the e-reader, when he'd sworn he hadn't been thinking about his scars when he'd made that crack about having enough souvenirs.

I believe you.

Just like that?

Yes. Because I trust you. And then, in that tone of wonder, she'd said them again, those words that held more import now than he could have ever imagined. *I trust you.*

He sat there until dawn. And when the first light streaked the eastern sky, he finally got to his feet. He looked up at his towering, silent companion. The one who had made him face it all himself.

Who had, in fact, been a help after all. Because that was the only way to do it.

"Thanks, buddy," he murmured.

And then he headed home.

CHAPTER THIRTY-THREE

R iley wiped at eyes that were burning so badly she wanted to claw at them instead. She hadn't cried this much since...ever. Even the night Gracie was conceived—she refused to denigrate it with the reality of how it had happened, not when it had resulted in the greatest joy of her life—she hadn't cried like this, because it had soon morphed into anger, and then into a determination to take something good out of what had happened to her. A determination that she wouldn't take the sperm contributor's actions out on an innocent child. A determination to stand up to her mother, who had pushed so hard to get her to follow the path she wanted.

Not that it had been easy. Standing up while fighting the nightmares and fear that haunted her had not been easy. It had been years before she'd been able to talk to a man she didn't already know with any kind of calm. But those years had been spent with Gracie, and her amazing, wonderful child had been more healing than any therapy. There were times when she had the thought she should be thankful it had happened, because a life without her child's bright, sweet, loving presence would have been hollow and cold.

She almost wished she had to work today. At least then she'd be forced to pull herself together. She had been making progress until Gracie had emerged from her room this morning. Since she had refused to talk to her since they'd left Dragon Hill, Riley had braced herself. But Gracie had merely pronounced that she was going to spend the weekend with her friend Christy, because she didn't want to be around her anymore. The plans, Riley discovered, had been made last night, including Christy's mom coming to pick her up. Normally, Riley would have put a halt to such a thing done without her input, knowledge, or approval, but at this moment she couldn't find the energy. Christy was reliable enough, and she'd met her mother a couple of times, so she let it go. And now the small apartment seemed cavernous, huge in its emptiness. She wandered it in the worn T-shirt and shorts she slept in, wondering how many monstrous mistakes one person could make in a single life.

When the knock on the door came, she thought Gracie must have forgotten something. Or maybe—hope flared—changed her mind about hating her mother. But then she remembered the way her little girl had looked back at her, arms crossed in front of her angrily, and with a glare said flatly, "You should have known better."

No, there would be no forgiveness from that quarter for a while. Because her little girl, her clever, loving, wonderful little girl was, as she was so often, utterly right. So it was with a dull ache still in her chest that she got up and went to answer. She didn't even look through the peephole because at this moment she didn't care. She simply pulled the door open.

And then stood there staring in disbelief.

Flynn.

She knew she must be gaping. And she laughed at herself for her first thought being what a perfect bookend for this most special time of her life; he'd first seen her looking like hell, and now at the end that's what he was seeing again. Tousled hair, eyes reddened, old, tired T-shirt and shorts...and nothing else. She couldn't even find it in her to be embarrassed about that.

When she didn't speak, he finally did. Gruffly.

"Is Gracie here?"

Relief flooded her. He wasn't going to turn his back on Gracie because of what she'd done. And again her daughter's last words echoed in her head. *You should have known better.* Yes, she should have.

"I...no. She's with a friend." With a tremendous effort, she met his gaze. "She didn't want to be with me. She was too angry." He looked disconcerted at that. She swallowed and added, "With every right. Just as you have."

"I'm not."

She blinked, drew back. "You're...not? Angry?"

She saw him let out a breath. "Can we not do this at the front door?"

"But I told you Gracie's not here."

"I didn't come to see Gracie. I asked if she was here because I don't want her to hear...this."

So he was going to tell her exactly what he thought of her. That's why he sounded so odd.

Get it done. Let him say it, then it will be over and you can pick up what's left and go on. You've done it before, more than once, you can do it again.

"Come in," she said stiffly, standing aside.

And the moment he stepped across the threshold, the

apartment went from vast to tiny again. Flynn simply was too much of a presence not to fill it. Her heart sank a little more when he sat down on the worn couch; clearly this wasn't going to be short enough for him to do it standing.

She walked over and sat in the single chair. Braced herself. And waited. And when his first question came, it was the last thing she'd ever expected.

"Who's Regina?"

She stared at him. How had he known that murmured name from a half-asleep Gracie had meant something? And why was that the first thing he asked?

"Who is she?" he repeated when she didn't answer.

"She was a famous musician from Italy back in the 1800s. One of the very few women to ever play the violin in public back then. My mother idolized her."

"And so?"

With a heavy sigh, she gave up. "She named me after her." *And I never thought Gracie would remember that.*

"So...Regina is you."

"Was."

"And Riley?"

"My father's middle name."

"And West?"

"My grandmother's house was on West 55th Street."

She half expected him to ask where, since there was no 55th Street, west or otherwise, in Wild Oak. But he didn't. What he did ask, in a totally different tone, was, "Why did you need to hide?"

Leave it to Flynn to ignore what she'd done to him and focus on what was done to her. She quashed the spark had her hoping that meant he still cared. "Does it matter?"

"Yes."

She sighed. "If you're looking for a way I wasn't stupid, there isn't one. I believed a man I shouldn't have, and paid for it."

"Will you tell me what happened?" he asked, now in a quiet voice that seemed somehow more dangerous than his gruff tone.

Her gaze shot to his face. She couldn't read his expression, but had the feeling more than an enemy or two had folded before that steely stare. Which meant she had no hope at all. But she'd already decided to tell him whatever he wanted to know. She owed him that much.

She sighed again. Marshaled the words. They came out in a burst. "The man who raped me was the son of an important man in L.A. I was young, fresh out of college and newly back home, in a suburb of the city. I'd seen him a couple of times, just for coffee, before I got suspicious. Then I found out he was engaged, and broke it off. Turned out no woman was allowed to say no to him. He wouldn't tolerate it. He came after me the next night."

Flynn had gone very still. She saw his jaw clench. And the certainty of who this man was flooded her, which only pounded home how wrong she'd been in those few moments, how badly she'd insulted him.

She made herself go on. "By the time I found out about Gracie, they were married. My mother wanted me to terminate the pregnancy, but...I couldn't. It sounds crazy, but...I could sense Gracie's presence, long before I ever felt her move. My mother was so angry at me I couldn't stay with her. But Gran...she understood. She took me in when I was at such a loss. Sheltered me. Was with me every step of the way, including when Gracie was born. She adored her only great-grandchild, and did everything she could for us. Including

Gracie's trust fund, and leaving me the house where she and my grandfather had lived for years."

"'Cars don't have grandparents,'" he said slowly.

As he quoted Gracie's words, the memory of that day with the car shot vividly through her mind. She'd obviously betrayed herself yet again to him, when she'd felt the stab of pain at her little girl's joking words. And as usual, Flynn hadn't missed it.

"Go on," he said, his voice still gruff.

She gave him a weary look. "You can't really want to hear all this."

"I have to hear it."

Her burning eyes stung again; did he really mean he had to know why she'd made that horrible assumption, accusing him of something too evil to be forgiven?

It's penance. Just finish it.

"Her...father found out later his wife could not have children. But obviously he could."

Flynn drew back, staring at her. "He came after...Gracie?"

She nodded. Then, with a flare of remembered anger, she said, "As if I'd turn her over to a rapist to raise."

"So you ran?"

"I had no choice. I told you they were important, but they were also rich. I couldn't afford lawyers to fight, and even then I knew they'd only be able to hold him off for a while. Gran had died by then, so I sold the house to give us running money. We went to San Diego, but...he had friends there, and found us. He tried to grab Gracie."

She'd thought his expression harsh before, but it was mellow compared to the look on his face now. "Let me be sure I have this right. He cheated on his fiancée, lied to you, raped you, knew you'd gotten pregnant but did nothing, offered no help, had no contact, until he decided he wanted Gracie? And then he followed you and tried to kidnap her?"

She nodded. "We had to run again. This time, I literally blindly stuck a pin in a map. And came up with Wild Oak."

"Why didn't you go after him? He was legally responsible—"

Riley laughed sourly. "I told you who he—they—were. I grew up hearing about his family. My mother admired them. She didn't believe me when I told her about the rape, because what woman would ever turn him down? Except a stupid fool like me. Then she thought I was an even bigger fool for not trying to lure him away from his fiancée. Finally, she went on a tirade about what an idiot I was being, to keep Gracie. 'You'll be giving up your dreams! Your career. All you've worked for. You can't be a single mother and do what you're meant to do. You'll waste the talent you were born with.' The subtext being, of course, that that blessing had come directly from her."

"Your musical talent."

She shrugged. "She was a frustrated concert orchestra player. She wanted the glamour and success she never got vicariously."

"Through you."

"Yes."

"But you didn't?"

"I loved music, and loved playing. I didn't care about the rest."

"Is that why you taught?"

She nodded. "I wanted to share the love of the music."

He lapsed into silence, and she tried not to squirm under his steady gaze. She wondered how many times, when he'd been in uniform, that he'd had to simply wait out the enemy.

And her stomach churned at the idea that he might think of her that way now. Finally, she broke.

"What else do you want to ask?"

"Open invitation?"

"I owe you any answer you want."

"You don't owe me anything, Riley. Or should I say Regina?"

"I've gotten used to Riley. I like it better. And it's a tribute to my father, who always understood when my mother—who chose the other name—never did." She steadied herself with a breath. "And I owe you more than I can ever repay. Among many other things, for what you've done for and with Gracie." She smiled sadly. "Who may never forgive me, either."

He was silent for a long moment. Then, unexpectedly, he said, "Do you remember when you accused me of thinking you were a helicopter parent?"

She remembered every second of every minute with him. Including the ones from last night that she wished she could forget. "Yes."

"I was thinking it. But now I know I was wrong. You were protecting her as only someone who's known the worst can."

"Yes."

There was another long pause. Then he took a breath and said, in rather choppy bursts, "I could...teach her. How to resist, to fight. Enough to maybe get away. If she ever had to."

Riley stared at him for a moment; once more he'd startled her. "But...she's so little!"

"There are ways to use that. Low center of gravity, against a top heavy opponent. Her quickness. And the element of surprise."

"I...you'd do that?"

"The worst part would be having to acknowledge to her

that she might need it sometime. I don't like that, her having to face that so young. But would it make you feel...safer?"

"If she at least had a fighting chance? Of course it would. I've thought about getting her lessons, as soon as I could afford it."

"My only price is your forgiveness."

Now he'd stunned her into silence. And it was a full minute before she managed to respond. "*My* forgiveness?"

"For thinking you were too protective."

She stared at him, wondering how he had somehow turned this all around. She was the one who should be groveling, begging his forgiveness, and he was asking for hers?

Her thoughts were tumbling, chaotic, until one thing solidified. Her gaze narrowed as she turned it over in her mind. "Is this how you do it with Gracie?"

He raised a brow at her. The unscarred one, as usual; she was convinced now he simply couldn't raise the other. Which somehow made the expression even more potent.

"Is this how you get her to...understand? By giving her...not explanations, but simply making her think?"

"That depends," he said, sounding a bit wary. "Are you going to be mad if I admit I'm using the same tactic on you as on an eight-year-old?"

"No," she said, "I'm going to embarrassedly admit it's probably necessary. Because if I was better at it, I never would have had that moment of doubt. I would have trusted you no matter what popped into my head."

Something shifted in his intense gaze then. "After what happened to you...how can you trust any man? And why did you trust me at all?"

"Do you think all women are like your mother and your former fiancée?"

He drew back. Frowned. Clearly thinking, as he'd made her do. "You're not," he said. Then that brow went up again. "Turnabout?"

"Sort of." She sighed. "I wanted to trust you, because of how you were with Gracie. Not to mention, you've got some dynamite references." She took a deep breath. "I once swore to myself I would never again trust as much as I'd trusted...that man. And I was right. I don't trust you that much." He went very still before she finished quietly, "I trust you more."

"Ahh, Riley," he said, the words coming on a long exhalation.

And then he was on his feet. Startled, she jumped up herself. He covered the distance between them in one long stride.

And pulled her into his arms.

CHAPTER THIRTY-FOUR

Crazily, it was harder to hold her like this than he would have ever imagined, now that he knew. He'd thought about it, hell, dreamed about embracing her and more, much more, but now that he knew what had happened to her, he felt as if he were holding some fragile, delicate piece of glass that had been shattered and glued back together. He couldn't not notice she wasn't wearing much, but neither could he let it send him reeling out of control. Not with Riley. Not now.

Still, he could no more let go of her than he could stop breathing.

And then he heard her say, as if she were fighting back tears, "I'm so sorry, Flynn. I was so wrong and I—"

He tightened his hold. "Stop. I understand. Now that I know, I'm amazed you didn't take me out right there."

"As if I could."

"Honey, you could cut my heart out with a look."

He hadn't meant to admit that, but doubted he could have held it back.

"Can you forgive me?"

He searched for the right words. He'd learned a lot about forgiveness from Shan and Juliette, because Shan had had a lot to forgive. But as bad as their situation had been, it wasn't as ugly or difficult as Riley's had been.

"For what? For loving Gracie that much? For a few seconds of thinking your worst, most haunting nightmare had come true? There's nothing to forgive, Riley. I only reacted the way I did because I didn't know."

"I think I knew that. That's why I had to tell you." She lowered her gaze. "And if knowing this...changes how you feel..."

"Changes?"

"Some men can't handle it."

"Misnomer," he said gruffly.

That made her look at him again. "What?"

"If they can't handle it, don't call them men." He saw something change in her expression then, a flicker of relief. "I'm sorry, Riley."

"Don't. I don't want your pity. I don't want you with me...only because you feel sorry for what happened to me."

He pulled back slightly, stared down at her. "I could say the same to you."

Her eyes widened. "Pity? For the most—"

He held up a hand to stop her. "That's not why I said it. I'm only sorry for my reaction. And for those pitiful excuses for men who would blame you for what happened. Believe me, pity is the last thing I feel, after what you've done to keep Gracie safe, and build a life for yourself and her."

"Not much of one," she said, sounding rueful.

"We'll talk about that later. Right now, you just have to tell me one thing."

"What?"

"What do you want?"

She met his gaze then, steadily. "Don't you know?"

All the things he thought he read in her eyes started his pulse hammering and his body heating. But this was not something he could take for granted. With Riley, he couldn't assume he was right. He had to know.

"I won't guess, Riley. Not at this, not with you."

"Then I'd better make it crystal clear," she whispered.

And then she was kissing him, fiercely, thoroughly, and every response he'd been fighting since the first time he'd held her, even though she'd been dizzy and sick, kicked to life. And this time they won, because Riley was indeed making it crystal clear what she wanted.

Him.

She wanted him.

She deepened the kiss, as if she wanted to devour him. As if his mouth—even his scarred mouth—held the key to her world. And her hands, God her hands were sliding over him, over his ribs, down his back, and then across his belly. He felt a tug, but didn't realize it had been her pulling free his shirt until he felt that stroke across his belly again, only this time it was her slender fingers across his bare skin. Fire erupted, billowed, surged, and he forgot how to breathe.

And then she changed direction and slid her hand toward the waistband of his jeans.

"Riley," he said, or tried to, it came out pretty rough. "Slow down."

She leaned back enough to look up at him. "Second thoughts?"

His jaw tightened as his body screamed at him to quit asking questions and take what she was offering. But he couldn't do that. Because once a man had taken what she hadn't offered.

"Not me. You," he said, his voice tight now. "Because in another ten seconds, I may not be able to stop."

"Thank you for your care, but I'm sure." She reached up and cupped his face. The scarred side. And the move ripped words out of him.

"You know how rude and crude guys joke about going to bed with a looker and waking up with a troll? Well, it's the woman who thinks that with me."

He felt her go very still. "You need to find a better class of woman, then, if that's all they see. Is that really what you think of me? That I'm that shallow? That I really am like your fiancée, or your mother?"

He let out a long breath. "What I think," he said with an effort, "is that there is no better class of woman than you."

"What matters to me, Finnbar Flynn, is the man you are. Not the wrapping." She added flatly, "I've had enough of pretty outsides hiding ugly insides, thanks."

She meant it. He couldn't doubt it. A sudden thought hit him. "Have you...been with anyone? Since, I mean?"

She lowered her gaze then. He saw her mouth—God, that mouth—twist at one corner. "I...tried. Once. It didn't go well." Then she looked up at him again, and what glowed in those beautiful eyes of hers melted him to the core. "But he wasn't you. I've never felt anything like this."

"I didn't know there was anything like this," he said, his throat tight.

"Then what are we waiting for?"

"I didn't come here...planning for this. Or prepared for it."

It seemed to take her a moment. And then she answered.

"I've gotten birth control shots regularly. If I get pregnant again, it will be intentional."

A contemplative expression crossed her face, and in that instant, he somehow knew what she was thinking. A cascade of possibilities, of future hopes and dreams careened around in his head. Dreams he'd never dared dream, hopes he'd never dared to unleash.

He reined them in. Focused on the here and now. His gut wanted to sweep her up in his arms and carry her to the nearest bed. But he didn't do it. He let her take his hand and lead him down the hall, like some housebroken pet. Because it had to be clear, especially this first time, that this was her decision. And God help him, if she changed her mind, he was going to have to find the control to stop. No matter when it was. If he had to personally pay for that other cretin's offense, so be it. What mattered now was Riley. Only Riley.

Her bedroom was simple, with only a double bed and a dresser. It was almost painfully tidy, except for the mirror above the dresser. That was festooned with drawings that had Gracie's stamp all over them. For all her brilliance elsewhere, here she was a typical eight-year-old.

Some men might find it off putting, the overwhelming presence of a child here. He didn't.

And then Riley was pointing, to a drawing that was a little bigger than the others. It was of a man in what he guessed was supposed to be camouflage, although the colors were a bit bright to serve the purpose. And across the chest was a row of ribbons and medals in equally bright colors. Including a fairly accurate representation of a Purple Heart.

And beneath the drawing his name was scrawled in Gracie's tidy hand.

"She loves you, Flynn," Riley said softly.

He couldn't deny it. Wouldn't. "And I love her." *And you. God help me, and you.*

He wanted to run. This was too much. Worse than any mine field. But he couldn't. Not after what she'd said, she'd think it was because of what had happened to her.

He wasn't sure what to do next. And he knew some of his old buddies, the ones that had known him before, would laugh their asses off at that. *Hang out with Flynn and, pretty as he is, there are always some extras.* It hadn't been a lie. And jerk that he'd been, he'd used it. If he went without, it was by his choice. And it had never been real. Any of it. It had been the surface, the exterior they'd been attracted to, neither knowing nor caring about anything else.

Gracie had never cared. His scars were unimportant to her.

They were, he finally had to believe, unimportant to Riley. Because she'd been through too much of her own hell for them to matter. In her way, she was as scarred as he was, only hers didn't show on the surface.

When she reached for him, when she tugged at his shirt again, this time upward, he made no move to stop her as she pulled it off. When she trailed her fingers over his bare chest and downward, he couldn't stop himself from sucking in a breath, but he didn't move. He closed his eyes for a moment, but that seemed to only increase the intensity of the feel of her hands on him.

When she reached for the zipper of his jeans, it took everything he had in him not to move. She fumbled, obviously unused to this. And the resulting, lingering touches as she tried to maneuver was driving him to the brink of insanity.

"Help me," she whispered.

It was all he needed. He was out of the jeans and everything else as fast as he could manage. And when he straightened up and saw she'd pulled off her own thin shirt, saw that what he'd already known was true, she wore no bra underneath. And then she slipped down the equally worn shorts, and he realized she truly had had nothing else on. She'd probably been so upset about Gracie she hadn't cared.

It was his last rational thought. And it took every bit of control he'd ever learned in a tough, sometimes brutal life to keep from grabbing her, from pulling her against him so he could feel every inch of that silken skin. His gaze slid over her, the soft fullness of breasts tipped with nipples the color of the pink flowers that lined the dragon's secret lair, lingered on the curve of her hip, that spot that seemed the perfect place for his hands, and his fingers curled into fists as he fought the need that was nearly overwhelming. Something had to give, and he spoke.

"God, you're beautiful."

He saw her cheeks flush. "Says the man who could be a statue of the male ideal."

He opened his mouth to say something like "A cracked one, maybe." But something in the way she was looking at him stopped the words on his lips.

The smile she gave him then made him feel as he had when they'd pinned that bronze star on him. Unworthy, a little embarrassed, but proud.

"Thank you for not saying what you were thinking." He blinked. She held his gaze. "Whatever joke you were going to make about the scars, but didn't."

He stared at her. She'd read him so perfectly he was rattled now. Rattled enough that he was thinking about that as she led him to her bed. In a moment when he would have assumed he'd be thinking only of at last easing this ache that consumed him, he was thinking about how Riley West knew him better than even the men he'd been under fire with.

And then he was lying beside her, her long, naked body against his, and it blasted almost every other thought out of his fevered brain.

Almost.

But still—fool that he was—he had to give her one last out.

"We can still stop."

She moved slightly, caressing ready flesh with one silken thigh. "Doesn't feel like you want to stop."

He went very still. Then he raised up on an elbow to look at her. "I can't control my response to you, Riley. Never could. The only thing I can control is what I do, or don't do, about it."

Unlike the predator who took away your right to say no.

She looked at him steadily. "And you would. I know that. You're everything a man should be, Flynn." Then, almost shyly, she added, "You don't really want to stop, do you?"

"God, no. But...Riley it's been a long time for me, too. I want to make this good for you but—"

"It's already been better than anything I've known, Finnbar Flynn. So don't you be worrying about that."

He didn't even wince at her use of his full name. "I just need to be sure."

"I'm sure that more than anything else in the world right now, I want you."

He let out a long breath. And then he let go of her. She looked startled. He dropped back on the bed, his hands knotting into fists at his sides. He lay there for a moment, knowing what he was letting himself in for, but knowing it had to be this way.

"Then take me," he said hoarsely.

Her eyes widened. Her gaze slipped down his body,

lingering at his straining erection before returning to his face. "Flynn," she whispered, then stopped.

"Nothing," he said, "*nothing* happens here that you don't want."

"But...what about what you want?"

"What I want is whatever you want to give, Riley. Everything you want to give. Give," he repeated with emphasis.

"Good," she said softly. "Because what I want to give is everything."

She started with a kiss so long and so deep his body almost ended it right there.

And he knew he'd underestimated what he was in for.

RILEY KNEW SHE HAD, if anything, understated the fact.

Flynn wasn't just her idea of the male ideal, he was more. Because while the physical aspect—including those scars whose only importance was as a symbol of the hero the man was—was nothing short of breath-stealing, it was who he was, the man inside, the mind, the heart, that had made her fall in love with him.

The admission, even made silently, made her shiver inside. Or maybe it was simply the feel and taste of him under her hands and mouth. Or the way he responded, the sounds he made when she kissed him here, the way he went rigid when she licked him there.

He'd meant what he'd said. He'd handed the reins to her, and now he was hers to explore, to learn, to savor. And as she'd hoped—no, as she'd known—with Flynn, it was different. There was no hesitation, no wondering if she was going to be hit with hideous memories at the worst moment. Because what she felt for him wasn't even in the same league. It was so much more, it bore no resemblance at all to anything she'd ever known. It was as if she'd crashed ugly on a bicycle as a kid, but was now an adult with a smooth, powerful, beautiful car to drive. They both involved getting from here to there, but one had ended badly, and this one...she didn't want to end at all. Ever.

Yes, she loved him. And since she couldn't quite say it out loud to him yet, she proceeded to try her best to show him. She traced every long, strong line of him, repeating whenever he gasped, lingering whenever he groaned, deepening whenever he went rigid. When she reached that particularly rigid part of him, she hesitated, not because she didn't want to stroke him but because she was having a little trouble breathing at the thought of this sizeable male flesh sliding inside her. At the same time her body clenched, low and deep, as if he were already there.

Hunger exploded inside her, fed by the certainty that this would be as it should be, freely given, hungrily wanted, and laced throughout with genuine feeling. Even if he didn't love her as she loved him, he would be as careful with her as if he did, because that was who he was.

He'd already proven that by doing nothing she hadn't asked for, by word or gesture. When she'd had to, simply had to feel his touch on her breasts, she'd had to take his hands and put them there. Once she had, he'd shivered as he cupped them gently, running his thumbs over her nipples and sending fire streaking through her to pool moltenly in that same low, deep place. When she'd had the same need for his touch in that place, she'd slid his hand down her body, and savored the moment when she'd truly realized how ready she was by the way his fingers slid over flesh slick with wanting him.

When he growled a gruff warning at her that he was at the breaking point, she straddled him, and began to lower herself slowly. This was new to her, both the position and the power of the wanting. Her own gasp echoed his as she began to take him in. He filled her, stretched her, but without pain or fear. It felt delicious, and she wanted more. And more. And when she was full, she began to slide on him, up and down, barely aware that the little cries of pleasure she heard were her own.

It caught her unaware, that moment when her body gathered itself. She felt the tightening, the lift, let out a little moan as it built. And then, for the first time, Flynn touched her without her asking, stroking her where they were joined, once, twice, and her body clenched fiercely around him and her world exploded. She cried out, maybe screamed, then moaned his name over and over as wave after wave of blissful sensation swept through her. She heard her own name in his voice, but rough, almost hoarse as he bucked beneath her, driving himself to the hilt inside her.

And when she collapsed atop him, there was no thought in her mind except that this was Flynn and only he could have done this for her. Brought her home. Made her safe.

Safe.

Flynn.

Later, when they lay in the darkness and she'd asked him to simply make love to her without her having to ask, he had done it with the same gentle care that even when his much bigger body loomed over her, she'd felt not even the faintest echo of that long ago night. And the feel of him, the weight of him, the size of him as he slid into her, practically had her clawing at him so quickly did she hit the peak.

Much later, when he'd been still long enough she thought him asleep, she whispered, "I love you, Finn Flynn." She knew in an instant she'd misjudged, because he stiffened. She stifled a sigh. "You can pretend I didn't say that if you want."

"I'll pretend you didn't say that stupid name," he said softly next to her ear. "The rest, I'll keep."

As declarations of love went, she'd take that one above any other. Because it was so very Flynn.

CHAPTER THIRTY-FIVE

"**Y**ou'll have to go get her," Riley said. "She won't have anything to do with me."

"She'll get over it." He gave her a sideways look. "I did."

"After a long talk with the guardian of the gate?"

"He's a good listener."

She smiled. That Riley smile that sent a shiver down his spine, to several points south, one in particular. After last night, even as often as they'd made love—because there was no doubt in his mind that's what it was, he'd had enough pure sex to know the difference—he could have taken her right back to bed.

But there was something else that took priority at the moment. "Let's go get your girl," he said.

"No." He drew back slightly. "She's made her feelings pretty clear. So let's go get *our* girl."

Warmth burst inside him. Completely different, yet no less powerful than the fire she'd lit in him last night. "Yes," he said, a little roughly. "Let's go get our girl."

The house Gracie was staying at with her friend was only a

couple of blocks from Matt's and Kelly's neighboring places. Riley had called ahead to Christy's mom to let her know, and tell her to tell Gracie that Flynn was coming. But when they arrived, she insisted on staying in his truck—they'd brought it because she'd said Gracie was mad enough that if she saw her car she probably wouldn't even come to the door—so he walked up to the door alone. And when Christy's mother opened it, he'd barely gotten two words out when Gracie raced in from the other room, shouting his name.

"Flynn!" She threw herself at him, and he swept her up, holding her close. "I was so scared I wouldn't see you again, I told her you would never, ever hurt me, but sometimes she's just so stupid about things and—"

"Whoa. Stop right there, Gracelyn." The use of her full name did it. She stopped. Stared at him. "Your mother is not stupid. She thought you were...hurt. She misunderstood something, because of something that happened to her a long time ago."

"What?"

He shook his head. "We'll get to that, sometime." She needed to know, eventually. But with luck, maybe they could stall that for another twenty years or so. "What you need to remember, always remember, is that she loves you more than herself, and if you get hurt, it makes her feel like...like you felt when those boys were hurting Brody."

The child's eyes widened. "Oh. That felt bad. Really bad. I wanted to hurt them right back."

"I know."

"But you fixed it, Flynn. Can you fix Mom, too?"

He cleared his throat. "Uh...I think we've made a good start." *Last night.*

"So she doesn't think you hurt me anymore?"

"She knows I didn't. Wouldn't. Ever."

"She should have known before," Gracie said, with such a stern expression Flynn paradoxically wanted to smile.

"Let it go, Gracie. I did."

She studied him for a moment, with that fierce intensity of hers. "Will it go back to like it was before?"

"Better, I hope." He was already wondering how Shan would feel about a couple of additional residents for Dragon Hill.

Finally, Gracie nodded. "Okay." She made a face. "I didn't like being mad at her."

"Because you love her, too."

"And you," Gracie said easily.

Flynn took in a deep breath, looked into those eyes so like her mothers', and said it. "And I love you both."

He wasn't sure the little girl got the full significance of that admission, but she would. She would.

And it was the strangest feeling he'd ever had, when they stopped for lunch at the diner, and decided to stay and eat there because Gracie never had. It was a strange feeling, as if they were already a family.

A family. Had he really thought that?

"My, but you can certainly tell she's yours," the waitress said as she handed out menus and smiled at all three of them. Gracie looked up curiously. "She has your eyes and your hair," the woman explained, looking from Riley to Flynn.

As the woman walked away, Flynn felt dumbstruck, and couldn't speak. Gracie, seated between them in the semicircular booth, looked at her mother, then at him, then at his hair. Then she pulled a strand of her own around to where she could look at it. And then she smiled widely. "I do!" she crowed. "It's the same color!" She looked up at him, her eyes wide with delight. "Do you think I got it because I'm supposed to be yours?"

Flynn swallowed, then again because his throat was so tight. "Gracelyn West, you'd be mine if your hair was purple."

Gracie snorted with laughter. "Ew. No thanks."

She went back to reading her menu, and Flynn shifted his gaze to Riley. She hadn't made a sound, but two solitary tears were streaking down each cheek. Flynn reached out and wiped them away with the back his fingers. Riley grabbed his hand before he could pull it back, turned it over and kissed his palm, sending a shiver through him.

He pondered the gravity and the intensity of his own verbally staked claim the entire trip to the McLane house to pick up Jimmy the next Sunday afternoon. Which was an oddity in itself; of all the things he never would have expected to find himself doing, it was picking up another kid for a play date in the new park. But Matt and Kelly had some wedding planning to do, and Gracie had insisted Jimmy could spend the day with them, since they'd planned a picnic anyway.

Of course, that arrangement had happened when the entire Wild Oak Bunch had descended upon him when he hadn't answered any calls or texts for a week. He hadn't really done it on purpose, he'd just been...busy. And still not quite used to having anybody give a damn.

He'd been marveling at that before realizing that it was not quite 7:00 AM Saturday morning, Gracie was on the couch with Brody, still sound asleep—he needed to carve out some space for a room for her—and Riley was in the kitchen fixing breakfast, still in the blue shirt of his she'd slipped on after they'd lingered in bed for one last exploration of each other before they gave in to the day.

He saw Riley and Gracie's presence register on every face.

"Uh..." He couldn't find a single word.

Riley had looked up, and her eyes widened. Her gaze shot to his face.

"About time," John and Jen said in unison.

"Amen," echoed Jake, while Rachel merely grinned.

"Riley," Juliette said with a grin, as Shan bent to pet Brody, who was clearly excited at all the new company, "I can't tell you how glad I am not to be the newbie in this group anymore."

Riley blinked. "Got any more eggs?" Kelly asked her. "It's going to take a lot to feed this bunch."

"I...there's another dozen in there," Riley said, sounding a little stunned.

"Good," Jen put in. She handed little Ryan to John. "Here, hold your son while I help Flynn's lady."

Flynn's lady. Damn, he liked the sound of that.

"We need more bacon," Matt's Uncle Lew said after peering into the refrigerator.

"Hadn't planned on feeding a battalion," Flynn muttered, finally remembering how to speak.

Gracie finally stirred, and sat up on the couch, rubbing at her eyes. She stared at the suddenly full room, uncharacteristically speechless and clearly wondering if she was still asleep and dreaming.

"Hi, Gracie," Shan said cheerfully. Then, "We have a lot of bacon. I'll go get some."

"Hey," Matt said, "send Jimmy in if you see him. He went up to see the dragon."

Shan waved in assent as he trotted down the steps. Gracie was still staring. "What's going on?" she finally asked, looking from her mother to Flynn and back.

"I think," Riley had said, sounding nothing less than

amazed, "we're having company for breakfast."

And right about then was when Jimmy had burst in, hadn't seemed at all surprised to see his classmate here, had been delighted to meet Brody, and Matt had joked about being glad to have more people to spread around babysitting.

"We're not babies!" Jimmy and Gracie had declared in unison, making everyone in the room laugh.

And so now, the next day, here they were in the shade of one of the oaks of Wild Oak Park, watching the two kids hopefully wear themselves out on some of the unique equipment Shan had devised and had built. The puppy had already been worn out, and was snoozing on the corner of the blanket.

"Flynn?"

He turned to look at Riley. Her expression seemed too serious to match up with watching two kids play. "What?" he asked, cautiously.

"Will you tell me something?"

"What?" he asked again, even more cautiously.

"I'd like to hear this once. Only once."

He blinked. That was an odd way of putting...whatever this was. "What?"

She reached up and cupped his face. The scarred side, as she usually did. "How it happened."

He hadn't expected that, although he'd guessed she would ask eventually. He just hadn't expected it here and now, in this relaxed, almost family type moment, them on a blanket on the grass with Gracie and Jimmy playing some sort of king of the mountain thing a few yards away. But then it hit him. What better time than this? When he had everything he'd never dared dream of within reach?

"We were on an HVT exfil in a port town near—" He stopped, started again in plain English. "We'd captured a high value target, a man who was directly responsible for the deaths of thousands, not to mention the beheadings he did personally, on video. We were on our way out. Things started to go south when our vehicle was blown up before we got back to it. His people were closing in. Only choice we could see was to grab a boat we saw tied up at a nearby dock. We got clear, but our prisoner decided he'd rather meet his god than face what was coming. He went over the side."

Her eyes widened. "And you went after him," she whispered.

He shrugged. "Stupid, really. He was secured and wouldn't have been able to swim. And I was still in full gear. But we'd already lost Ryan Manetti getting the guy, and damned if I was going to let that be for nothing." He grimaced. "During the struggle, we got up close and personal with the boat's propeller."

He heard her suck in a breath. "Dare I hope he's dead?"

He hadn't expected that, either. But he should have. Riley West was no shrinking violet. She was as tough as she had to be, because she'd had to be.

"Let's just say what happened to him was an appropriate payback for what he'd done to others. That prop caught his neck. Completely."

She stared at him for a moment. He thought he might have gone too far. So many back home, even if they understood in generalities what terrorists were like, couldn't seem to take in the true cruelty and heartlessness of their actions. And then something shifted in her gaze and when she spoke, it was with a coolness that rivaled any operator he'd ever worked with.

"I hope you didn't bother to look for his head."

Flynn couldn't help it. He burst out laughing. He grabbed

her and pulled her tight against him. She laughed with him, and that was the most glorious of all.

"I love you," he said simply.

"And I you, Finn Flynn."

He was so far gone he didn't even wince.

THAT NIGHT, back at the flat, as she'd taken to calling it, Riley remembered the story he'd told her as she stopped at the third photo in the stack Gracie had been going through before falling asleep. It was a measure of how completely Flynn had accepted the child as part of his life that he didn't withhold anything from her.

Rile stared down at the image captured in time, years ago. A young man in camouflage, turned so that she couldn't read the name on his uniform. It didn't matter, she knew who he was, even if it was a decade ago. He was twenty-eight or so in this shot. He was grinning. He was vibrantly alive.

He was absolutely stunning.

He could have graced the cover of any men's magazine, in a tux, in workout gear, or heaven help the women of the world, in swim trunks. She could imagine him on the big screen, sending female hearts around the world into flutters.

"As you can see," Flynn's voice, his tone dry, came from close enough behind her she almost jumped, "I should have left the swimming to the SEALs."

He didn't sound angry that she'd looked, so she turned to face him. "You know, I wondered once, how a man who was raised by a mother who walked out on him for such a preposterous reason ended up the man you are. But now—" she gestured at the picture "—I think I get it."

He blinked, and one brow, the mobile one, lowered. "What?"

She nodded at the image. "He's beautiful. Stunning, in fact. But he's also the kind of man who could, if he wanted to, slide through life on those incredible looks." She held his gaze steadily as she went on. "You wouldn't be the man you are, if you hadn't gone for that unplanned swim. And it's the man you are now that I love."

He growled something unintelligible. Riley didn't care that she couldn't understand, because in the same moment he swept her up into his arms and headed for the bedroom.

CHAPTER THIRTY-SIX

"**I** did some digging," John said.

Flynn looked at his best friend warily across the table. This did not bode well. "Into what?"

John hesitated, and that alone told Flynn how explosive this might be. When Jen had insisted he and Riley and Gracie come for dinner tonight, he'd suspected it was more than just more welcoming Riley into the fold. Apparently he'd been right. He had the feeling he would be glad that Gracie was in the other room, entranced with little Ryan.

"Your father," John finally said.

Flynn blinked as he drew back sharply. "What the hell?"

"There are things you should know," Jen put in quietly.

"Is he dead?" Flynn snapped.

"No," John said.

"Too bad."

"Then I shouldn't tell you that he walked out on your mother soon after that day at the hospital when she walked out on you? Or that right after that, he got sober, and has stayed sober ever since?"

Flynn stared at him.

"Or," Jen put in, "that he would have come to you long ago, except he feared you would just throw him out, because he didn't stand by you when he should have?"

"I'll give you the string of adjectives he had for your mother, but not in mixed company," John said. "And the string he had for himself for not getting out—and getting you out—long ago was even worse."

Flynn gave a slow shake of his head. "And you just...did this. On your own. Without asking me. Without asking if I even gave a damn if he was dead or alive."

"No, he didn't." His head snapped around as Riley quietly spoke. "I asked him if he could find him."

Flynn had always heard the phrase about someone's jaw dropping, but he'd never experienced it until now. "You...asked him?"

"She did," John answered. "With the proviso that if he hadn't changed, I'd say nothing. So it's up to you now, buddy. Say the word, and we'll set up a meeting. Or don't, and it's never mentioned again."

Flynn didn't know how he felt. Didn't know what to think, what to feel. And he sure as hell didn't know what to say. So he said nothing. And it took Gracie about two minutes after they'd pulled out of John's driveway to realize something was up.

"What is it?" she demanded.

"Nothing you need to worry about, honey," Riley said, the first time she'd spoken since the moment she'd admitted she had been the one to put John up to this.

"Flynn's all tense. You're worried. So I'm worried. Did you do something wrong again?" she demanded of her mother.

Flynn felt Riley's gaze. "I don't know yet," she said softly. "I only know I meant to help."

"It's not...about us, is it?" Gracie's tone had changed, and the note of anxiety that came into her voice stabbed through the lingering shock of what had just happened.

Flynn steadied himself and reached back to grab the child's hand. "It is not about you, Gracelyn, and your mother's right. You don't need to worry about it."

The child relaxed, taking his word since he'd given it with her full name, and she knew now that was the equivalent of an unbreakable vow for him. And the pure simplicity of that was still a wonder to him.

To reassure her, he put Gracie to bed himself that night, in the small bedroom they'd added, carving the space out of the great room that was a bit smaller now, yet felt more perfect than it ever had.

And when he and Riley went to bed, when she quietly asked if he was truly angry at her, he had no words to answer. And he slipped the leash that night, more than he ever had with her. He'd taken her almost wildly, and in the instant when what was left of his functioning mind warned him he was going too far she growled fiercely in his ear, "Don't you dare stop. I'm not fragile anymore, thanks to you. Quit holding back."

And he didn't hold back. He let go, driving his body into hers with a force he'd never allowed himself before. And, to his amazement, she seemed to revel in it, urging him on more and more until she practically screamed his name as her body clenched around him, hurling him over the precipice into free fall.

Much later, after his pulse had slowed and he'd regained his breath, he stared at this woman he'd come to love, but had the feeling he still didn't quite understand. She met his gaze, held it, with more nerve than most enemies he'd ever faced. And when she spoke, it was with a quiet ache in her voice that made his gut knot.

"You have a chance, Flynn. I never had the chance to say what I wanted to say to my father. You do."

"Your father was a different story."

"Yes. And from what John found, yours is trying to rewrite his story. But he can't finish that without you."

"You really want me to do this."

"I want you to be able to put it behind you, one way or another. I don't want you to ever wonder. Or regret, as I do."

"And if I meet with him and end it for good?"

"Then so be it. It's your call."

And then this woman who had brought him so much, who had given him so much, made slow, sweet love to him, in the way she had always done, and when she rose atop him and lowered her body to his, she held his gaze. And he knew from her look that she was showing him this purposely, this opposite from the way he'd taken her. And her words, in that low, caressing voice that made him shiver, proved it.

"It's all a part of us, Flynn. Both ways. All the facets. Everything we want, and nothing we don't. But that means...exploring the options."

She leaned forward and her mouth trailed over him, exploring some options that sent fire leaping along every nerve. And he wondered how he'd ever been lucky enough to end up with the one woman in the world who could make perfect sense of everything that had happened and would ever happen to him.

And it was that, in the end, that had made up his mind. And why he found himself in the Kelleher building two days later, opening the door to Shan's private meeting room. It was occupied by one man, yet it might as well have been a crowd for all the emotion Flynn felt churning inside him.

His father had changed. A lot, for the six years it had been since he'd meekly followed his wife out of that hospital room.

I'm afraid, Mrs. Flynn, some of the scarring will be permanent. There's only so much even modern plastic surgery can do.

You're saying my son will be disfigured forever? He'll be this...hideous thing?

It will be better than it is now, but—

Never mind. Thank you, doctor.

She'd turned on her heel and walked away without a backward glance for that son who had nearly died. Just like Riley's mother had turned her back on her and Gracie.

Another image formed in his mind. A surprising one. Funny, he hadn't really remembered until this moment that his father had protested, tried to call her back. But when she'd ignored him, he'd followed her. Had he even looked back? Flynn couldn't remember.

But the man he saw now, staring out of the window of the tenth floor meeting room, was very different. He was less...puffy. Lean, in fact. Flynn assessed him with the ease of years spent calculating the strength of an adversary. And the old man looked a lot more fit, a lot stronger than he had six years ago. And not so old.

He turned away from the window as Flynn closed the door behind him. "I still don't know why I'm here, Mr. Kel—" The man stopped. His eyes widened. Eyes that were clear, and bright, and his own hazel. "Finn," he breathed.

"Did you really tell my mother she's an ugly, selfish, self-absorbed, and utterly inadequate bitch?"

Patrick Flynn drew himself up and met his gaze head on. "I did. And it was too kind."

Flynn's mouth twitched. "I would have liked to have seen that."

"And you should have," his father said frankly. "I should have done it that moment, in that hospital room. I shouldn't have let her leave, I should have thrown her out."

"Maybe the window?"

"Too high up. She would have had time to get on her broom."

To his own utter amazement, Flynn nearly laughed. He'd totally forgotten his father had had a sharp sense of humor.

"Witches don't have quite the bad rep they used to," he said.

"She's the older version," Patrick said. And then, with a pointed look, "And all the plastic surgery in the world can't stop that from showing."

And then he did laugh. His father's gaze changed, his eyes glowing with what Flynn couldn't deny was pure joy. As if having made him laugh was all he'd ever wanted in life.

Flynn sat down on the leather couch, remembering now the time when that had been true. His father sat in the chair opposite him. And the things Flynn had always wondered about, the questions he'd never had the chance to ask, why he'd married her, and more, why he'd stayed, came pouring out. And the man answered them all, quietly, with nothing showing in his face but gratitude for the chance.

And by the time Flynn was feeling more than a little scoured out, his father ended it quietly.

"I can only say I was what I haven't been for almost six years, and never will be again. A drunken fool. And even the rare times when I was sober, I was still a foolish drunk. If I hadn't been, I wouldn't have stayed with her as long as I did."

He's got the biggest power of all. Forgiveness. Hadn't Shan and Juliette taught him that? And hadn't Riley pounded the lesson home in the most painful—and sweetest—of ways?

"I think," Flynn said slowly, feeling the pain of years sliding away, "maybe you have that backward. You didn't stay because you drank, you drank because you stayed."

Those pair of hazel eyes, so familiar, widened. Then, softly, he said, "I'm not nearly as tough, as strong, or as wise as my son is."

"Wise? No. I borrowed that."

"Borrowed?"

He nodded. And then, feeling as if he'd finally set down a burden carried for far too long, he stood up. "Come on...Dad. I'll introduce you to owner of that wisdom. She's why we're here at all."

His father got to his feet. Steadily, without a waver. "It would be an honor. Son."

CHAPTER THIRTY-SEVEN

There was no more amazingly beautiful sight to her than Finnbar Flynn tonight. And it wasn't simply because of the custom-tailored tuxedo Shan had insisted on having made for him, even though it took her breath away to see how he looked in the formal wear, broad-shouldered, slim-hipped and ever powerful. No, it was much more because he wasn't hiding. He wasn't looking away from people. He wasn't even turning his head so they only saw the unscarred side of his face.

"Nice to see, isn't it?" John said from beside her. "Flynn being in your face with his face, and to hell with you if you don't like it?"

"Yes," Riley said, and it was heartfelt.

"It's because he has you, and Gracie," Rachel Stone said from her other side. "He can take on anything now."

They truly had welcomed her, this Wild Oak Bunch. At first, for Flynn's sake, but now she felt for her own, as well. And so here she was, at the annual gala fundraiser for the Wild Oak Children's Cancer Clinic, Shan's most important project, wearing a long, formal black gown she couldn't have imagined owning mere months ago.

She'd been nervous that first day, the day with the roses, about meeting the man Flynn worked for, the man some called the billionaire of Dragon Hill, others simply Mr. K. But he'd been not just kind but as generous with everything as his Juliette had been. Besides insisting she come play the piano whenever she wanted, he'd helped her set up the website she'd surprised Flynn with, for Flynn Landscape Design. And Juliette had taken a ton of photos for it, with permission from all the Wild Oak Bunch, including famous artist Jake Stone and Shan himself, to use shots of what he'd done for them.

Shan had also been generous about the fact that he'd now acquired an energetic eight-year-old and a dog as tenants, saying only, with a loving smile at Juliette, that he hoped they'd add to the population soon. Given his history, and how much he'd loved the little boy he'd lost, Riley was amazed at his resilience.

She was a little amazed at her own. But it was thanks to Flynn that she'd regained so much. And healed so much. The night of Gracie's conception was a distant memory now, blunted to near insignificance by the joy and pleasure she found with Flynn.

Who was now walking toward her.

"Come with me for a minute?" he asked.

"To the ends of the earth," she answered, and got that beloved smile again. Then, teasingly, she added, "Although maybe not tonight. I did promise Shan I'd play."

"And I wouldn't deprive these donors the joy of that," he promised. "I just need to...give you something."

Riley's brow furrowed at his tone. He was always giving her things—flowers for no reason, or sheet music for a song she'd mentioned she liked, and never mind the way he spoiled Gracie with just about anything she wanted. But he'd never sounded quite like this.

He led her out into the hallway outside the banquet room of the Wild Oak Hotel. He reached into the jacket of his tux and pulled out a large envelope. "Shan just gave me this," was all he said.

Her brow furrowed as she opened the envelope and pulled out the sheaf of papers. Something legal, obviously, that was immediately apparent from the format. She scanned the front page quickly, seeing only the unfamiliar names of attorneys. But then a name at the bottom caught her eye and she gasped. Her gaze shot to Flynn's face. His expression was pure satisfaction.

"Flynn...what?"

"The Kelleher Company has some top-notch lawyers on staff. This might not be their usual area of expertise, but they made it clear who and what—as in rape charges—he'd be dealing with if he fought this. And the name Shan Kelleher carries an incredible amount of weight." He smiled. "In other words, they scared the crap out of him. And the friend who tried to help him kidnap Gracie in San Diego."

She looked back at the pages in her hands, unable to quite process the words, the legalese. "Does this mean...what I think it means?"

"It means that the sperm contributor can never even look sideways at Gracie again. He's relinquished any and all claim to her, in perpetuity. Plus he'll be fattening up her trust fund quite a bit. Not that she'll need it. Shan's already got his heart set on funding anything she wants to do."

She looked up at him again. "I...you did this?"

He shrugged, as if it were nothing, this resolving of the one remaining dark shadow that hung over her life. "Oh, and there's a medical history there, in case there's ever an issue. Doesn't look like it, the scumbag was healthy." He grinned at her then, and her pulse rocketed. "But from what they found, the brains sure didn't come from him. That was all you, honey."

She flushed, but managed to hold his gaze. "Why? I mean, I know Shan would do anything for any of the Wild Oak Bunch, but why did you ask him to?"

"I wanted you free, Riley. I don't ever want you afraid, or even looking over your shoulder again." He smiled again, and her heart practically turned over in her chest. "Unless it's at me, of course."

"God, Flynn..."

"You can take your life back now. Do whatever you want. Take Shan's offer to fund a world tour. You're that good."

"I could teach again?"

He smiled at that. But he already knew she didn't have any desire for the glamour, the spotlight. "You could. You can take your name back, too."

"I like my name now."

For a moment he went very quiet. Then, his voice low and a little rough, he said, "Does that mean you wouldn't want to change it...again?"

Her breath jammed up in her throat, and for an instant, the room seemed to spin. "Are you...asking me to?"

"I think Riley Flynn has a nice ring to it."

"So do I." It came out breathless, because she was still having trouble with that lump in her throat.

"You sure you want to tie yourself to beauty and the beast stories for the rest of your life?"

"Hush with that stuff. All I want is the happily ever after part."

He pulled her into his arms, into a hug so fierce and strong and warm that she felt safer than she ever had in her life.

"I love you, Riley. I think I have since you charged to Gracie's rescue despite being half-dead on your feet."

"And I love you," she whispered. "You're the man I never believed existed."

A long, silent moment spun out before he said quietly, "I think Gracie Flynn has a nice ring, too."

She looked up at him, her eyes wide. "You want to...adopt her?"

"Would you let me?" He grimaced. "I have no clue about being a father. It's not that I don't want to. I'm crazy about her, but I don't know how."

Her chin came up. "Did you know how to...fire a rocket launcher before you joined the Army?"

He blinked. "Uh...no."

"All right, then. Besides, you're already perfect with her. So I'd say you have every clue."

"You think she'd want it?"

"How can you ask?" It burst from her. "She adores you, so much. Almost as much as I do."

He lowered his gaze then, but she got her precious smile once more. Then, with a glint in his eye she'd come to know in these happy days, he lifted his gaze back to hers.

"I don't know. She'd end up Gracelyn Flynn. It's a bit...rhyme-y."

"It's like Finn Flynn, so she'll love it." He smiled at that, and the happiness in it let her tease him. "So will I. I'll get to introduce my daughter and husband, Gracelyn and Finn Flynn."

He made a choked sound, but it wasn't laughter as she

expected. Instead, to her surprise, she saw his jaw clench and moisture sheen his hazel eyes. "I think," he said, swallowed, then went on, "I think that's the most wonderful thing I've ever heard." He drew in a deep breath, and said with a solemnity that touched her so very deeply, "Twice now, the life I knew has ended. The first time was...awful. But this, this new life you and Gracie have given me, makes up for it all."

When she sat down at the piano on the small stage a few minutes later, she simply knew she couldn't put a finger wrong. It was as if every note was powered by the love burgeoning in her heart, and boosted by the love of the people gathered closest in the crowd, the Wild Oak Bunch, all smiling at her, and at Flynn. She abandoned her planned playlist and tackled every complex piece she could remember, filling the room, until even those who hadn't been listening at first stopped their chatter and began to stare in awe.

But she ended it with that simple, swelling, uplifting song from a child's movie, and it seemed so appropriate, for she had regained the childlike optimism she'd once thought lost forever. And it was all because of one man, who had given her a future free of running away, free of fear. And while Gracie would never know the kind soul who had been Riley's father, she would know a grandfather, who had declared her more than worth every minute of the six years of his fight for sobriety.

When she finished, applause began, grew, and soon filled the room, with the loudest coming from that group to the right, the gathered Wild Oak Bunch, all of them. That unlikely bunch that had found their way to the kind of friendship few ever found. That bunch that had welcomed her so generously, and had gone from accepting her for Flynn's sake, because they loved him, to accepting her for her own.

A movement drew her attention, and she had only a moment to focus and truly see, because an instant later her vision was blurred with tears. But she knew the image would be with her the rest of her life.

The image of a tall, strong, indomitable man, tenderly holding the child who adored him, and he adored in turn. Gracie leaned into him, resting her cheek against his, heedless and truly uncaring about the scars that only meant to her that her soon-to-be father was the bravest man in the world.

And Riley knew the luckiest day of her life had been when she'd stuck a pin in a map and ended up in Wild Oak.

THE END

ALSO BY JUSTINE DAVIS

OPERATION SOLDIER NEXT DOOR
OPERATION ALPHA
OPERATION NOTORIOUS
OPERATION HERO'S WATCH
OPERATION SECOND CHANCE
OPERATION MOUNTAIN RECOVERY

SINGLE TITLE ROMANTIC SUSPENSE
DANGEROUS GROUND
DANGEROUS GAMES
HIGH STAKES
NIGHT FIRES
AVENGING ANGEL

Dear Reader,

If you've enjoyed the entire Wild Oak series, thank you! If you're beginning with this book, I hope you'll go back to the beginning and see how the Wild Oak Bunch came to be.

Readers often ask me about the genesis of a particular series, and I'd like to share the story of beginning of this one. First of all, the horses are real. They were on display in the lobby of a lovely California inn near Santa Rosa, and I was awestruck at the pure energy in this work of art. Those amazing creatures swirling up out of a huge chunk of redwood were stunning, and became the inspiration for the first book of the series, STACY'S HORSES. And in tribute I set the series in a fictional but similar area.

Although I say series, and it is one, in the beginning I had no intention of doing one. This was simply a story I had to write, whether it ever ended up in reader's hands or not. But once STACY'S HORSES was done, a secondary character began to nag at me. I should have known then that I had not spent my last day in Wild Oak, and sure enough, yet another character stepped up, then another and another.

So here we are now, with a five book series that has taken a few years to come to fruition. Thank you so much for taking this journey with me!

Justine Davis

PS: Dare I mention that there's another inn stuck in my mind, a quiet little place on a secluded island that has a rather unique history and an even more unique occupant? More to come!

ABOUT THE AUTHOR

"Some people call me a writer, some an author, some a novelist. I just say I'm a storyteller." –Justine Davis

Author of more than 80 books, (she sold her first ten in less than two years) Justine Davis is a five-time winner of the coveted RITA Award, including one for being inducted into the RWA Hall of Fame. A fifteen time nominee for RT Book Review awards, she has won four times, received three of their lifetime achievement awards, and had four titles on the magazine's 200 Best of all Time list. Her books have appeared on national bestseller lists, including USA Today. She has been featured on CNN, taught at several national and international conferences, and at the UCLA writer's program.

After years of working in law enforcement, and more years doing both, Justine now writes full time. She lives near beautiful Puget Sound in Washington State, peacefully coexisting with deer, bears, a pair of bald eagles, a tailless raccoon, and her beloved '67 Corvette roadster. When she's not writing, taking photographs, or driving said roadster (and yes, it goes very fast) she tends to her knitting. Literally.

www.justinedavis.com

http://justinedavis.com/newsletter.html